The Girl at the End of the Line

Also by Charles Mathes

The Girl with the Phony Name
The Girl Who Remembered Snow

THOMAS
DUNNE
BOOKS

The Girl at the End of the Line

For Stan and Michael —
In memory of a perfect time
at the Deerhill Inn
With very best wishes,

Charles Mathes

St. Martin's Press ✦ New York

THOMAS DUNNE BOOKS.
An imprint of St. Martin's Press.

THE GIRL AT THE END OF THE LINE. Copyright © 1999 by Charles Mathes.
All rights reserved. Printed in the United States of America. No part of this
book may be used or reproduced in any manner whatsoever without written
permission except in the case of brief quotations embodied in critical
articles or reviews. For information address St. Martin's Press,
175 Fifth Avenue, New York, N.Y. 10010.

Library of Congress Cataloging-in-Publication Data

Mathes, Charles.
    The girl at the end of the line / Charles Mathes. —1st ed.
        p.   cm.
    "Thomas Dunne books."
    ISBN 0–312–19887–6
    I. Title.
PS3563.A83543G53   1999
813'.54—dc21   98–46784

First Edition: April 1999

10   9   8   7   6   5   4   3   2   1

For T.P.C.,
Who was my very first girl,
and for Arlene,
Who is my one and only

"Comb your hair, it looks like a bird's nest," whispered Molly O'Hara, grabbing her sister by the sleeve of her T-shirt and locking Nell's green eyes with her own. "And stay away from oyster plates, you hear me? We've got twenty-six and that's enough."

Nell replied with a wink and a grin in the early morning light but didn't say a word. This was hardly surprising. She hadn't spoken since she was eight.

A slow rustle swept through the restless crowd, the kind of sound the summer wind blowing makes through a stand of loblolly pines. Grim-faced men ground out cigarettes on the slate walk. Women with skin the North Carolina sun had cured to old-wallet perfection licked lipstick off their lips and checked their watches. A young man in a chartreuse shirt tittered and waved his long fingers in the air, indicating either that he found the tension unbearable or that he needed to dry his nail polish in a hurry.

Suddenly the door of the big old house opened, and the crowd surged through as one. Molly grabbed her sister's hand, not so much to protect her as to haul her inside ahead of the others.

Three competent-looking ladies, all blondes, were sitting at a card table in the entrance hall. Their tired eyes filled with a mixture of awe and terror as the mob of early birds swarmed past them and into the house.

It had taken the women weeks to price and advertise the property that the late Miss Edna Gerritze had acquired over a long lifetime. It would take only two days for the dealers, the decorators, and the public to strip the house clean, the way maggots strip the carcass of a dead fox. Already the madness that was a tag sale had begun.

"It's mine," declared a deep voice.

"I saw it first," replied a shrill one.

Crash.

One of the tag sale ladies jumped up from her chair and scurried toward the noise, but Molly knew that the combatants would already have fled the scene of the crime in search of undamaged booty. She was an old hand at this, starting from the days when she had bought Depression glass with baby-sitting money to sell from a begged table at the Clark County Flea Market. Now, at twenty-eight, Molly O'Hara owned Enchanted Cottage Antiques on Porcupine Road at U.S. 29 and by her calculation had been an antique dealer half her life.

Across the room Molly caught a glimpse of her sister juggling three Noritaki teacups and shot her a furious look.

Nell casually plucked the cups out of the air and deposited them back on a table. Molly's sister loved showing off and never dropped anything, but Molly hated the attention she drew to herself with her antics. Since Nell didn't talk, the apologies and excuses were always Molly's to make, and these took time. Time was money at a tag sale. They were here to work.

With a practiced eye Molly took in the cluttered panorama as she walked briskly from room to room: umbrellas and flowerpots; birdcages and end tables; once-precious pictures whose only value now lay in their frames.

The late Edna Gerritze's dining room was piled high with tableware. Unfortunately the "silver" was commercially produced plated stuff. The candlesticks were cheap glass reproductions. Even the two sets of Sunday dishes—one modern Lenox, the other hideous Limoges—weren't anything a savvy dealer would ever consider.

This was the sort of stuff you found at tag sales, Molly knew. At least it was what you found here in Pelletreau, North Carolina, though there were still treasures to be had. Even the best tag sale ladies missed things occasionally, which was why Molly had roused Nell before dawn today to get here before the doors opened. By ten o'clock a sale was so picked over that any real bargains were gone.

Molly turned her attention to the glassware, which was laid out on a sideboard across from the china. The estate suddenly began to look a little better. Molly recognized a dozen pieces of pattern glass, which had surely come down in the Gerritze family; it was already clear from the contents of the house that the deceased had simply accumulated her worldly goods, not collected them in any conscious manner.

Molly nonchalantly ran her fingers through her short brown hair, then flicked the rim of a Seneca Loop pattern goblet. It produced the dull noise: soda-lime glass. The price of the goblet in her hand was reasonable, but Molly already had too much pattern glass. It might be years before she could sell an ordinary piece like this one. She put it back on the table.

Another flick with her fingernail on a Waffle-and-Thumbprint pattern celery vase sent an unexpected thrill down Molly's spine, a thrill she never tired of. The glass rang like a tiny bell. It was "flint," as pre–Civil War lead glass was called. This piece was priced as cheaply as the others but could easily bring a hundred dollars from a collector.

Leaving the rejects on the table for other dealers to pick through, Molly brought her prize back to the front hall. Her sister was just coming down the stairs with an old radio, an RCA Victor in a red plastic case.

Nell was four inches taller than Molly's five feet one and three years younger. The family resemblance between the girls was still obvious, however. Though Nell's figure was more curvaceous, both of them had green eyes, upturned mouths, and too-small noses. They shared the same brown hair, cut short with bangs, and the same porcelain complexions that had to be kept out of the summer sun. Even their eyebrows, which were too thick to be pretty but which Molly refused to pluck, were similar.

But there the resemblance between the girls ended.

While Molly was intense and driven, a gregarious chatterbox so impetuous that she kept a packed suitcase in her van so that she could take off at a moment's notice, Nell was unhurried in her actions, uncertain of what she wanted and entirely mute. Her moods swung crazily. One moment she was impish and full of mischief, the next she could fall into an inexplicable sullenness that lasted for hours. Though Nell had the body of a woman, she seemed to have the mind of a child. She could do complicated tasks like ringing up sales on a cash register or baking a pie, but the simplest interaction with anyone other than Molly was all but impossible for her.

It was as if Nell had slammed some inner door against everybody in the world but her sister. There was no mystery as to why she had done so, why she had withdrawn from everything and stopped speaking. Seventeen years ago, when she was eight, Nell had seen something that no one should have to see, certainly not a little girl. There was no way she was going to grow up to be normal.

Molly checked the price tag as Nell laid the radio on the card table in front of the blond salesladies.

"Good girl!" she exclaimed, patting her sister on the shoulder and placing her precious celery vase down next to Nell's find.

There was big nostalgia for old radios, and they might be able to quintuple their money on the one Nell had just found if the right tourist wandered into the shop. As much as Molly loved her sister, she wouldn't have brought Nell along if her eye for bargains wasn't almost as good as Molly's own.

Nell was already bounding back up the stairs. Molly left her business card on top of the radio so the ladies could keep track of her purchases. Then she hurried back into the house, which had gotten crowded in the last fifteen minutes as more people had arrived. The feeding frenzy had begun in earnest.

Molly elbowed her way into the late Edna Gerritze's living room, hoping to find something everyone else had overlooked. As usual she was the shortest person in the room, but that fact never stopped her. What she lacked in height and reach, she made up for in speed and determination. Antiquing was a kind of warfare, and Molly would take on Arnold Schwarzenegger for the right piece of printed fabric.

A couple of women were fighting it out in front of the curio cabinet, though Molly didn't see anything particularly exciting— just the usual china birds and silk fans. The young man in the chartreuse shirt was wrestling with a *Gone with the Wind* style lamp.

There was a nice mahogany breakfront that nobody seemed to be looking at, probably because it was so big. Molly checked the price tag—quite reasonable for a piece like this, but it would be hard to sell and a bitch to get home. Molly passed.

In the kitchen a young couple was inspecting the refrigerator, probably because they couldn't afford a new one. A gaggle of old ladies—civilians, not dealers, judging by the sweet, kindly look of them—poked through assorted tea strainers and juicers. In the back hall a greedy-eyed bald man scooped up mason jars like they were filled with jewels. A collector? Or was he just someone into canning preserves?

By the time Molly made it back to the front hall, Nell had returned from upstairs and was putting a large cardboard box down next to their other purchases.

"What did you find?" said Molly eagerly, coming over and fingering through the contents. Her excitement quickly evaporated, however. The box was full of old theater programs. The Chattanooga Civic Light Opera presents *Show Boat*. Tennessee Williams's *Summer and Smoke* at Playmakers of Chapel Hill.

"What are we supposed to do with these?" she exclaimed. "You know nobody wants this kind of stuff. What's the matter with you?"

Nell's pretty smile collapsed and she looked away. Molly immediately felt guilty. It wasn't her sister's fault if she sometimes got confused or carried away.

"Come on," Molly said in a conciliatory voice. "Let's take them back upstairs. I was just going up."

When Nell didn't move, Molly picked up the heavy box by its cutout handles and struggled up the stairs with it. Nell finally followed, looking confused and a little hurt. Molly deposited the box on the landing at the top of the stairs—there was no point in worrying exactly where it had come from—and started into the upstairs hall.

"See if you can find some baskets," she said over her shoulder. "We could sell a million of those nice old peach baskets, like the kind you found up in Leightonville. You know the ones I mean?"

Nell stared back with an unreadable expression. Molly didn't wait for an answer—she knew there wouldn't be one. She walked into one of the bedrooms, a typical old lady's room with a mahogany bedstead, crocheted comforter, and heavy curtains that smelled of lavender.

By the time Molly had satisfied herself that there were no valuable perfume bottles among the late Edna Gerritze's dressing table bric-a-brac, the hallway had begun to fill up with browsers from downstairs. Nell was still where Molly had left her, however, squatting next to the box they had brought back upstairs, leafing through a theater program.

"Will you please put that down?" said Molly in exasperation, marching over and taking the program out of her sister's hands. "We don't have time to waste today. We have to see Grandma before we can open the shop. Now, please, sweetheart, go down and see if you can find something I missed. Go on."

Molly dropped the program on top of the others and waited as Nell reluctantly made her way down the stairs. What was the girl thinking? Molly shook her head and checked her watch. It had stopped, of course.

Molly cursed under her breath and knocked the cheap timepiece against the bannister railing. Grandma had given both her and Nell watches when they were teenagers. Grandma was too poor to afford good ones, and Nell had thrown hers away years ago. Molly couldn't bear to hurt the poor old woman's feelings, however, and buy a replacement. Grandma looked for the watch every time Molly visited—at least she had until recently.

Molly spent another ten minutes checking out the remaining second-floor rooms, then came back downstairs to settle up. There were presently only two tag sale ladies on duty ringing up purchases at the card table in the front hallway. Molly went to the more benign-looking one: a small-boned woman with bronze-colored hair and lips no thicker than chives. Her name tag proclaimed to the world that she was LILLIAN of THREE BLOND LIQUIDATORS.

"Let's see," said Lillian the Liquidator, tapping a calculator. "You've got the glass vase, the radio, and the oyster plate."

Nell smirked and gave Molly a little pat on the back. Molly felt her face go red. So what if she had happened to find another oyster plate in an upstairs bedroom? This one was different than all their other ones. Besides, the price was too good to pass up.

"I'll need your resale number," said Lillian the Liquidator. "And we take only cash, no credit cards or checks."

Molly took her wallet from the back pocket of her jeans and counted out the bills. The third tag sale lady had now come back into the hall from the house and was taking her place at the card table. She was the oldest of the trio, a wrinkled blonde not a day under seventy. Something stopped her before she sat.

"You okay, honey?" she asked in a quivery voice, looking over Molly's shoulder to where Nell was standing. "You need a drink of water or something?"

Molly turned around in time to see her sister cover her face with her hands. Nell's amused expression had suddenly changed to one of sheer terror. Her eyes brimmed over with tears. Her mouth opened as if she were screaming, but no sound came out. She took several steps back until she was against the wall and began to shake violently.

It was happening again. Nell was having another one of her attacks. She had had them on and off since that terrible day so long ago. Months had passed since her last attack, however. Molly had almost begun to believe that they were a thing of the past.

"She's all right," said Molly, rushing over. "Just leave her alone. She'll be fine in a minute."

Molly put an arm around her sister's shoulders and gently stroked the back of her neck. That sometimes worked when Nell got like this. What had brought it on? The crowded house? Oyster plates? Too many blondes?

"Did I say something wrong?" said the elderly tag sale lady, looking concerned. "I just thought she looked a bit peaked and asked if she wanted some water."

"Do you want us to call a doctor?" piped in Lillian.

"Thanks, but that won't be necessary," said Molly. "My sister just gets like this sometimes. A nervous condition. It's nothing to worry about. She's perfectly okay. I need a receipt for those things."

The ladies returned to the paperwork, occasionally glancing nervously at Nell. Molly led her sister over to the door, stroking her neck and speaking to her in a gentle voice. After a few moments, Nell dropped her hands from her face and stopped shaking.

Molly dug into her pocket for a tissue and wiped the tears from her sister's cheeks. Then she held Nell out at arm's length and scrutinized her.

"You okay now?"

Nell nodded her head.

"What was it?" Molly asked. "What frightened you?"

Nell didn't answer. She smiled weakly and slipped out of Molly's hands. Then she opened the front door of the house and ran out across the lawn in the direction of their van.

Molly didn't try to stop her. She returned to the card table and finished up the details of their purchases. An overwhelming sense of guilt descended on her, as it always did after one of these episodes.

Why did Nell still have these attacks? Why wouldn't she speak after all these years, even to Molly? The doctors all said that there was nothing physically wrong with her voice. Molly had always feared that Nell was just angry. Angry at her. She could hardly blame her sister for that. After all, what had happened to Nell that day had been Molly's fault.

"That wasn't much of a sale, huh?" Molly said later, when she had loaded the morning's treasures into their ancient minivan and they were on the road back home. "But can you believe how they had that radio priced? Those poor women didn't have a clue what they had. We're going to sell it to some fool Yankee for a fortune, you just wait and see."

Nell nodded, then stared silently out of the window at the strip malls and red clay that passed for scenery in their part of the world. Molly rattled on, as was her nature. The van made more than its usual quota of creaks, knocks, and groans. It had taken to stalling out if you drove it for more than a few hours a day. Molly knew that she'd have to replace it soon—maybe at the end of the summer, if she could put together enough money.

It was another twenty minutes before they had driven back across the spread-out old city of Pelletreau and pulled into the unpaved drive of Enchanted Cottage Antiques. There was parking for up to six cars in front next to a stand of oak trees, but Molly drove the minivan around back and parked under the carport by the rear door. The day was already getting hot, but that was hardly unusual for North Carolina in July.

Molly got out carrying the celery vase and the oyster plate. Nell followed Molly inside with the radio. They deposited their haul on the round maple table in the little kitchen at the back of the shop. It was ten after nine according to the cuckoo clock out front—early, but there was still a lot to do.

"I've got to take care of business before we see Grandma," said Molly, resetting her watch and giving it a good wind. "You go on upstairs and get ready. I won't be but a minute. I thought you were going to comb your hair."

Nell had sat down at the table on one of the cathedral chairs that Molly liked too much to sell. She didn't move.

"Come on, honey, we've got to get going," Molly said gently.

"And please put on some lipstick. You look like an iceberg lettuce. You don't want to scare Grandma, do you?"

An image of their beloved grandmother the way she used to be flashed into Molly's mind—a big woman sitting in an easy chair, sewing dresses for rich ladies. She would sit there like that ten hours at a time, seven days a week sometimes.

One of Molly's clearest memories from her childhood was of a six-year-old Nell, a Nell who was still a normal, happy little girl climbing into the old lady's expansive lap and stopping Grandma's needlework with her tiny hand.

"One day I'm going to buy you a great big house, Grandma," Nell had promised, her eyes wide and earnest. "And you'll never have to work again."

Grandma had smiled her sad smile, clearly not believing that it would ever happen, not believing that she would ever have anything but a two-room apartment in downtown Pelletreau.

Even then, even before the tragedy that had befallen them all, hers had been a hard life, but until three months ago Grandma had still smiled her resigned smile and sung funny old songs in her big, raucous voice. Then she had had the stroke that had put her in the Pelletreau Charitable Nursing Home. Now it was Molly who tried to smile and do the singing.

"Nellie, what are you doing?" asked Molly, coming out of her reverie only to find Nell lost in one of her own. "Where are you?"

Nell still didn't move or make eye contact with her sister. She looked deep in thought, like she was trying to remember something, something very important, but very lost.

"Go on," said Molly, coming up behind her sister and squeezing her shoulders. "Git."

Her expression unchanged, Nell rose and wandered through the kitchen archway into the back hall. Molly listened until she heard footsteps going up the stairs to the bedroom they shared over the store. Then she brought out the ledger in which she kept track of purchases.

In her tiny neat handwriting, Molly entered the information for the celery vase, the radio, and the oyster plate.

The cuckoo clock out in the shop chirped its quarter hour reminder that cuckoo clocks didn't sell. If someone didn't buy it soon, Molly was going to bury the damn thing in the backyard. The shop fell silent again.

Molly closed the ledger and replaced it behind the sugar jar. She sat for a moment, enjoying the silence and the unfamiliar sensation of being alone.

Another image from childhood drifted into Molly's mind. She and Nell were at their grandmother's tiny apartment again. Their mother had often left the girls with her when she had to do something in the city. Nell was coloring with a crayon in a coloring book. Grandma was sewing, as she always was.

Suddenly the old woman's face grew dark with unmistakable rage. She took the garment in her hands and tore it in half, threw it on the floor. Molly was terrified. She had never seen her grandmother so angry, even when she argued with their stepfather after Sunday dinners.

But Nell wasn't frightened by Grandma's unprecedented outburst at all. She looked up from her coloring book with a stern look and shook her finger at the old seamstress.

"Temper, temper," she chided in a mild little voice.

Grandma's face had melted into a smile. She cut another piece of cloth and returned to her thankless work.

Nell had been such a brave, smart little girl, Molly remembered. But this morning at the tag sale she had been a mass of terror. Why? It couldn't have been just what happened seventeen years ago, that was ancient history. What had set her off this morning? What had she seen?

The kitchen was getting too crowded, Molly thought glancing around the room, trying to shrug off the guilt that began to overwhelm her again.

There were books everywhere—under the table, lined up against the walls, blocking the hall. Molly might not have had a lot of formal education, but knowledge was survival to an antiques dealer and she was probably better read than many PhDs. There were even books in the oven, a 1940s-vintage gas behemoth.

That probably explained why Nell hadn't baked any pies lately, Molly realized. Nell's apple pie was something directly from heaven. But this wasn't the time to worry about her lack of library space. Or about Nell. Or about pies. Molly stretched and headed for the stairs.

Upstairs, Nell was sitting on her bed, staring at a small white booklet in her hands. She had made no move to comb her hair.

"Oh, for pete sake's," Molly exclaimed. "Next time I cut your hair I might as well do it with the lawn mower if you can't keep it combed. You want Grandma to think you're some kind of semi-human creature from the swamp? What am I going to do with you?"

When Nell didn't look up, Molly went over and took what she was reading out of her hands. It was a "Playbill" from the Booth Theatre in New York City. The late Edna Gerritze had apparently been to Broadway.

"Oh, this is marvelous!" Molly exclaimed. "My baby sister's a thief now, too. You stole this from that box at the sale this morning, didn't you? What did you do? Stick it under your shirt when I wasn't looking? Are you going to start knocking over Seven-Elevens next?"

Nell reached for the program, but Molly pulled it away.

"I should make you take it back to those people. If it weren't so far away I would, I swear. You know how we feel about shoplifters. You should be ashamed of yourself. What's so darn interesting about this thing anyway?"

But what was so interesting was right on the cover—a beautiful young woman in an elegant white gown. Molly's mouth dropped open as she read the caption beneath the picture of the strangely familiar-looking actress.

Margaret Jellinek in *Without Reservations*

It was Margaret Jellinek, their grandmother. Margaret Jellinek, the seamstress.

". . . and to think Grandma never said a word about it, never let on that she ever did anything but dressmaking!" marveled Molly, trying to keep her eyes on the road and at the same time catch a glimpse of Margaret Jellinek's picture on the cover of the "Playbill" in Nell's lap. "I didn't think she even liked the theater. Remember when I did that play in high school and told her I wanted to be an actress? Remember what she said? No, don't say it—I don't want you using that kind of language!"

Nell scratched her cheek and nodded. Molly crossed Highway 5 and turned down Moffat Road, talking all the while.

"I mean, Grandma must have been a star. Did you see all her credits in the program, all those other plays she'd been in? They don't put your picture on the cover if you're just some walk-on from the chorus, you know. Why didn't she say something? That's what I don't understand. Unless she was ashamed, maybe. Ashamed that she lost her big Broadway career and had to work her fingers to the bone making dresses for people in Pelletreau, godforsaken North Carolina, just to stay alive."

Molly reached over and playfully punched her sister on the shoulder.

"And if you hadn't found that program we never would have known a whit about it, you clever thing. You steal anything else, and I'm going to break your arm."

Nell grinned. Molly turned into the drive of the Pelletreau Charitable Nursing Home and parked in the drab little lot. Then she got out of the van and came around to Nell's side. Nell had made no move to open her door.

"Of course, we can't put Grandma on the spot about it," Molly chattered on, "not with her the way she is right now. We'll have to bring it up casual-like, when the moment is right. 'Oh, and speaking of the weather, look what Nell happened to find the other day. We didn't know you were a famous Broadway actress. My, what a pleasant surprise.' "

But Nell wasn't listening. Her face was suddenly full of panic. She glanced around like a frightened animal, then stared at the floor. Molly opened the door.

"Are you okay?" asked Molly in a quiet, serious voice. "Is it happening again?"

Nell shook her head, but didn't look up.

"Is it this place?"

Nell nodded, still looking at the floor.

"It's okay," said Molly with a sigh. "I understand. You don't have to come in with me, if you don't want to. I'm not going to make you."

Nell raised her eyes, hopefully.

"It's just that she's got nobody but us," said Molly, "and it's been practically two weeks since our last visit. I think she's pretty lonely and miserable. I know I would be."

Nell took a deep breath, then nodded. Looking grim, she got out of the van.

"Thanks," said Molly, reaching back inside for the theater program, then locking the doors. "We won't stay long, I promise."

They crossed the parking lot to the nursing home entrance.

Molly didn't want to admit it, but she wasn't looking forward to seeing Grandma any more than Nell was. Not like this, not the way she was. Besides, Molly was puzzled and hurt that Margaret Jellinek hadn't said anything about her stage career. It had never occurred to Molly that Grandma would have kept secrets from her. They had always had a special relationship. With their mother dead, the girls were all the family the old lady had in the world, as she was always reminding them.

Grandma must have had her reasons, Molly knew, but the cat was out of the bag now. Molly was determined to find out all the details of Margaret Jellinek's life in the theater. Of course she probably wouldn't learn much today, she knew. The therapist had said it might be months before Molly's grandmother would be able to hold an intelligible conversation. But she would pry out the whole story, sooner or later. Once Molly got her mind set on something, she never gave up.

At the busy reception desk a stern, pasty-faced woman in rhinestone-studded glasses was talking into the phone. The other receptionist—the sweet, black girl who knew everybody's relatives by name and always seemed happy to see them—must be off today. Pasty-faced Mrs. Springer didn't know anyone and obviously didn't care to.

Molly fought down an urge to dodge the ritual check-in entirely and just go up to the room. The Pelletreau Charitable Nursing Home's *security* was little more than an annoying formality.

"Molly and Nell O'Hara to see Mrs. Jellinek," she said obediently, however, when the woman finally put down the phone.

"That other man still with her?" asked Mrs. Springer, who had a voice like a frog.

"What other man?"

"Redheaded gentleman," croaked Mrs. Springer. "Asked for her room number earlier."

"Who was he?"

"Don't recall the name. He was wearing sunglasses and had a bushy mustache. Said he was a friend of hers. The limit's two visitors per room. He still up there?"

"Oh, *him,*" said Molly, wondering who it could be. "No. He left."

"Okay, y'all can go up then."

"Thanks." Some security.

Molly led Nell to the elevator. The hallway was a sickly pea-green and badly in need of a paint job. She made it a point to keep her eyes straight ahead and hoped that Nell would follow suit.

Modesty was no longer a high priority for many of the resident old folks. The last time they had been here Molly had come back from the drinking fountain to find a little old man outside his room regaling Nell with tales of the shoe business. He was buck naked beneath his robe, and his robe was hanging wide open. Nell had found the whole thing hugely amusing—though perhaps hugely wasn't the right word to describe what she had seen.

Molly pressed the button for the elevator and waited for it to arrive, wondering who her grandmother's visitor could be.

She had thought she knew all Margaret Jellinek's friends. None of the men had much hair left at all, let alone red hair and bushy mustaches. A son, perhaps, paying respects for someone too old and sick to come herself? Or did Grandma have other secrets besides her long-lost career? Was this some old beau? Some guy who liked loud, older women like Grandma? Molly smiled at the thought of it, trying to ignore the odors of medicine and decay in the hall.

When they got to the little room on the second floor the door was closed. Molly opened it, half expecting to find an unfamiliar man sitting by her grandmother's bedside, holding a bouquet of flowers, and making the kind of awkward small talk that visitors made with sick people.

There was no visitor, however. The lights were off. Margaret Jellinek lay in bed flat on her back under the covers, her pillow on her chest.

Molly turned to Nell.

"Sssh," she whispered, putting a finger to her lips. "She's asleep."

Nell shrugged uncomfortably and stared at the pillow on her grandmother's chest. With a smile, Molly gently picked up the pillow and went to place it under Margaret Jellinek's head.

Instantly she knew that something was terribly wrong.

"Grandma?" she said in a voice so small it frightened her.

There was no answer. Molly grabbed the call button next to the bed and pressed it repeatedly.

"Go get someone," she said after a moment when no one came.

Nell looked from side to side, but didn't move.

"Get the nurse! Now!"

Nell darted out of the room. She returned a few moments later, pushing an annoyed-looking aide in front of her, but it was too late, of course. Molly had known from the instant that she touched her grandmother's head that Margaret Jellinek was dead.

eeee

The funeral was three days later.

More than two dozen old people and Nell and Molly in dresses their grandmother had made for them stood at graveside under a tent against the morning drizzle. All around them the green grass was crowded with white gravestones, some older than the Civil War. A rented clergyman spoke of the Resurrection and Eternal Life.

Margaret Jellinek had never had much use for religion. Neither did Molly, but she thought it wouldn't have been fair to her grandmother's friends not to have a service and let them say goodbye. There hadn't been a service for Molly's mother seventeen years ago, and it still seemed like her death was unfinished business.

"I'm so sorry," said Mrs. Hoyt, another seamstress, afterward.

"It was a blessing," said Mrs. Siegrist, the pharmacist's wife. Mr. Siegrist nodded sad agreement.

"If there's anything I can do," declared Mrs. Onckelbag, for whom Margaret Jellinek had made dresses for thirty years, "please let me know."

As the crowd began to disperse, Tessie Haimes, Margaret Jellinek's neighbor and best friend, made her way to their side.

"How are you girls holdin' up?" she asked in her sugary North Carolina drawl, squeezing Molly's arm.

Tessie was a round little woman with curly bluish hair and deep dimples in both cheeks that made her look like an ancient Shirley Temple. She had worked most of her life in a fishmarket, but always smelled of face powder and English soap.

"We're fine, Tessie. Thanks for coming."

"Maggie would have liked this. All her friends. The two of you."

"She would have hated it, and you know it," said Molly. "She would be yelling at me for wasting the money. She once made me promise to bury her in a tin can in Wheatman State Park."

"Oh, she was just carryin' on," tittered Tessie, waving her lacy handkerchief in the air and shaking her head. "You did the right thing. It was a real nice service."

"Thanks."

"Hi, Nellie," Tessie said, turning her attentions to Molly's sister. "You're lookin' real pretty. How are you, sweetheart? You remember me? Tessie?"

Nell shrugged out of Tessie's attempted embrace. She had always been agitated around Grandma's friends, especially when they tried to touch her—as practically all of them had tried to do today.

"That's okay, honey," said Tessie, not taking it as a personal rejection, the way some people did. "I know you're upset 'bout losin' your grandma. I understand."

"How about you, Tessie?" asked Molly in an amiable voice. "How are you doing?"

"Oh, I'm all right," sighed the old lady. "I should have expected something like this, I guess. Was it another stroke?"

"The doctor at the home thought it probably was. That or her heart. He said that in her condition she could have gone at any time."

"And here I was convinced she was gettin' better. Last time I saw Maggie, she was beginnin' to growl again, just like her old self. She even told me to shut the hell up when I started talkin' about the damned Republicans—I swear I understood every word she said."

"She was something else," said Molly, smiling. "Did you know she was an actress once?"

"Really? She never said nothin' 'bout that to me. Here in Pelletreau?"

"On Broadway, almost fifty years ago."

"No!" squealed Tessie. "You're funnin' me."

"It's true. Nell found a program from a big New York City theater with her picture on the cover."

"Well, if that don't beat all. It's possible, I s'pose. Maggie never would talk about her life before she came South, and she certainly was a dramatic individual. Always making grand pronouncements in that big ol' voice of hers. And y'all didn't know?"

"Not a thing."

"Your mama never said nothin'? Evangeline was just a baby when they came to Pelletreau, but surely Maggie would have said something to her over the years. She never passed it along?"

"If she did, I don't remember," said Molly.

"No, of course not. Whatever happened to my brains? You was just a little girl when Angie got . . . when your mama passed away."

Molly suddenly noticed a white Mercury Sable parked across the drive. The driver wore sunglasses and had rust-colored hair and a thick mustache, but as Molly looked over, he lowered his face and pulled into the line of departing cars.

"What is it?" asked Tessie, trying to follow her gaze.

"Do you know who the man in that white car is?" said Molly, wondering why he hadn't gotten out and come over for the service. He seemed to match the description of Margaret Jellinek's visitor that last day.

"What man?"

"It doesn't matter," said Molly with a shrug. "He's gone now. Well, anyway. Thanks again for coming, Tessie."

"Listen, Molly, honey," said the little woman, lowering her voice and leading Molly away from the gravesite to the back of the tent. "Maggie gave me somethin' for you, somethin' she wanted you to have when she was gone."

Tess dug deep into her enormous handbag.

"She gave it to me that day she got sick, before the ambulance came. Maggie had it on a chain around her neck. She just pulled it right off. Broke the chain. Her head was hurtin' her something awful, but she knew what was happenin'. Kept talkin' 'bout how people was always gettin' robbed in hospitals and such places."

Tessie pulled her pudgy hand out of the handbag. She opened her fingers triumphantly beneath the shelter of her ample bosom to reveal a ring that took Molly's breath away: a large, deep green stone entwined in a thick golden band.

"It's beautiful," said Molly, stunned.

"I didn't want to take it, but Maggie made me," said Tessie, pressing the ring into Molly's hand. "You know how stubborn she could be. Said I could give it back if she got better, but if not, she wanted you to have it. Then the ambulance came and took her away."

Nell came over for a closer look, her curiosity apparently overcoming her reluctance to be in clutching range of Tessie.

Molly studied the ring. The thick band was crafted to look like the stem of a flower. It was deep yellow in color and surprisingly heavy for its size. The clear green stone was square-cut and perfectly faceted.

Molly's field was antiques, not jewelry. The ring looked expensive, but she was well aware that jewelry was a trap for the unwary. Things often were not what they appeared at first glance to be. Still, a bold, well-crafted piece like this had to be worth a few hundred dollars to somebody, Molly knew, even if it was just costume jewelry. If it was real . . . well, she couldn't even guess at a price. Her appraisal expertise was strictly limited to antiques.

Who could have given Margaret Jellinek such a thing? wondered Molly—she surely wouldn't have bought a ring like this for herself. Grandma just wasn't the sort of woman who was interested in flashy jewelry, even if she could have afforded it, which she couldn't. She had barely been able to buy herself a new toaster oven when the old one broke and had even shared a telephone with Tessie to save money. Other than a small savings account and the drab furniture from her apartment, there had been no assets for the nursing home to take before admitting her.

Molly turned the ring over and looked on the inside for lettering that said 14K or GOLD-FILLED or some other clue that could tell her something about it. What she found was a faint mark that seemed to read SC & P.

"I guess it's pretty valuable, huh?" said Tessie's faraway voice.

Molly snapped back to the present. She had forgotten for a moment where she was. Nell was staring at her with a quizzical look. Two cemetery workmen were standing by the open grave, waiting to get on with their business. The sky was gray. The rain had finally stopped.

"Did Grandma say where she got this ring?" asked Molly.

"No," said Tessie. "Just that she'd had it since before she got to Pelletreau. I figured maybe it was from a beau, but then of course, I'm just a hopeless romantic. Y'all don't have any idea?"

Molly shook her head.

"Maybe it was an heirloom. Something from her family. Did she ever talk about them?"

"Not really," said Molly, flustered. "Grandma didn't like to talk about the past. She said all her family were dead."

"Well, I'm just glad you have it now, honey," said Tessie, reaching over and patting Molly's hand. "That's the important thing, that's what Maggie wanted. I'm surely gonna miss her. Look, I better scat before I get all weepy again. You girls take care of yourselves, you hear?"

Tessie wrapped her arms around Molly and kissed her fervently on the cheek, as if she were kissing a precious child farewell.

Nell endured a hand squeeze. Then they watched their grand-mother's best friend scurry back to her big old Pontiac and drive slowly off.

"What do you think?" Molly said to Nell, holding up the ring, when Tessie was out of sight. "I know I shouldn't be thinking about money at a time like this, but I can't help myself. I've been a dealer too long, and this looks real to me. Then again, what do I know about jewelry?"

Nell didn't answer. She looked at the ring, then stared at the grave, her eyebrows scrunched together in thought.

"It's turning out that there was a lot about Grandma we didn't know," said Molly in a sober voice. "First she's this big Broadway actress. Now she has a ring on a chain around her neck that nobody's ever seen, but that she leaves to us as some kind of legacy. Do you leave your grandchildren a fancy-cut piece of glass?"

Nell didn't look up.

"I don't much feel like going home right away. Maybe we should show it to Oscar, what do you think?"

Nell didn't say what she thought. But she started walking toward their van.

eeee

When Oscar Winnick moved down from Detroit in 1961, he had been the only black jeweler in Pelletreau.

Molly knew that he had had some trouble at first. Older deal-ers had told her that Oscar's first store downtown was firebombed and that he had marched to Selma with Martin Luther King. Oscar himself would never talk about those days, however, and things had changed a lot since then, even in North Carolina.

Oscar now lived in a cheerful Victorian house in what used

to be an all-white suburb and helped out three mornings a week at the jewelry store in Pelletreau's most fashionable mall that his son had taken over from him. As far as Oscar was concerned, he was just another senior citizen, though there weren't many eighty-year-olds who taught themselves Greek all winter then spent the summer working eight hours a day in their vegetable gardens. Since his wife's death a few years ago, Oscar's garden had grown to the size of a small farm.

Molly had known Oscar since she was sixteen years old. She had bought a box lot of odds and ends at a country auction and had found a strand of pearls hidden inside a leather change purse. Molly couldn't wait to cash in on her good fortune, and Oscar had been the only jeweler open on a Sunday.

Her *pearls* had turned out to be plastic. Oscar had been nice about it, however, and had shown her how she could tell phonies herself by running them across her teeth. They had been friends ever since. Oscar still kept his hand in the jewelry game even in semiretirement. He still gave Molly a fair price for what she brought him and good advice whether she wanted it or not.

Molly found him digging up radishes in his backyard half an hour after she had laid Margaret Jellinek to rest. He knelt on a tarp against the still-wet ground; a little dampness never stopped Oscar.

"My condolences about your grandmother," he said in his precise baritone as she and Nell approached.

"How did you hear about that?" asked Molly, surprised.

"The obituaries. These days, they're about the only part of the paper where I can read about people I know."

"Thanks, Oscar. She was a nice lady. You would have liked her. I'm sorry you two never met."

"I'm sorry, too," said Oscar, brushing black soil from a clump of radishes and tossing them into a waiting bushel basket. "You and your sister look real pretty. Don't think I've ever seen you in dresses before."

Molly winced. She had always hated grown-up clothes.

"And you're not going to again anytime soon," she declared. "We just came from the cemetery. I have something I want you to look at."

"Wash your hands first. Nell, too. Come on. I'll take you inside."

Oscar took off his gloves and threw them in the basket with the radishes, then stood and headed for the back door.

"This is important, Oscar," protested Molly, following.

"So's washing your hands after you get back from the cemetery," said Oscar, holding the door for her and Nell. "Old Jewish custom."

"Funny, you don't look Jewish."

"In the jewelry business you meet a lot of Jewish people, and you come to respect what they have to say. At my age I'm practically a professional funeral-goer, and I can tell you for a fact that it's a good thing, psychologically speaking, to wash your hands of death. Sanitary, too. Bathroom's by the front stairs."

"I know where it is," said Molly, reaching into her pocket. "But you look at this in the meanwhile."

Molly placed the ring on the kitchen counter and followed Nell through the door to the hall.

When they returned, Oscar was squinting at the green stone through a loupe and shaking his head.

"Where did you get this, Molly?" he said, strangely sober and very businesslike.

"It was my grandmother's."

"I see."

"It's glass, right?" sighed Molly.

"Hardly. It's the best emerald I've ever seen."

"An emerald!"

"You'll have to give me a little time to raise the money if you want to sell it."

"What's it worth?"

"To me, about forty thousand dollars."

Molly opened her mouth, then closed it. Nell held a hand to her forehead and collapsed theatrically into a chair at the kitchen table. Oscar's mutt, a playful little hairball named Pythagoras, attempted to revive her by licking her hand.

"You're kidding, aren't you?" Molly finally managed.

"All right," smiled Oscar. "You drive a hard bargain. Forty-five. And that's my best offer. Interested?"

"I don't know," stammered Molly, glancing at Nell. "We have to think about it."

"Up to you," said Oscar, handing her back the ring. "You might be able to get more from a dealer in a bigger city."

"You know we wouldn't give it to anyone but you."

"Well, I appreciate that, because you know I intend to make a profit on you. A small one, of course. You did okay this time, kid."

Molly tried to smile. None of this made any sense.

When she had first come to Pelletreau, Margaret Jellinek had barely been able to feed herself and her daughter. Molly clearly remembered the horror stories of hunger and privation that her mother had told about her own childhood in order to get them to eat their vegetables. There must have been truth to some of those tales. Now it appeared that Margaret Jellinek had had a forty-five-thousand-dollar emerald ring on a chain around her neck all that time.

"Do you have any idea where this ring might have come from originally, Oscar?" Molly asked.

"There was an SC & P mark on the inside, pretty worn, but I could still make it out."

"Yes, I saw that. What does it mean?"

"It was the retailer's mark. Scanlon, Carrier and Polk, the Boston equivalent of Tiffany. They went out of business about thirty years ago."

"Boston, Massachusetts?"

"Of course, Boston, Massachusetts. You don't get stones like this and high-quality custom settings in Boston, Arkansas. That any help?"

"Not much," said Molly. "But thanks anyway, Oscar."

Molly didn't know anything about Margaret Jellinek's childhood except that she had grown up in New England. The fact that the ring had come from Boston seemed to connect it to her youth. Was it an heirloom? Had it been a present from a suitor? Unfortunately if the store had been out of business for three decades there would be no way to trace the original purchaser.

"Well, just give me some time if you decide you want to sell," said Oscar. "Like I say, I'll have to make some calls to raise that kind of money. You might put it somewhere safe in the meantime. It really is a beautiful stone."

Forty minutes later the beautiful green stone that hung like a fruit from a golden stem was in the safe-deposit box at Pelletreau Trust and Savings, alongside various family papers, the deed for their house, and the passports Molly kept ready for the Mexican vacation that she planned to take with Nell some day.

Molly hadn't said a word during the whole drive from Oscar's house—perhaps some kind of a record for her—though Nell didn't appear to have noticed.

Since their mother's death Molly's life had been an endless scramble for money. Yet even with twelve-hour days and seven-day weeks she was barely able to keep their heads above water. Plunging property values in Pelletreau had decimated Molly's equity in the house. Any cash she had left over after paying the bills went back into inventory, which seemed to move more and more slowly these days. Margaret Jellinek's funeral had all but wiped out their cash reserve.

Suddenly, however, Molly had a ring that she could sell for enough to turn everything around. A ring that was the only thing left of her grandmother. A ring Maggie Jellinek had apparently refused to part with, no matter what.

"You don't think she stole it, do you?" Molly asked in a quiet voice, finally putting into words what had been bothering her since Tessie had pressed the ring into her hand at the cemetery.

Nell raised an eyebrow and scrunched her lips into one of her famous don't-be-an-idiot looks.

"But it just doesn't make any sense!" Molly exclaimed, as she turned the van into the driveway of Enchanted Cottage Antiques. "Grandma was about as sentimental as an Otis elevator. I don't care whether that ring was a family heirloom or party favor from the Shah of Iran, you know she would have sold it in a minute to feed herself and Mom unless there was one hell of a good reason why she shouldn't. And if it was so important that she shouldn't sell it, how can we?"

Nell wasn't paying attention, however. She was staring out the window at a white Mercury Sable that had turned down Porcupine Road behind them and now continued on, down the road in front of the store.

Molly caught only a glimpse of the man behind the wheel as the car sped away. He was wearing sunglasses. A red-haired man with a bushy mustache.

"There it is again!" exclaimed Molly, glancing out the front window. "A white Mercury Sable."

Nell was sitting by the cash register, brushing epoxy onto the two halves of the broken foot of a nineteenth-century ironstone creamer. She didn't look up from her delicate work.

"Either they've got a white Mercury Sable convention around here somewhere," said Molly, "or I've been seeing the same car all week. I just wish the road weren't so far away so I could see who's doing the driving. Do you think it's that same man with the red hair and the mustache?"

Molly instantly regretted her words. She hadn't meant to say so much. There was no point in troubling Nell with her irrational worries. Not Nell, of all people.

"Of course, it is a pretty common car. It's probably not him at all. I'll bet you think I'm nuts, don't you?"

This time Nell did look up—and nodded enthusiastically.

Molly and her sister hadn't been out of the shop for several days now, trying to adjust to a world without their grandmother in it, living on the peach cobblers, country hams, and tuna-noodle casseroles that Margaret Jellinek's friends had thoughtfully dropped off.

Summertime was tourist time, and there was enough traffic heading toward Charlottesville on U.S. 29 to assure a small but steady stream of customers into Enchanted Cottage Antiques. A few people had actually bought things, mostly ten-dollar odds and ends, but Molly had also sold an American Empire mahogany chest of drawers with a heart inlay on the black splash. It had been in the shop for years and Molly had despaired that anyone would ever take it off her hands. Miraculously a Yuppie couple had left a four-hundred-dollar cash deposit on it yesterday and promised to return with the four-hundred-dollar balance when they picked it up tomorrow or the next day on their way back to Atlanta.

Despite the prospect of being a little ahead for a change, Molly had been having a hard time keeping her mind on business. Margaret Jellinek's emerald ring kept burning a hole in her pocket. What they could do with forty-five thousand dollars! But how could they sell something like that without knowing why Grandma had held on to it all these years?

The ring wasn't the only thing that was troubling Molly. She was also worried about the way they had found their grandmother at the nursing home. The picture of Margaret Jellinek in her bed, her pillow on her chest, kept flashing in Molly's brain like a neon question mark.

Why, Molly wondered, if Grandma were having another stroke, would she have taken her pillow out from beneath her head and placed it on her chest? It made no sense. Throw it on the floor, yes, but would she have had the strength to do even that if she were dying? Certainly no nurse would have put a pillow on a patient's chest. If anything, a nurse would have plumped the pillow up and put it where it belonged.

So, why had Grandma's pillow been on her chest?

Of course, dying people did inexplicable things, Molly knew. Maybe Grandma had just wanted to lie flat. Maybe she had gotten the pillow out from under her head and rested it on her chest until she could decide what to do with it. That made sense.

But the image of Margaret Jellinek, cold and dead, with the pillow on her chest wouldn't go away. Molly couldn't stop thinking about it.

Other pictures kept springing into Molly's head, too, ones that were alive, almost like a little movie. Hands taking the pillow out from behind Margaret Jellinek's head and forcing it down over her face. A brief moment of struggle, then stillness. The hands discarding the pillow, its work done, and leaving it where it falls, there on Margaret Jellinek's chest.

Who would do such a thing?

There was only one candidate. The man who had been with her right before she died. The redheaded stranger with the bushy mustache—the man who may have shown up again at the cemetery driving a Mercury Sable and who might have driven by the house a dozen times over the last few days. Had he somehow found out about the emerald ring worth forty-five thousand dollars that was supposed to be on a chain around Margaret Jellinek's neck? People had been murdered for much less; nothing at all had been taken from Molly's mother by her killer. Except her life.

"I can't believe I'm being so paranoid," muttered Molly to herself, glancing out the window again. The road was empty. The afternoon heat rose off the pavement in waves, making the trees across the street shimmer like a mirage.

"Where's that program you found?" Molly asked, walking over to her sister. "The one with Grandma's picture?"

Nell nodded toward the counter. She had finished her repair and was bracing the creamer with pieces of Styrofoam so it could dry. Her hands were sure and steady.

Molly reached under the counter for the "Playbill," wishing she had her sister's patience, and stared at the picture of the young Margaret Jellinek on the cover.

"I've got to do something to get my mind off Mercury Sables," she announced. "I need a project, something to do with my idle little brain, or I'm going to crack up. What do you say we find out about Grandma? About the ring, maybe, and about her being on the stage?"

Nell rolled her eyes. She'd been down this road with Molly's projects before. Once they had spent an entire day mixing snails, quicklime, and Gruyère cheese to test out a glass-mending recipe that Molly had found in an old book. Another time Molly had dragged Nell off in the middle of lunch and driven all the way to Lancaster, Pennsylvania, just to learn more about the Amish name, Zook, which she had found impressed on a spoon.

"You know who might know something? Clyde, that's who. I'm going to call him."

Calling Clyde was just the sort of mad, impulsive thing that would make her feel better, more in control. Nell, however, scrambled off her chair and intercepted Molly before she could pick up the receiver. She shook her head furiously.

"It's okay," said Molly. "He can't do anything to hurt us anymore."

Nell shook her head again and clenched her fingers around Molly's hand. Molly had to pry them off.

"Will you cut it out? You're just being silly. There's nothing to be afraid of. I can handle Clyde, I promise. You want to find out about Grandma, don't you?"

Nell stared at Molly for a few more seconds, then returned to her chair. The fear was still evident in Nell's face, mixed with unconcealed anger at Molly, who paid it no mind. Sometimes you just had to act, and this was one of those times. She looked up Clyde's work number in the phone book and dialed.

"Pelletreau Fuel and Lumber," answered a voice on the seventh ring.

"Clyde Cole, please," said Molly. Did he still work there? Was he even still alive? She hadn't spoken with Clyde for years.

"Who wants him?"

"His stepdaughter. Molly O'Hara."

A few minutes later a gruff, too-familiar voice came on the line.

"Well, if it ain't little miss antique dealer. To what do I owe this honor?"

The palm of Molly's hand was suddenly damp against the telephone receiver. She fought down a wave of disgust. Maybe this hadn't been such a great idea, after all.

"Hello, Clyde. How have you been?"

"What's it to you?"

"I'm just being polite," she said.

"Save it. What do you want?"

Clyde had been the main suspect that terrible Saturday afternoon seventeen years ago. Molly had come home from the movies and had found her mother sprawled on their living room floor, a thirty-eight-caliber hole in the center of her forehead.

Clyde's alibi was unshakable, however: he had been at Cousin Hecker's American Tarheel Bar and Grill, drinking with the boys. Six drunkards and Cousin Hecker himself had sworn to it. So had a pair of off-duty cops who had gone to the bar to watch a baseball game on TV.

Hearing the perpetual sneer in his voice, Molly once again felt the same revulsion and helplessness she had experienced as a child. When she asked him to turn down the television so she could study, he would laugh and order her to fetch him another beer or just blow cigarette smoke in her face. If she ever expressed excitement over anything, he would make fun of her and call her names.

Clyde had been the girl's legal guardian after their mother's death. Until Nell turned sixteen and Molly was able to get them their own place he had insisted on "raising" them himself. That he hadn't any talent or feeling for the job didn't matter—all he knew was that Molly and Nell were his property.

"Grandma died," she said simply.

"Yeah, I heard. Can't say I'm really sorry. She was always a mean old bat. You gonna tell me what you want?"

"I wanted to ask you some questions about her," said Molly, ignoring the insult.

"About the old lady? What would I know?"

"Did she ever say anything to you about her career on the stage?"

"Her what?"

"Her stage career," said Molly. "She was a big Broadway actress."

"Yeah, right," snickered Clyde. "What are you, nuts?"

"No, really. Did she ever—"

"Come on," barked the cruel voice. "That worthless old lady never did nothin' in her whole life. I'm in the middle of a job here, for Crissakes. Anything else you want to know?"

"No, that's all," whispered Molly.

The line went dead.

Molly slowly placed the phone back in the cradle. Nell shot her a look that at the same time said both, "I told you so" and "what now?"

Molly knew that she deserved the I told you so, and she already had an answer to the what now?

"We're going to see Daddy," she said simply.

— ᥫ᭡ ᥫ᭡ ᥫ᭡ ᥫ᭡ —

Molly's mother had thrown Tim O'Hara out of the house shortly before Nell's fourth birthday. A month after the divorce became final he had married a woman whose family owned a candy company in the Moorehaven suburb on the east side of Pelletreau.

Molly had not seen her father since then, but she knew where he lived. Moorehaven was the wealthiest part of town, and Molly often came here to yard and garage sales—rich people were the ones most likely to be selling quality things, and surprisingly often they didn't understand the value of what they had. Molly had made it a point to find his big white house on Daisy Hill Lane long ago. She and Nell had driven past many times, but had never had the courage to knock on the door.

Today was different.

Even Nell, normally so shy, didn't hesitate to get out after Molly drove up the long driveway and parked the van in front of the big, beautiful house.

Molly straightened her clothes. Nell reached into her pocket for a comb, which she ran nonchalantly through her hair, as if she did so on a regular basis. They looked briefly at each other and shared a pair of nervous smiles. Then Molly knocked three times on the frame of the screen door at the same time that Nell pressed the bell.

After a moment a woman came out.

She was about Nell's height, an attractive brunette with full lips and an athletic figure. She wore spotless tennis whites and two-hundred-dollar running shoes. Her wristwatch was a gold Rolex.

"Yes?" she asked with a smile perfect enough to persuade people to change their brand of toothpaste to hers.

"Hi," said Molly. "I'm Molly O'Hara. This is my sister, Nell. We'd like to speak with our father, please."

The woman stepped back as if hit in the face. Her smile never wavered, however. It seemed actually to grow even wider if that were possible. And whiter.

"Certainly," she said after a moment, barely moving her lips. "I'll tell him you're here."

The woman went back inside. After a moment Molly could hear raised voices, sounds of a man and woman arguing. After another moment a man came out and closed the front door behind him.

He looked almost exactly as he did in her memories and in the snapshots of a smiling teenager that Molly had found in a shoebox after Evangeline O'Hara Cole had been murdered: a thin man, about five feet ten inches tall, with a weak chin and a scraggly mustache. He was dressed in khaki pants, a yellow polo shirt, and brown loafers without socks. He didn't look exactly thrilled to see them.

"Hi," he said in a cautious tenor, his eyes darting from Molly to Nell. Then he glanced over his shoulder back at the house. "I'm Tim O'Hara."

"I'm Molly. This is Nell."

"Yeah, my wife told me. You're Angie's girls."

"That's right," said Molly softly, too proud to point out the fact that he had had something to do with their existence as well.

"So what can I do for you?" he said, trying to find a suitable place to park his hands. He tried several combinations of under his armpits and behind his neck before settling for the pockets of his pants. "I'm sorry I can't invite you in, but Susan is just making dinner now. That's my wife. Susan."

"Of course," said Molly, struggling to contain her disappointment. "I understand."

Making dinner—what a great excuse not to invite in your daughters whom you haven't seen in over twenty years. Nell just stared wide-eyed at Tim O'Hara, her expression a blend of uncertainty and startled recognition.

"Look," said Molly, coming to her sister's rescue, "we don't want to take up too much of your time. There are just a few things I thought you might be able to help us clear up about Grandma. You know she died."

Tim O'Hara stared back blankly.

"Margaret Jellinek," said Molly. "Our grandmother. She died last week."

"Oh, Maggie," he said, looking almost relieved. "Yeah, right. Dead, huh? Sorry about that. My condolences."

"There are some things we don't understand, and we thought you might remember."

"Well, I was sort of persona non grata with Maggie," he said. "She was pretty pissed when Angie and I eloped. I don't know that I can tell you much."

"Did you know that she was once an actress?"

"Yeah? I never heard anything about that."

"Do you know where Grandma lived or what she might have been doing before she came to Pelletreau?"

"No," answered O'Hara. "You really would do better asking somebody else."

"What about Grandma's marriage?" asked Molly in a measured drawl. "Did she ever talk about that?"

O'Hara broke into a strange, unpleasant chuckle.

"Oh, sure," he said. "That was the whole problem. Between Maggie and me, I mean. Maggie ran off with a guy her family didn't approve of when she was a teenager, see? Dick Jellinek was his name. Richard Jellinek. He walked out on Maggie when Angie was just a baby. Deserted them."

"I never knew that," said Molly, surprised.

To her Richard Jellinek had always been just "Bride's Father" on the yellowing copy of Angie O'Hara's marriage license that Molly kept in the safe-deposit box. Grandma had never even mentioned her ex-husband's name, let alone that she had fallen out with her family because of him or that he had deserted her. At last they were finally getting somewhere.

"That was why Maggie was so furious when Angie and I eloped, I guess," O'Hara went on. "The old lady had wrecked her life by running off with a man, and she thought that Angie was going to do the same with me."

Obviously Grandma had been right.

Tim O'Hara smiled guiltily, like a taxpayer who had just admitted too much to an IRS agent. Molly glanced over at Nell, who seemed confused and uncomfortable. She alternated staring at the ground and stealing peeks at her father, as if she expected he might suddenly give her a hug or break into song the way he used to when they were little.

"Did you ever hear anything about Grandma's family?" Molly asked, trying not to let her feelings show on her face.

"Well, they were rich, I know," said O'Hara.

"Excuse me?" said Molly.

"Yeah, the old lady got a little tipsy one night right after Angie and I got married, and let slip her folks were loaded. She claimed they owned a castle or something."

Molly couldn't speak for a moment. The notion that her grandmother had grown up wealthy was like hearing that an umbrella had once been a rose.

"Why didn't she go to them when her marriage broke up?" she said finally.

"Yeah, that's what Angie wanted to know," said O'Hara. "But the old lady wouldn't say. She was too proud, I guess. Too stubborn."

Molly shook her head with disbelief. Had Grandma really lived in a castle? She had always told Molly that all of her family was dead. Were there still relatives somewhere, wondering where she was? Molly looked over at Nell, but couldn't catch her eye.

"The more Angie thought about it, the angrier she got," continued Tim O'Hara. " 'You mean, I could have grown up rich in a castle instead of dirt poor in Pelletreau?' she hollered at Maggie once. 'You wouldn't have been happy, believe me,' Maggie yelled back. Angie barely spoke to the old lady for a year after that, she was so pissed."

"Poor mom," said Molly softly.

"Yeah," said O'Hara sympathetically—or was it pity? "It would have been just as well if she had never written to them."

"Mom wrote to Grandma's family?" asked Molly, amazed. "How did she find out who they were, where they lived?"

"Right before we split up Angie was over at her mother's and found an insurance policy in some old book," answered O'Hara. "It listed Maggie's father as next of kin: Mr. Something-or-other Gale and his address. So Angie wrote him a letter and poured her heart out."

"Gale," repeated Molly, turning the unfamiliar name over in her mind. "You can't remember his first name?"

O'Hara shook his head.

"Hey, this was a long time ago."

"Where did they live?"

Tim O'Hara waved a manicured hand, and smiled his lopsided smile.

"The address was up North somewhere. New England, I

think. I never knew exactly. All I remember is that their name was Gale."

Molly looked over at Nell. Her sister was staring at the ground, her face without expression. Hadn't she understood a word that Tim O'Hara had said? Their mother had reached back and touched the past, had connected with Grandma's parents, the family that none of them had ever known existed—the Gales!

Tim O'Hara glanced again at his watch, not noticing the tears that had welled up inexplicably in Molly's eyes.

"What happened then?" she asked.

"Nothing," said O'Hara with a shrug. "Maggie's father never answered. Your mom wrote a few more times. Never heard from anyone."

He looked over his shoulder at the closed front door of the beautiful house and shifted his weight from side to side.

"So. Is there anything else I can help you with or is that about it?"

"That's about it," murmured Molly. "Oh, one last thing. Do you know if Grandma had any good jewelry? We've been looking around but haven't found anything."

"Fat chance," he said with a laugh. "Rich parents or not, Maggie didn't have diddly-squat. Why would you think she had any jewelry?"

"Oh, it's just that most women have a little jewelry. It doesn't matter."

"I'm sorry I can't invite the two of you in for dinner," said O'Hara. "We just . . . well, we weren't expecting company."

"Oh, we have to run anyway," said Molly with an artificial smile. "But thanks. You've been a lot of help."

"If you'd like some candy, I've got a few boxes of samples in the front closet that I can let you have."

"No, that's okay."

"Okay, then," he said, extending his hand. "Thanks for stopping by."

Molly awkwardly shook his hand. When he offered it to Nell, she turned and ran back to the van. Tim O'Hara grinned weakly, opened the door and scuttled back into his big white house.

Molly walked slowly back to the van. Nell was already sitting there in the passenger seat, her chin propped up between her hands. Her eyes were wet with tears.

"Oh, Nellie," said Molly reaching over to try to comfort her. "Don't do that. He's just an idiot."

Nell pushed Molly's hand away again and sobbed soundlessly.

"Some family, we've got, huh?" said Molly, starting the engine. "Daddy's a jerk. Clyde's a Neanderthal. Our long-lost grandfather, Richard Jellinek, was a rat, and our rich Yankee relatives, the Gales, were so mean that they wouldn't even answer Mom's letters."

Nell slumped in the seat and rubbed her eyes, but didn't look over.

"You know," said Molly, "the more I think about this, the madder I'm getting. Why couldn't Grandma just go back home after her marriage broke up and give Mom a chance to have a life? Would it really have been so hard to admit she made a mistake? We didn't know her at all, Nell. Not at all."

The van began making the grinding noises it did when it was unhappy. Molly slowed down. Nell wiped her eyes, slumped in her seat and stared out unhappily at the wealthy suburb's big landscaped houses. They drove for a minute in silence, then Molly started talking again, as if she had never left off.

"The Gales must have loved Grandma once," she declared. "She was their daughter, after all. And they were rich, so they were probably the ones who gave her the ring. Maybe Grandma still has brothers and sisters or nieces and nephews who would want to know what happened to her. To Mom. To us even, if they knew we were alive."

Nell looked over at Molly for the first time, her questioning eyes reflecting a lifetime of pain and hurt and helplessness.

"It would be nice to have a real family, wouldn't it?" said Molly.

Nell's upper lip trembled. She reached over and touched Molly on the arm.

"I'm getting an idea," said Molly with a familiar look in her eye.

Nell pulled back her hand. The last time Molly had had that look in her eye they had wound up driving a hundred miles to buy a player piano from a lady in a shopping mall.

"Oh, come on, don't be a such a chicken," said Molly. "You know it makes sense. There must be some Gales left up in New England somewhere, and there's no reason why we can't find them. Grandma was a big Broadway actress. There must still be records that can tell us where she came from originally. All we have to do is get to New York and do a little research."

Nell looked heavenward.

"Come on, Nellie. Don't you want to know about the Gales? Don't you want to know about Grandma's big stage career?"

Nell shook her head an emphatic no.

"Don't you want to find out about the ring?"

Nell shook her head again.

"Can you really walk away from our last chance at having someone else in the world who cares whether we live or die?"

Nell frowned.

"Then it's settled," said Molly. "I knew you'd see the light."

Nell pointed at Molly. Then she mimed holding the wheel of a car. Then she pointed her finger at her chest, and then at her temple and turned it slowly. You. Drive. Me. Crazy.

"I love you, too," declared Molly happily. "We'll just follow Grandma's footsteps back to New England and present the Gales with two brand-new relatives. It may be fifty years too late, but maybe, just maybe, we'll end up with the family that Mom always wanted. At the very least I'll bet they'll invite us in for a cup of coffee!"

e e e e

"Hello?" Molly announced, pushing open the screen door of Taffy Hupperman's house. "It's us."

Taffy's living room looked as if it hadn't been cleaned since Molly's last visit, two months ago. Dust bunnies the size of Chihuahuas roamed the hardwood floors, occasionally colliding with abandoned articles of footwear. The furniture was draped with dirty laundry of all description. Every surface displayed Taffy's collection of used Chinese takeout cartons, which in quantity rivaled Molly's collection of oyster plates.

"Taffy? Are you home? Why do you leave this door open? There's a serial killer on every block these days, don't you watch television? Taffy?"

"Does someone call?" boomed Taffy, emerging from the kitchen waving a turkey leg like a magic wand. "Why, can it be the young O'Hara girl? By God, yes! Accompanied by her factotum and sibling, Little Nell, she of the smiling Irish eyes and bosom as white as the driven snow."

Taffy was a little bit taller than Nell and several times as wide. She had dead-mouse blond hair, tiny teeth, and a face that would be pretty if she lost a hundred pounds. She wore Farmer-Brown coveralls that totally obscured her figure while doing nothing to conceal her girth.

"Why don't you lock your door?" said Molly, hands on her hips.

"Oh, shut up, you little pork chop," said Taffy, brushing past Molly and draping a fat arm around Nell's shoulder. "I want to say hello to my friend, Nell. How are you, honey? You been a good girl? I haven't seen you in a dog's age. Come over here, there's someone I want you to meet."

If sound had come from Nell's mouth it would have been a giggle, judging by her expression. Molly rolled her eyes and wished again that she had someone other than Taffy who she could come to at times like this. A visit with Taffy was like Alice's trip down the rabbit hole. Or a production conference with some over-the-top movie queen from the heyday of Hollywood. Taffy turned to the kitchen door.

"Oomba-lapa-tu!" she yelled, waving her turkey leg. "Oomba-lapa-tu, queen of the jungle! Get your royal ass in here this instant. I want you to meet my oldest friends in the world."

A moment later a young woman of about Molly's age and height entered the room. She had a strong, pointed chin, short hair, and was dressed in neatly pressed red slacks and a patterned top. She was built like a stop sign and looked more like a bank teller than a jungle queen.

"Oh, great Oomba-lapa-tu," extolled Taffy with much exaggerated bowing and scraping, "may I present the short but difficult Molly O'Hara and her enchanting sister, Nell."

Oomba-lapa-tu strode briskly over and shook Molly's hand. She had a grip like a clamp.

"My name isn't really Oomba-lapa-tu," she announced in a brisk, businesslike soprano. "It's Alice Markham. Taffy just thinks that Alice is too plain a moniker for the likes of me. Hence the Oomba-lapa-tu routine. Pleased to meet you."

Then she shook Nell's hand, repeating her greeting exactly.

"Show plain old Alice here how you can fly, honey," said Taffy to Nell. "You can still do it, can't you?"

"Leave her alone, Taffy," protested Molly, seething with determination and resolve after her meeting with Tim O'Hara. "We're here for a reason and don't have time to waste. I need a favor."

"Oh, hush up, runt," said Taffy, pushing Molly out of the way as if she were some insolent extra on the back lot. "Come on, Nell. Show Alice your trick."

Molly opened her mouth to protest, but held her tongue. It was usually better just to let Taffy talk herself out than try to fight. Nell grinned and cocked her eye at the high ceiling to make sure she had enough room. Then she centered herself on the hardwood floor, kicking away an empty plastic cup.

The room fell silent in anticipation. Nell bent her knees, swung her arms out in front of her twice and jumped up into the air. In the next split second she curled into a ball, flipped over neatly, and landed squarely on her feet in the exact place she had launched from.

Taffy clapped her hands in delight.

"Very impressive demonstration," declared Alice heartily, rushing over and shaking Nell's hand again. "Thank you, Nell, was it? I greatly enjoy gymnastics. Do you train professionally?"

"She's a natural, been flipping all her life," said Taffy, putting her arm around Nell, who beamed. Nell actually liked Taffy, for some reason that Molly had never understood.

"Taffy . . ." began Molly again, but Taffy paid no attention.

"You want to learn some new words, Nell, honey?" she said. "See, Alice, Nell doesn't feel much like talking these days, do you sweet 'ums? But I still try to teach her useful words in case she ever changes her mind. Say 'mousse au chocolate,' honey. Say 'periodontist.' Say 'lesbian.' "

"Taffy . . ."

"Lezzzzzzzzzbian," repeated Taffy, buzzing like a bee. "Isn't that a fascinating word, lezzzzzzzzzzzzbian? Now show us how to juggle."

Taffy picked up a paperback science fiction novel and a balled-up sock from the floor and tossed them to Nell along with the turkey leg.

"Taffy!" said Molly.

"She doesn't mind, do you Nell?"

Nell obviously didn't. She juggled the items happily until Molly marched over and batted them out of the air.

"Okay, Taffy, you've demonstrated dominance. We all bend down and kiss your feet. Now I need a favor."

"A favor, she needs," said Taffy, throwing a hand theatrically into the air. "I don't see her for months, but when she needs a favor, who does she come to? She comes to saintly Taffy Hupperman, that's who, the Ford Foundation of unemployed scientists. All right, shrimpboat, what'll it be? And don't ask for money. 'cause I don't have any."

"Well, you will soon," said Molly. "I'll pay you seven dollars an hour, off the books, if you go over and mind the shop for a few days. Nell and I have to go out of town."

"Big money."

"It's more than you're making now."

"And when do you expect me to begin this odious tour of duty, if I may be so bold as to inquire?"

"Tomorrow. You can stay at our place tonight, if you like, so you won't have to schlep over in the morning."

"Forget it!" exclaimed Taffy, sticking her nose into the air and giving a symbolic sniff. "Oomba-lapa-tu and I have important things to do."

"Like what? You're never doing anything when I come over here, except maybe eating. Why aren't you calling labs or working on your résumé? You've been out of work since February. Your unemployment can't last much longer."

"I am closely monitoring several important soap operas," sniffed Taffy, "and the jungle queen's presence is required each and every day at Daddy's odious insurance agency. We are otherwise engaged."

Molly looked at Taffy's great hulk of a figure, trying to see the wide-eyed little girl who had lived next door when they were eight, the girl who had been with Molly at the movies the day Evangeline O'Hara Cole had been murdered. Though her body had enlarged beyond recognition and she was now entitled to be called "Doctor" by virtue of a PhD in chemistry from the University of North Carolina, Taffy's manner was just the same. She still had to be courted and wooed, like a pussycat up a tree, to do the smallest thing. No wonder she couldn't keep a job.

"There's a little television at the shop that you can watch at the register," said Molly. "And your father still handles our insurance, so the shop will be of great professional interest to Oompa-Poompa-choo."

"Oomba-lapa-tu," corrected Taffy. "From the Sanskrit, meaning, 'she who clips the crusts from her Wonder Bread and knows how to Mambo.'"

"Come on, Taffy," cajoled Molly. "You can raid the refrigerator. We've got three pies, homemade by little old ladies, that you're welcome to. There's a whole cooked ham. Don't you want to spend some quality time with Alice in a place that isn't a pigsty?"

"Are you insinuating that I am a less-than-adequate housekeeper?"

"Yes!"

"Well, I can't argue with that," muttered Taffy. "Why can't you just close up, if it's just for a few days?"

"Because I have people coming with cash money to collect an expensive chest of drawers, that's why."

"Then wait a day to leave. Can't you wait a day?"

"No, I can't, you lazy bum," said Molly. "Everybody is always waiting a day and then another day, because there's always something else to grab your energy if you let it. And then the urge passes and you never do what you wanted to do, and you never have a life."

"Oh, I get it now," said Taffy, nodding smugly. "This is one of your little spur-of-the-moment adventures. When did you decide to make this trip? Ten minutes ago? I swear, Molly, you are so immature. Why don't you just go home, take a nice bath and eat a few pints of ice cream? Tomorrow whatever this is won't seem so important."

"I know that, which is why we are going tonight. Will you do it, Taffy? Please?"

"Oh, all right," said Taffy with a deep, tortured sigh. "Just one more station, I suppose, on the road to my personal cross."

"Thank you. Now you can take us to the bus station."

"The bus? Why aren't you driving?"

"Because the van is ten years old and has been making noises louder than your stomach. I'm not taking the chance."

"Good, then you can leave it with me. My own vehicle is otherwise indisposed."

"You mean repossessed?"

"Whatever," said Taffy. "I don't know why I put up with you."

"Ditto," agreed Molly.

"You're really an impossible girl."

"Likewise, I'm sure."

Half an hour later they were at the old-fashioned brick bus

station in decaying downtown Pelletreau. Through the chainlink fence by the squat building, Molly could see the lineup of shiny buses that were still the cheapest way to get out of town.

It was a little past seven. Molly had called and found a bus leaving within the hour that would get them into New York City by morning. Molly was uncomfortable about being away during peak tourist season, but at least Taffy would be minding the store. With any luck she wouldn't scare away too many sales.

"You take care of this van, you hear me, Taffy?" said Molly as she got out carrying their trusty "escape" suitcase, packed with essentials for both of them. It hadn't seen action since an auction in Tennessee last fall. "Let her rest for a while when she starts making noises. And drive carefully."

"Oh, relax, you ridiculous creature," said Taffy taking over the driver's seat and, adjusting the rearview mirror so she could admire her greasy curls. "Taffy knows how to make an engine purr, doesn't she, Alice?"

"You know which one is the house key?"

"Yes, yes, yes."

"The Nicholsons are the people coming for the chest," said Molly. "Be sure you get four hundred dollars cash, that was the deal. You shouldn't have any trouble, though. They were nice folks, and I've already got another four hundred dollars of their money, so they can't get away."

"Don't worry," said Taffy with a yawn. "It's not like I haven't ever done this before."

"I'll call you at the shop when I know when we're coming back so you can pick us up," said Molly. "We shouldn't be too long. Not at New York prices."

"Okay, okay," said Taffy. "Anything else, oh, great half-pint pain-in-the-ass?"

"Let me know if you happen to notice a red-haired guy with a bushy mustache hanging around."

"Who is he?"

"I'm not sure, but I'd like to find out. He's driving a white Mercury Sable."

Taffy rolled her eyes.

"Women," she muttered.

"Very pleased to have made your acquaintances," declared Alice Markham, aka Oomba-lapa-tu from the van's passenger seat, tapping two fingers to her eyebrow in some kind of insurance-agent salute. Taffy waved a fat hand at Nell and demonstrated how she made engines purr by screeching away from the curb in a cloud of burned rubber.

Nell waved happily until the van rounded the corner and sped out of sight. Molly was pleased to see her sister so carefree for a change, though she herself suddenly wasn't so confident anymore.

"We're doing the right thing here, aren't we, Nell?" Molly said, almost whispering, her mind suddenly flooded with second thoughts.

Nell nodded her head and smiled brightly. Whatever doubts she had had were obviously long gone. Why shouldn't she be eager to get away after all that had happened over the last week?

Molly bit her lip. When she left Tim O'Hara she had felt so certain about going to New York and tracking down Grandma's past. Now she just felt foolish and unprepared.

"I mean, maybe Taffy was making sense for a change," Molly said. "I do get crazy and impulsive sometimes, and we end up spending a lot of money we don't have. I don't know how much we can really find out in New York about what Grandma was doing half a century ago. And even if we do ever find the Gales, they might not want to see us. Or they might all be dead. I must be crazy."

Nell reached over and gently took Molly's hand in hers. Her palm was soft and warm, her touch gentle.

"Taffy was right," said Molly unhappily. "If I had any brains I'd just go home, have a bath, and eat a few pints of ice cream."

With her other hand Nell picked up their suitcase. Then she turned toward the bus terminal and tugged Molly's hand.

An image of Margaret Jellinek, dead in the nursing home with a pillow on her chest sprang again into Molly's mind. A second image superimposed itself, the nightmare image of her mother with the little hole in her forehead that had haunted Molly since she was eleven. Two wasted lives. What would Molly and Nell make of theirs?

Nell gave another tug on Molly's hand. Molly felt her doubts drop away. She let Nell pull her off to finish what she'd started.

No matter where the road might take them, it began in New York.

Four

"Will you come out of there, please?" said Molly to the closet. "I know you can see me through the keyhole, Nell. Come on."

The door finally opened. Nell was seated cross-legged on the floor of the tiny closet. She grinned and pulled herself up by the door handle. Nell still liked to hide in closets and see the world through the keyholes—especially when she was in unfamiliar places. The Gotham Arms Hotel in New York City was about as unfamiliar as places got.

Molly returned to the bathroom and finished drying her face with the thin hotel towel. The room they had taken was tiny and ridiculously expensive, but at least it was comparatively clean.

When they had left Pelletreau last night, Molly had actually thought about trying to pack all they needed to do in New York into one day, thereby saving the money they would need to spend on a hotel room. Fourteen hours of trying to sleep in a reclining seat on a speeding bus, however, had cured her of that fantasy.

One or two nights in a hotel wasn't going to bankrupt them. Whether they could dig out fifty-year-old stories from a city that could hide all of Pelletreau in a vest pocket was another matter.

A gray sliver of Big Apple loomed menacingly outside the room's sealed window.

Over the years Molly had heard about New York from dealers who came up to the big antique shows at the passenger piers. She had even bought a guidebook at the bus station last night and read it from cover to cover. A city was a city, she had told herself, having been to Charlotte—which was quite a big and sophisticated place— Richmond, and Washington, D.C.

Looking out the bus window this morning as New York had grown like Oz out of the dawn, however, Molly knew she had been wrong. The traffic-filled elevated highways that climbed toward the gleaming towers of Manhattan were like tiny trails of ants approaching a steel forest. Even from a distance New York was bigger, faster, and louder than any place Molly had ever seen. Up close it was positively frightening.

Just the five-block walk this morning from the Port Authority bus terminal to Forty-seventh Street where they had found the hotel had been intimidating.

The morning sidewalks had been thick with weary prostitutes and streetwise kids, bicycle messengers and dog walkers, secretaries in summer dresses and grim-faced men in business suits—everyone revved up to triple speed. Panhandlers swarmed on every street corner, shaking paper cups full of change like rhythm instruments. Wild-eyed tourists, half of them speaking foreign languages, pointed out mounted policemen and porno theaters to one another and recorded the whole erratic scene with video cameras.

It had been a relief for Molly when she and Nell had finally escaped into the relative calm of the Gotham Arms. Nell hadn't seemed to share Molly's discomfort. Bright and confident, she had gawked at the gritty skyscrapers and laughed soundlessly as she nimbly dodged the dump trucks, taxicabs, and city buses that vied for dominance in complicated pollution and noise competitions.

"Don't you want to sprinkle some water on your face?" said Molly, glancing at her watch, which miraculously was working. "And change that blouse, it looks like you slept in it. Which you have."

It was nearly eleven. There was no point in hanging around the hotel. Somewhere in New York there had to be records of Broadway performers and Molly was determined to find them. The sooner they got started, the sooner they could get back to Pelletreau.

While Nell washed up and changed her clothes, Molly checked the thick phone books in the night table for the names of the other cast members from the *Without Reservations* program on the off-chance that at least one of them might still be around. None of them had listings, however. Nor was there a listing for her grandfather, Richard Jellinek—not surprising after all these years.

Ten minutes later Molly and Nell were downstairs in the lobby—as bright, bustling, and full of polished brass and marble as their room was dull and threadbare.

"How do we get to the Booth Theatre?" Molly asked a harried-looking desk clerk. The Booth was the theater where Margaret Jellinek had starred in *Without Reservations,* so many years ago. If it still existed, the Booth was the logical place for Molly to begin tracing her grandmother's footsteps back in time.

"Forty-fifth Street," replied the clerk without looking up. "Turn right when you get out the door, then right again down Broadway."

Molly thanked him, though he didn't seem to hear, and walked with Nell out of the air-conditioned lobby onto the crowded street. It was like walking into a wall of wet flannel. No wonder the hotel had vacancies in July—it was almost as hot and humid here as it was in North Carolina and there was not a tree in sight to provide any shade.

At least New York didn't look so gray from street level, Molly consoled herself, as they made their way to the corner and into the colorful madness that was Times Square. The blazing morning sun sharpened everything to crystal clarity: the electronic billboards and turn-of-the-century buildings; the neon lights; the seething, honking traffic, and, of course, the people.

Molly had never seen so many people, thousands of them. Young and old. Beautiful and hideous. Black, white, and every shade in between, all animated with unknowable cares and hopes, plans and worries. It was a strain just to walk down the street, through so many unfamiliar faces. She instinctively drew close to her sister to protect her, but Nell didn't seem to need help. Her eyes burned with excitement, her head eagerly darted back and forth to take in the overload of sights. It was Nell who turned onto Forty-fifth Street and led a disoriented Molly to the box office of the Booth.

The turreted theater sat catty-corner on the walkway known as Shubert Alley in the shadow of a behemoth hotel across the street. Its marquee was filled with the names of actors Molly didn't recognize. Nor had she heard of the show, though it was obviously a hit. A line of people snaked out of the theater and onto the sidewalk.

"I guess we'll have to wait," said Molly, surveying the scene and making a quick decision not to barge right up to the ticket window. Not only did she have good manners, but most of the people in line had hard New York faces that promised significant bodily harm to anyone who tried to cut in. Their Yankee-accented conversations were rapid and knowing.

". . . if they've already sold all the orchestra seats to the brokers, I'm calling the Attorney General. It's such a racket. . . ."

". . . but the *Times* loves it, and that's all that matters to me, though I think their critic's a jerk. . . ."

". . . and then she bit him, right on the ass. I swear to God, Shakespeare ain't what it used to be. . . ."

After twenty-five minutes Molly finally reached the barred ticket booth.

"Date?" said the clerk.

He didn't look the type to be asking her out. If there was such a type.

"I'd like some information about a play that was here about fifty years ago," she said.

"I'd say you're about fifty years too late."

"You don't have information about your productions?"

"Sister, the only information I got is that we're sold out weekends until December and most of what's left during the week is mezzanine and side seats."

Molly was neither surprised nor overly disappointed. She had figured the theater for a long shot but had had to try.

"Is there a good library near here that you would recommend that has information about Broadway shows?" said Molly, switching to the next stop on her list of research options. "We're from out of town."

Before the man in the booth could answer, half the people in line seemed to be talking to her at once.

"Fifty-third street, across from MOMA."

"Don't fool with branches, lady. Go to the main library at Forty-second and Fifth, the one with the two lions and all the tourists out in front."

"You're all nuts. She should try Lincoln Center."

"She wants opera?"

"No, she wants the Library of Performing Arts. And that's at Lincoln Center!"

A murmur of agreement rippled through the crowd. Molly wasn't expecting New Yorkers to be so helpful, especially after a long wait in line. But they were. The man behind bars couldn't sell another ticket until Molly had been thoroughly briefed on how to get to Lincoln Center and had passed a quiz.

Molly and Nell walked up Broadway as instructed—the one Samaritan who had recommended the Eighth Avenue bus had been shouted down. It was a beautiful day in spite of the heat, and walking in New York wasn't like walking anywhere else.

An endless sea of pedestrians flowed up and down Broadway dressed in every fashion and color imaginable, from white-belted tourists to half-naked beggars. A babel of languages joined the car horns and sirens in the strange symphony that was the city.

In a second-floor window dancers were rehearsing in front of a wall of full-length mirrors. The streets were pocked with marquees advertising legendary musicals and popular television shows among storefronts filled with cameras and calzones, salamis and sofa beds. The air crackled with excitement.

At Fifty-ninth Street Molly and Nell had their first New York City lunch—hot pretzels and frankfurters from street vendors—and stopped to pet a weary-looking horse, one of many attached to hansom cabs at the curb in front of the park.

On the other side of Columbus Circle, Broadway widened into two lanes and ran diagonally into a neighborhood that felt completely different than the area from which they had come. Here, the buildings were newer, more residential, and not as tall as the ones in Times Square.

Abruptly the street opened again into another plaza, and the white marble and glass buildings of Lincoln Center spread out to the left. According to a sign they were at Sixty-fourth Street. They had covered twenty blocks in what had seemed like no time at all. Molly suddenly understood why the people at the theater had insisted that she and Nell walk. Walking in New York was so entertaining it was a wonder that the city hadn't figured out a way to tax it.

The Library of the Performing Arts was a comparatively small structure at the rear of the Lincoln Center complex, wedged between Julliard and the Metropolitan Opera. A million-dollar Henry Moore sculpture lazily sunned itself in a reflecting pool out in front. Inside, however, the library had the same atmosphere of purposeful doing, the same kind of people, and the same smell as probably every library in the country.

Molly suddenly felt more at home—libraries were an antique dealer's best friend and she had spent countless hours in them over the years. A helpful clerk at the front desk quickly directed her and Nell to the fourth floor. A few minutes later they stepped out of the elevator and entered a room of books surrounded by glass walls.

The Billy Rose Collection was a small, quiet space done in the same 1960s architecture that characterized the whole Lincoln Center complex. Bookcases ran along one wall. Five long wooden tables with seats numbered from one to sixty filled the center of the room. A few researchers sat in red 1960s-style chairs. The only evidence that the room had anything to do with theater were a few models of stage sets in white lucite boxes on top of the card catalogues.

"We're looking for information about someone who appeared on Broadway a long time ago," Molly explained to the librarian, a thin bearded man in his thirties. "Where should we start?"

Five minutes later Molly and Nell were in assigned seats perusing the spread for *Without Reservations* in the appropriate year's *Theatre World Annual*. It was as easy as that. The reference book was packed with information about the show, including the same cast list of eight actors as in the program Nell had found, plus three more production photos. In each photo a young and beautiful Margaret Jellinek dressed in odd, old-fashioned clothes struck a different pose as various cast members looked on.

Tingling with excitement Molly read the brief description of the story:

> The family of a dying girl keeps the seriousness of her illness a secret from her. When Linda Blake (Margaret Jellinek) learns the truth, she decides to spend her last days on a whirlwind tour of Europe rather than finish the promising symphony she has been composing. Her heartbroken fiancé (Tuck Wittington) and parents (Lillian St. Germaine, Arthur Page Anderson), try to talk her out of leaving, but it is only the noble sacrifice by her faithful cocker spaniel, Alexander The Great, that finally shows Linda the true meaning of life.

As she read further, however, Molly's excitement turned to disappointment. *Without Reservations* had previewed in Boston and tried out in New Haven and Philadelphia before opening in New York City at the Booth on Thanksgiving Day. It had closed that same Sunday, having played a total of five performances on Broadway.

"Well, you're bound to have some failures in a big Broadway career," Molly whispered to her sister.

Nell nodded absently, leafing through the current issue of *Backstage,* the showbiz weekly, that somebody had left on the table. She had long ago learned to amuse herself at libraries while Molly was digging out obscure facts about this antique or that.

Molly turned to the brief biographies of "Popular Broadway Players" included at the back of the *Theatre World*. Margaret Jellinek wasn't listed. Nor was Tuck Wittington who played her fiancé in *Without Reservations,* or the actors who played the Doctor, Aunt Tillie, Gramps, and Bart the Handyman. Only the parents—Lillian St. Germaine and Arthur Page Anderson, who were married to each other in real life—rated mention. Each had numerous Broadway credits, including plenty of Shakespeare.

Apparently you had to be pretty well established to get a bio, Molly realized, which meant that Margaret Jellinek must have been something less than a full-fledged Broadway star when she had won the lead in *Without Reservations.*

Of course, there was nothing wrong in being a newcomer, Molly told herself—or to star in a show that didn't have a long run. Anthony Quinn had starred that same year in a play that hadn't lasted even as long as Grandma's. And he hadn't rated a bio, either.

"Wait here," said Molly to Nell, then walked over to the card catalogue and filled out call slips for any archival materials that might be available for *Without Reservations.* She also picked up more *Theatre World* annuals for the years before and after *Without Reservations.*

Two hours later Molly had pieced together the whole story of her grandmother's Broadway career. It was not what she had been expecting.

From the dates in the reference volumes it was clear that Margaret Jellinek must have managed to land a part in the chorus of a Broadway musical almost as soon as she had arrived in New York at the age of seventeen. To Molly's surprise Richard Jellinek had been an actor, too. He had made his debut in the same musical—his name had appeared right next to Margaret's in the chorus listing.

"We're from a whole theatrical family, how do you like that?" Molly had whispered to her sister, who didn't seem impressed.

The Jellineks had performed in various shows over the next

six years—sometimes together though usually apart, sometimes in the chorus of musicals, sometimes in walk-on roles in straight plays. One musical in which both Margaret and Richard had sung and danced had gone on to a three-year run, but the Jellineks had both left after only a few months for small speaking parts in other shows that quickly closed.

Then, when Margaret Jellinek was twenty-three by Molly's calculations, she had landed her first leading role: Linda Blake, the doomed young composer in *Without Reservations*. Calling her performance a failure was too kind a word, however. Molly's grandmother had bombed.

"Last night at the Booth Margaret Jellinek may have given the worst performance not only of this disappointing season, but possibly in the history of the world," wrote the critic from the *Herald Tribune,* capturing the spirit of the reviews.

No one was spared. The playwright was ridiculed. Tuck Wittington, who was making his Broadway debut in the play was savaged (one reviewer called him a "shaky-voiced pipsqueak"). Arthur Page Anderson and Lillian St. Germaine were chided for betraying their talents by participating in such garbage. Even the dog was panned.

The brunt of the blame, however, was heaped on Margaret Jellinek, whose role had to carry the show. Brooks Atkinson said it all in his review for the *Times*:

> *Without Reservations,* which opened at the Booth Theatre last night seemed to conjure up not the spirit of Edwin Booth, the Prince of Players, for whom the theatre is named, but that of his infamous brother, John Wilkes. After enduring three hours of Margaret Jellinek's pathetic screeching and yowling, I was ready to shoot Lincoln, myself.

Molly closed the box of reviews, unable to read any more.

No wonder Margaret Jellinek's name did not appear again in the *Theatre World* annuals after that year. How many people would be brave enough to show their faces in public after such a humiliation? Two years later she had made her way to North Carolina with her baby, Evangeline. Richard Jellinek's name had vanished from the Broadway listings at about the same time.

"She was hiding," whispered Molly to Nell. "That's what Grandma was doing in Pelletreau. She was licking her wounds and hiding where no one would have heard of that stupid play."

Nell looked up from a picture of Yul Brynner in the original production of *The King and I* and smiled a sweet, open smile. Did she understand, Molly wondered, what it meant to spend your whole life broken and fearful in a backwater town? Or did she understand too well?

"Come on," said Molly, picking up the folders and boxes that contained the evidence of Margaret Jellinek's shame. They took these to the return window, then walked back to the librarian's desk. Just because Grandma hadn't been a success didn't mean Molly was going to give up trying to find out about her.

"Is there some organization or association that professional actors have to belong to, somewhere that would have information about its members?" asked Molly, her stomach still in knots from the reviews.

"Equity," said the librarian.

"Equity?" repeated Molly.

"Actor's Equity. The union."

It hadn't occurred to her that actors would have their own labor union, but why not? A union was perfect.

The address for Actor's Equity ironically turned out to be on Forty-sixth Street, just across Times Square from the Gotham Arms Hotel.

As they left Lincoln Center, Nell reveled again in the noisy, crowded streets. Molly tried to sort out her feelings. Her anger at her grandmother had dissipated after reading the reviews, but so many questions were still unanswered. Where had Margaret Gale originally come from? Why had Richard Jellinek deserted her and his child, and what had happened to him? Why hadn't Grandma sold the emerald ring?

At least they were making progress, Molly thought ruefully.

"At the rate we're going we might be able to take the bus home tomorrow," said Molly, stopping as a traffic light changed from green to red. "Wouldn't you like that?"

Nell shook her head in a definite no, then nonchalantly jay-walked through traffic like all the other New Yorkers.

Twenty minutes later they had completed the descent back down Broadway and entered the Actor's Equity building.

The polished gray granite lobby wasn't crowded, but Molly immediately noticed that there was something different about the people who came and went: the way they moved, the way they spoke to one another, the way they looked.

Three tall, thin, and fit women in summer dresses swept past and walked up a staircase at the rear of the lobby. Suddenly Molly was conscious for the first time of the silly print blouses she and Nell had on, their worn blue jeans. Everyone here looked so to-gether, so full of sparkle, so . . . noticeable.

There was a podium directly in front of the lobby doors where one might expect to find an attendant or receptionist, but no one seemed to be on duty. Feeling out of place and uncomfortable, Molly walked over to the address board on one of the gray granite walls and looked at the many listings for different departments of the actors union, trying to figure out where to go.

A young blond woman came in carrying a straw basket from

which Molly could see the title on the playscript poking out. It was by David Mamet. The woman was not much taller than Molly and not exactly pretty, but she carried herself with the same confidence that everyone else in the lobby seemed to have. As she passed she gave Molly a quizzical but friendly look. Molly leaped at the invitation.

"Is there a main reception area for Actor's Equity?" she asked.

"Certainly," said the girl in a voice that was surprisingly rich, round, and resonant, considering her small size. "Up those stairs at the back of the lobby. Come on. You can follow me."

"Thanks," said Molly and fell in line behind her with Nell bringing up the rear.

At the top of the stairs it was crowded confusion, a hallway filled with poised, intense-looking people, some seated on the floor, some leaning against walls. Most were young, but there were a few middle-aged faces. On a door to the left was posted a sign that read, PLEASE BE QUIET, CALLBACKS IN SESSION. Inside somebody was singing at the top of his lungs. Everywhere were bulletin boards full of incomprehensible postings.

"Were you looking for something in particular?" asked the young woman who had given Molly directions.

"My grandparents performed on Broadway, years ago," said Molly staring over the girl's shoulder at a window marked TICKETS AVAILABLE where a crowd had gathered. "I need to find out some information about them, but I guess I'm in the wrong place. Is this some kind of box office?"

"Oh, they don't sell any tickets here," said the young woman following Molly's gaze. "We get comps."

"Comps?"

"Complimentary tickets. Producers like to paper the house with actors when there aren't enough paying customers, so they give us freebies. Actors make great audiences. We whistle and stamp for everybody on stage, figuring they'll do the same for us one day."

"Are all these people here for . . . comps?" asked Molly.

"Oh, no," laughed the girl. "There are job listings posted in the other room. There's some casting done here. But basically it's just a place where you can come in between auditions, check the boards, get off your feet, go to the bathroom, talk with your friends. They might have the kind of information you're looking for up in Membership, on the fourteenth floor."

She indicated a bank of elevators through an archway.

"Thanks," said Molly.

"Good luck," answered the young woman, disappearing into the crowded hallway.

Molly led Nell to the elevators, feeling more out of place than she ever had in her life. Everyone seemed to be staring at them in the same strange way—as if they were watching her but not watching her. Was it so obvious she didn't belong here? It was a relief when the elevator came and they got in alone.

It was only as they climbed to the fourteenth floor that Molly finally realized that the actors downstairs hadn't been staring at her at all—they were just aware of *her* looking at *them*. It was what their profession was all about, after all: being seen, controlling what you look like to other people, living your life in deliberate and perpetual self-consciousness. How did they stand it?

Before Molly could even begin to understand what being an actor must be like and why anyone would want to live that way, the elevator doors opened. She and Nell walked out into an open area with people lined up at a windows marked ACTOR'S CREDIT UNION on one side of the room, and a counter marked MEMBERSHIP on the other. Behind the counter informally dressed people sat at desks, typing and filing. It looked like an insurance agency.

Marveling at the strange new world she had landed in, Molly took her place in the short line with Nell beside her. After a few minutes they found themselves facing a pleasant, compact young man.

"Can I help ya?" he said in the deese-dem-and-dose dialect of New York.

He wore shiny pants that might have come from Kmart and had none of the sparkle of the people downstairs. Why was Molly surprised? Had she expected out-of-work actors to be staffing the membership office? Unions were businesses. They probably paid minimum wage and specifically avoided performers as being bad employment risks.

"My grandparents acted in Broadway plays years ago," said Molly. "I'm wondering if you might still have some information about them."

"You a member?"

"No, but as I said, my grandparents performed on Broadway, so I imagine they were."

Molly spelled Jellinek. The clerk poked a computer terminal in front of him, then shook his head.

"Sorry, we don't got no Jellineks registered with Equity."

"Maybe not now," said Molly. "This would have been almost fifty years ago."

"Well, then there's your problem. The computer don't go back before about nineteen eighty."

"What about records from before that? Where are they?"

"Yeah, people ax that sometimes, but we don't really need that kinda stuff. They're stored away, I don't even know where."

After a few more questions it was painfully apparent that the priorities of a union were a lot different than a library's. If Molly had been looking for a steamfitter or plumber who had once worked in New York, how much luck would she have had at those unions?

And even if Equity's old records could be found, the only information that had been recorded was the agent's name and a local address, not where they had come from originally.

"Your actors, they ain't so stable, see?" confided the clerk with a knowing look. "They move around a lot, so your fifty-year-old local address ain't gonna mean much."

"Can you look up some other names for me?" asked Molly, disappointed.

"Sure, but if it's more old stuff, we ain't gonna have it, probably. Like I say, we only keep track of active members."

Molly began reading off the cast of characters of *Without Reservations* in order of appearance. Gramps, Aunt Tillie, the Doctor, Bart the Handyman. None of their names appeared in the computer, either. Molly wasn't surprised. From their pictures in the program she knew that they had been older people fifty years ago. They were probably long dead.

"Here ya go," said the clerk, looking up triumphantly from his terminal. "We got Arthur Page Anderson and we got Lillian St. Germaine. They stopped paying dues back in eighty-one and eighty-three respectfully. I can't give you addresses because you ain't members, but their last contact was Ajax Bowles. Ajax Bowles, that's the agency."

"Do you know where I can find this agency?"

"Haven't the slightest," said the clerk. "We only keep track of actors, and only them that pay their dues."

"Ajax Bowles closed after Burt Wolfanson died of AIDS in the late eighties," said a woman who had stepped into line behind Molly and Nell. "Burt wasn't a bad guy. He used to send me out for commercials sometimes. You civilians?"

She looked strangely familiar—an attractive woman in her fifties who had obviously once been beautiful, though the harsh fluorescent lights now accentuated every wrinkle beneath her impeccable makeup.

"We're not in the theater, if that's what you mean," said Molly. "Our grandmother was."

Molly suddenly realized where she had seen the woman. It had been on television. She had starred in a series of singing tuna fish commercials when Molly was a teenager. Molly marveled at seeing her up close after all these years—her first celebrity in the flesh. The jingle even flashed into Molly's mind, a hypnotic ditty recounting how all ambitious tuna made straight for her sponsor's can, only to endure a rigorous audition process. Just like the fish downstairs.

"Do you happen to know any of these people?" said Molly, handing her the *Without Reservations* "Playbill." Perhaps an old performer might know more than an old computer.

The tuna fish lady scrutinized the names in the program.

"I really liked how you sang to the tuna," ventured Molly.

The woman sadly shook her head.

"I've done everything from Sophocles to Noel Coward over the past thirty years," she said with a sigh. "More than a hundred productions, and the only thing they ever recognize me for is three lousy commercials that I spent less than a week of my life on."

"Sorry," stammered Molly.

"Most of these people were before my time," said the tuna fish lady, returning the *Without Reservations* program to Molly. "You never heard of Arthur Page Anderson and Lillie St. Germaine?"

"Should we have?"

"Such is Broadway fame," sighed the actress. "They died years ago but were on top for quite a while. At least in New York. I did a Shaw play with them when I first came to town. Lovely people, real pros."

"Well, it was a long shot," said Molly. "Thanks anyway."

"And then there's Tuck Wittington."

"He's still around? You know him?"

"Oh, everybody knows Tuck," said the woman with a chuckle, shaking her head.

"But he wasn't in the phone book."

"Neither am I, and Tuck probably has lots more people he doesn't want to hear from than I do. But five nights and two afternoons a week you can find him right around the corner. He's playing in *Bank Street Story* at the Lyceum. Wait a minute while I finish my business here, and we'll go downstairs and see if we can get you comps."

Five

That night, after an hour of exploring, an attempted nap at the hotel, and a pair of eleven-dollar club sandwiches at a Times Square coffee shop, Molly and Nell made their way to the Lyceum, which was indeed only just around the block from Actor's Equity.

The old theater was gray with the grime of a century and dwarfed by a flashy modern skyscraper next door, but Molly loved the wackily elegant Beaux-Arts building on sight. It was like an overdone piece of nineteenth-century revival furniture, complete with Corinthian columns, Greek masks, ornate balconies, and windows wreathed with bellflower garlands and wedding-cake moldings. The lobby was a wonder of hand-carved oak and polished brass, the carved acanthus leaves and leaping dolphins testimony to a grander age.

The tuna fish lady had very kindly talked the people at Equity out of two tickets for the eight o'clock performance of *Bank Street Story*—Annie Oakleys she had called them because of the hole punched in the center of each. When the great woman sharpshooter and Wild West Show star gave out free passes, so the story went, she used to throw the tickets in the air and punctuate them with signature bullet holes.

Molly was immensely grateful—the seats would have cost them well over a hundred dollars—but the actress waved off her thank-yous with a sad, "Just forget about those commercials and remember my knowing smile when you watch Tuck eat the scenery tonight."

Things had already been going better than Molly could have dreamed. Now, thanks to the kindness of strangers, they were about to see their first Broadway play and meet, Molly hoped, a man who had known their grandmother in her youth. If their luck held Tuck Wittington would remember where Margaret Jellinek had originally come from. They'd be able to sleep late, check out of the hotel tomorrow morning, and still have the day to explore the city before catching the overnight bus back to Pelletreau.

She'd have to give Taffy a call tomorrow and let her know when to pick them up, Molly reminded herself, settling back in her narrow, black velvet seat as the Lyceum's houselights dimmed and the play began.

Bank Street Story had been running for more than a year, and it was evident from the opening curtain why it was a hit. His name was Mitch Wanders.

Molly hadn't seen the blond actor on the television police drama that had catapulted him to celebrity, but even she knew who he was. Now she understood why he was a star.

Wanders was a dynamic and sexy guy with a quiet reserve that was utterly masculine. Molly couldn't take her eyes off him. Nell seemed impressed, too, judging from the way she stared at the actor with her lips slightly parted and her cheeks ruddy. He had a clear baritone voice and eyes that were so light blue as to be almost freakish. Though their second-row seats were far off to the left, Molly could actually see the tiny beads of sweat form on the actor's beautiful face under the hot lights and smell his makeup.

Molly hadn't sat through a live play in a real theater since she was in high school. She was amazed at how exciting and immediate it was. She found herself thoroughly sucked in, horrified at what had happened to the little girl, but outraged to see the grieving Dr. Lewis, played by Mitch Wanders, forced to stand trial for her death.

The district attorney—whom Molly hated on sight—was a sarcastic bully who treated poor Dr. Lewis like a common criminal. The actor who played him had a craggy face with a ridiculous cleft in his chin, curly black hair, and a voice that Molly thought of as trumpetlike, even though he never raised it.

"Name three of your daughter's friends, Dr. Lewis," he snarled, his cruel dark eyes flashing.

"I . . . I don't know their names."

"But you know that she had friends?"

"My daughter was a wonderful little girl. She must have had friends."

"What time would you say that this wonderful little girl had available to be with these friends, when your wife spent practically every waking minute dragging her to health clubs, restaurants, and beauty parlors and burdening her with intimate details of your sex life?"

By the end of the play, the good Dr. Lewis didn't look so good anymore, and society as a whole had been convicted of sacrificing its children on the altar of parental neuroses and needs. In fact the only likable character left was the honey-voiced, puckish, adorable judge, played by the man whose credits in the program ran three times longer than anyone else's: Tuck Wittington.

Molly and Nell were waiting at the Lyceum's stage door around the block when the old actor emerged twenty minutes after the final curtain. Molly didn't approach until he had walked without incident through the crowd being held behind a police barricade.

"Mr. Wittington?"

"*C'est moi,*" he answered with a hopeful smile, like a cocker spaniel hearing its name called at dinner time.

He had taken off his makeup, and his old, well-lined skin was raw and pink-looking. Over his shoulder was slung a leather bag, almost like a purse. His strawberry blond hair had gone to white at the temples and the sideburns. He looked much smaller in person than he had in his black robes on the elevated judicial bench on stage. He stood maybe five feet five, but his slight frame carried forty or fifty more pounds than the "pipsqueak" who had made his Broadway debut in *Without Reservations* so long ago. His faintly British voice, once a shaky thing reviewers had laughed at, was now as deep and melodious as an old pipe organ.

"I'm Molly O'Hara and this is my sister Nell," said Molly. "We loved you in the play and we wondered—"

"Say no more, my lovelies," he said, taking her program from her hand and scribbling on its cover with a felt tip pen that he took from his pocket. "I am just heartened to see that there are those of your generation who can still appreciate an old thespian."

"Thank you," said Molly as he handed her back the autographed "Playbill." "Actually I wondered if we could talk to you for a moment about our grandmother . . ."

"What is the dear old party's name?" said Tuck, reaching for the program again.

"Margaret Jellinek."

Tuck's outstretched hand stopped in midair.

"Margaret . . . Jellinek? I knew a Margaret Jellinek once."

"You made your Broadway debut with her in *Without Reservations.*"

"Yes, I did. Good God. And you are that same Margaret Jellinek's granddaughter?"

Molly nodded. Tuck shook his head back and forth.

"Suddenly I feel time's wingèd chariot hurrying near," he said in a mournful voice. "Brontosaurus Wittington, the dinosaur of old Broad-way. So how is your ancient granny, whom I, God help us, remember only as a beautiful young woman?"

"She died," said Molly. "About a week ago."

"You really know how to cheer a fellow up, don't you?"

A chorus of squeals suddenly exploded behind them. Holding out programs and writing utensils and at least one piece of underwear, the crowd surged through the barricade toward the confident, grinning figure of Mitch Wanders, who had just appeared at the stage door.

"Oh, Jesus," said Tuck, rolling his eyeballs broadly enough to be seen from a block away. "It's Mitchell versus the great unwashed horde again. Let's get out of here before I regurgitate."

Nell's eyes lit up and she started back, obviously intending to join the crowd converging on Mitch Wanders. Molly grabbed her by the arm and dragged her along after Tuck, who was already to the corner of Broadway.

It was past eleven o'clock now, but the streets of Times Square were every bit as crowded as they had been at noon. A million neon lights lit up the Great White Way like a stage set, making the night sky far above seem unreal and irrelevant.

Tuck navigated surely through side streets thick with emerging audiences, chattering about plays in which he had performed in each theater they passed. By the time they came to rest in a restaurant on the other side of Eighth Avenue a few blocks up from their hotel, Tuck with studied nonchalance had dropped the names of half-a-hundred famous people he'd worked with.

"Ralph's" had looked like just a nondescript doorway from

the street, but inside was a cavernous space with exposed brick walls and menus scrawled with chalk on blackboards. The noise level was high and so were the customers' spirits.

Magnanimously greeting patrons and waiters alike, Tuck led Molly and Nell to a large table in a rear corner of the restaurant where several of the other cast members from *Bank Street Story,* and some of other actor types were already eating, drinking, and generally having an uproarious time.

"People," announced Tuck, tapping the round glass candle holder on the table with a fork and depositing his bag on a chair, "these are . . . what did you say your names were?"

"Molly and Nell O'Hara."

". . . Molly and Nell O'Hara, whose grandmother acted with yours truly in his Broadway debut back in the seventeen sixties. Please be kind to them. I'll be right back, children, I must say hello to Cameron."

Tuck bounced away and disappeared into the crowd at the bar. Nobody seemed to take much notice of Molly and Nell. The conversations around the table continued at high decibels. A few seats away the actor who had played the hateful district attorney nursed what looked to be scotch and stared at Molly in a way that made her skin crawl. After a few moments Molly couldn't stand it anymore. She turned to the woman next to her who had played the horrible Mrs. Lewis and tried to strike up a conversation over the din of the room.

"I enjoyed your performance very much."

"Thanks."

"It's a really good play."

"The *Times* thought so."

The woman seemed just as petulant and self-involved in real life as she had on stage. When Molly asked if the little girl who had played her daughter was scared about having such a mean mother on stage (in one particularly frightening flashback Mrs. Lewis had bent the girl's pinky finger back until she would say "I love you, Mommy"), the actress replied with a curt, "Realism is important." Molly looked around for Tuck, but he was nowhere to be seen. The DA actor continued to stare at her.

"Do you like being an actress?" said Molly, trying again with Mrs. Lewis.

"Actor. You wouldn't say doctoress or lawyeress. A person who acts is an actor."

"Sorry," said Molly. "Do you like being an actor?"

"To me," announced the woman, striking a pose as if everyone in the restaurant were waiting for her answer, "being an actor is the single most important contribution a person can hope to make in the world today. Actors are our storytellers, our spirit guides to the magical essence of life, our touchstones for the creative forces of the universe. By literally bringing themselves into the creative process, actors gift audiences with the most precious human experience available in our egocentric, antihumanistic society."

Mercifully a waiter arrived at this point and cut her off.

"What can I get you guys?" he demanded.

Nell pointed to a bottle left by an actor who had paid his check and exited just as they were getting settled.

"Right. Heineken for you."

"Me, too," said Molly, happy to see Nell order for herself for a change. Nell hardly ever tried to communicate with waiters or salespeople or anyone else for that matter, preferring to let Molly do it for her. Perhaps it was because when she did try, nobody in Pelletreau seemed to understand her. People here seemed a whole lot quicker.

"Two Heinekens," said the waiter, "anything to eat?"

Nell put her thumb and forefinger together and twisted her hand back and forth.

"Screwdriver," guessed the waiter not missing a beat, as if customers ordering in pantomime were a regular occurrence at Ralph's.

Nell shook her head and repeated the hand motion.

"Key," said the waiter after a moment and seemed to quiver with delight when Nell nodded her head. Then she touched her ear.

"Sounds like."

Nell dug into her pocket and went through her change until she found the coin she wanted.

"Dime. Sounds like dime. Rhyme. Time. Lime. Lime! Key lime pie!"

Nell nodded happily. Molly was amazed. And not just by Nell's sudden talkativeness.

"How can you want to eat lime pie when you're drinking beer? What kind of combination is that? You want to get sick?"

"Oh, leave her alone," said waiter. "She's obviously a very creative person. I suppose you want something conventional."

Nell folded her arms in front of her and grinned smugly.

"Yes, I do," said Molly. "Do you have pretzels or something like that?"

"We do, but you're an idiot if you have anything but the fried calamari."

"Of course, she'll have the calamari," declared Tuck in a sonorous baritone, returning to his seat next to Nell. "My treat."

"I don't even know what calamari is!" said Molly.

"Where are you from? The moon?" muttered the actor who played Mrs. Lewis, getting up and heading toward a friend at another table.

"North Carolina," murmured Molly. She had always thought of herself as smart and sophisticated. In Pelletreau, where barbecue was considered an art form, she was. Here among this crowd she felt like a hick.

"Trust me, bubee, you'll love it," said the waiter and escaped in the direction of the kitchen.

"What did I just order?" said Molly.

"Fried squid," said Tuck. "Very delicious. So tell me about Margaret. I truly am very sorry to hear about her passing. We were all so young then, so very young. I was fresh off the farm. Literally. Those were my salad days, and I but a spring lettuce. Tucker Aloysius Wittington, *Radicchio theatricalis*. The kiss Margaret and I shared in the play was actually my first from a representative of the opposite sex. So what was Margaret up to all these years?"

Molly explained diplomatically that her grandmother had lived a quiet life in Pelletreau. She told how they had come to New York after finding the program and what they had managed to learn at the library.

"Poor Margaret," Tuck muttered, remembering. "The critics really destroyed us."

With deep sighs and dramatic hand gestures, he recounted how well things had gone on the road for *Without Reservations—* the changes the playwright had made in Boston, the applause and curtain calls in Philadelphia, and then the silent Broadway audiences, the vicious reviews, the snickering.

"The producer had seen it coming, of course," Tuck said with a sigh. "That's why he opened on Thanksgiving—he knew he had a turkey and just hoped to feed it to a weekend of happy holiday audiences. But one was allowed to fail in those days, not like now when everything costs so much money. It was a truly creative time then, so many more productions, so much more energy. And what performers we had. My first play, and there I was, sharing the boards with Arthur Page Anderson and Lillie St. Germaine. There were giants then. Giants."

Tuck had ended this pronouncement with a hand thrown up theatrically, as if he were tossing a bouquet of flowers into the air or concluding a tango. Nobody else at the table paid any attention except for the DA character who sat a few seats away, quietly nursing his drink and watching Molly, who wished he would just go away.

The waiter returned with their food and drinks. Nell tore into her key lime pie. Molly tentatively tried a ringlet of her calamari and was surprised to find it pretty good, if a little rubbery.

"Tell me about my grandmother," she said, offering Tuck a piece that looked suspiciously like a tentacle—probably because it was one.

"Oh, Margaret was a darling," said Tuck, "very earnest, very nervous about her part, but funny, always joking around. She had a wonderfully raucous laugh—like a horse, I used to kid her. Then those reviews came out. I didn't see her much after that, except on stage. She hid in her dressing room until we closed, poor thing."

"Did she ever talk about her family, about where she had come from originally?"

"Not that I recall."

"She left us a ring with a big stone. Do you remember it? Do you know where she might have gotten it?"

"Have not a clue. Who could notice jewelry when there was Margaret to look at? She was dazzling."

So much for that, Molly thought.

"You know," Tuck went on, "when I first met Margaret she had stars in her eyes. It was amazing. I mean you could actually see them twinkle. I wouldn't have thought that a few bad reviews could destroy her, but you never know about people. Margaret really took it to heart. A few months after we closed, I ran into Dickie on the street, and he said she still wouldn't even come out of the apartment. Then they got divorced and I never saw her again."

"Dick Jellinek."

"Yes, that was before Dickie changed his name."

"Dick Jellinek changed his name?" exclaimed Molly.

"Of course. What kind of career could you have with a name like Jellinek in those days? And Maggie really was a laughingstock for years after we bombed so badly. I suppose Dickie got tired of people thinking about her when they saw him. So somewhere along the line he became Dick Julian, and did a lot better."

"You mean he kept on acting?"

"He was an actor, my dear," exclaimed Tuck. "What else would he do?"

So that was why Richard Jellinek had vanished from the *Theatre World* annuals, Molly realized. He had become someone else. Richard Julian.

"Dickie was a leading-man/best-friend type, quite a competent fellow," Tuck went on. "And very attractive. He and I even did a few shows together in the sixties, then Dickie was off in Hollywood for a while doing television dramas. But he was basically a creature of the stage and always made his way back to New York."

"Do you know where I can find him?" said Molly, excitedly. "Is he alive? Is he still working? I'd love to talk with him."

"Oh, Dickie hasn't been around for years and years," clucked Tuck. "God only knows what's happened to him."

"Maybe Equity would have an address or a contact for him," said Molly.

"Well, I know his agent was poor Burt Wolfanson at Ajax Bowles if that's any help."

"Not really," said Molly her heart sinking.

"You know who might know is Bobby Prince," declared Tuck, snapping his fingers dramatically (Molly suspected that everything Tuck did—down to and including setting his alarm clock and tying his shoelaces—he did dramatically).

"Is Bobby Prince an actor, too?" she asked.

"Oh, indeed. And just as beautiful as Dickie. His name was

originally Plotkin, as I recall. Anyway Bobby and Dickie were always up for the same parts and they became inseparable. I'd see them at the same auditions and the same bars. They were always hanging around together. If anyone would know what happened to Dickie it would be Bobby Prince. He's been retired for years, but I shall track him down and give him a call on your behalf this very instant. It's the least I can do."

"It's not too late to call?" said Molly. Her watch had stopped hours ago, but it had to be after midnight.

"Of course it's too late, but this is for old times' sake. Now who would have his number? Nick Lawlor? Suzy Winston? Chita? I'll have to check around."

Obviously relishing the prospect of waking half the people in New York, Tuck bounced up from his chair and headed toward a bank of telephones near the restrooms. Someone turned up the volume on the jukebox, which was blaring show tunes. A guy from another table came over and without a word pulled Nell off to a small open area where people were dancing. Molly nervously watched her go, then looked over to find herself alone at the table with the unpleasant actor who had played the DA in the play.

"Why doesn't your sister talk?" he said, taking a sip of his scotch.

"I'd rather not go into that if you don't mind," said Molly, trying to be polite. "It's very complicated."

"You're her keeper?"

No, she didn't like him at all.

"I'm her sister," Molly said evenly and turned away, using every ounce of body language she could muster to let the man know how she felt about him. It didn't work. He scooted over into the chair next to hers.

"You live together in North Carolina?" he asked.

"How did you know we're from North Carolina?"

"You mentioned it. Liz asked if you were from the moon. You said North Carolina, though I could tell anyway from your accent."

"I don't have any accent. Y'all are the ones with accents. Do you always listen to other people's conversations?"

"Sometimes. So how long have you been taking care of your sister?"

"What is this? An interrogation? The play is over. You're not really a courtroom lawyer, you know."

"I am, actually."

Molly gave this the look it deserved.

"No, it's true," he said, cracking a smile, the first one Molly had seen from him, onstage or off. "I was an assistant district attorney in Stamford, Connecticut. The woman who wrote the play you saw tonight served on a jury of a case I tried. When Longwharf first presented *Bank Street Story,* they couldn't find anybody believable for the prosecutor so she persuaded the producers to give me an audition. I hated my job and desperately wanted to change my life. They offered me the part, and I grabbed it. When the play moved to Broadway, I came along. My name's David in case you didn't read your program. David Azaria."

"Molly O'Hara. As I'm sure you've overheard. I enjoyed your performance tonight. Sort of."

"Thanks. Sort of."

They sat in awkward silence for a moment.

"So are you going back to being a lawyer when the play closes?" Molly said finally, just to get him to stop staring at her.

"Nope," he said. "Not that I like acting so much. The rehearsals are great, but after the first month of performances I was so bored I was ready to shoot myself. Then I started appreciating it from a deeper perspective. Doing the exact same sequence of actions, night after night, can be very Zen if you let it. Like the

Japanese tea ceremony. I'm using the time to learn more about the craft. Already casting directors are fighting over me for daytime TV, and I'm doing voice-overs."

"Voice-overs?"

"Narration for documentaries, commercials—that sort of thing. Eventually I'd like to direct, but already I'm making more money now than I ever did as a prosecutor. And having a lot more fun, which is the point, isn't it?"

"You mean you don't believe that being an actor is the single most important thing in the history of the world?"

He smiled again.

"I just prefer to spend my time entertaining people than sending them to jail. You still haven't answered my question."

"Which was?"

"Why is your sister your responsibility?"

"Because she's my sister," said Molly. "We don't have any other family."

"She lives with you."

"Yes."

"What about work?" asked David Azaria, taking another sip of his drink and staring at her with the same cold calculating expression. "What does she do when you're at work?"

"We work together. We have an antique shop. Look, why are you so interested in my sister and me?"

"What about dates? Does she go out on dates with you?"

"I don't go—" Molly stopped, flustered.

"You don't go out on dates," David said, finishing the sentence. "Have many friends, people you get together with?"

"Sure I have friends."

"Name a few."

Molly didn't say anything. Besides Oscar, who she didn't see socially, and Taffy, who she didn't see unless she had to, Molly couldn't think of anyone who even knew she was alive, except for the dealers who were her professional competition.

"In other words, you're sacrificing any chance to have a normal life so you can take care of your sister," said David in a surprisingly gentle voice. "Why?"

"I'm not doing any such thing. And I don't see how it's any of your business."

"I don't care if you lie to me. I'd just like to know why you're lying to yourself."

"Because what happened to her was my fault," snapped Molly, then brought her hand instantly to her mouth.

She couldn't believe she had told him. She'd never told anyone, not in all these years. And now she'd blurted it out to a stranger in a bar, a stranger she didn't even like.

"What happened to her?" he asked after a moment.

Molly shook her head.

"Come on," he pressed. "You want to tell someone. I can see it in your eyes. Who better than somebody you're obviously planning never to see again?"

Molly didn't intend to tell him anything. She was surprised therefore to hear herself talking.

"When Nell was a little girl she saw someone murder our mother, if you must know."

"How was that your fault?"

"Because she was supposed to be with me," said Molly angrily. "I was supposed to take her with me to the movies that day. But my friend Taffy didn't want to be bothered with my little sister and I let her talk me into leaving Nellie at home. If I had taken Nellie with us like I was supposed to, she never would have seen what she did."

David Azaria took a sip of his drink and continued to stare at her.

"How old were you when all this happened?" he said finally.

"Eleven," said Molly, wiping her eyes which had become moist somewhere along the line.

"How old are you now?"

"Twenty-eight."

"Seventeen years for going to the movies. Pretty rough sentence for a kid. I'll bet the guy who did it got less time."

"They never caught anybody."

"Sounds familiar. Professionally speaking I'd say you've paid in full for whatever blame is rightly yours for what happened to your sister."

"My life isn't some kind of punishment, Mr. Azaria," said Molly. "I love my sister. I'm the only real family she has. Somebody has to take care of her."

"Call me David," said David Azaria. "And it looks to me like your sister can take care of herself."

Molly followed his eyes to the dance floor, where a handful of people were executing wild and intricate dance sequences. A radiant Nell was matching the Broadway gypsies step for step. Where had she learned to dance like that, Molly wondered. When had she become so beautiful?

"You don't understand," whispered Molly. "She needs me."

"Can she dress herself?"

"Of course, she can dress herself."

"Can she feed herself?"

"She's a wonderful cook, but that doesn't—"

"Can she read and write?"

"Yes, but—"

"Maybe it's you that need her," said David, "not the other way around."

"That's the most ridiculous thing I've ever heard," sputtered Molly. "How could she make a living? Nellie can't even talk. And she gets terribly frightened sometimes, she has these . . . these fits. I don't know what would happen to her if she were alone."

"Well, she's never going to find out if you keep treating her like some little baby, is she? Plenty of people who can't talk or hear or even see make lives for themselves. If she had to, maybe your sister would do just fine on her own."

He fixed Molly with his huge, coal-black eyes. She met his gaze for a second, then looked away.

"You're crazy," she said. "And it's none of your business."

"How about going out with me sometime?" he replied.

"If you ever get to Pelletreau, North Carolina, you can give me a call."

"How long are you staying in New York?"

"We'll probably leave tomorrow."

"Then how about tomorrow morning? We can have breakfast. I cook. I'll make you French toast."

"Forget it," said Molly. "You're not my type. Maybe you could fix us up with Mitch Wanders."

"Us?"

"Nell liked him, too."

"Be my pleasure, only I don't think Mitch would be interested in either of you."

"Why not?" said Molly, defensively.

"He's gay as a goose."

"That's a miserable thing to say," exclaimed Molly. "Why would you say such a thing?"

"It's not a miserable thing," said David in a quiet voice. "It's just who he is. I don't think you'd like him either. Mitch is a stuck-up, obnoxious little shit who uses people like toilet paper. He's out with a different man every night of the week. He broke poor Tuck's heart."

"Tuck? I can't believe . . ."

"You can't believe that Tuck is gay? You really are living in a dream world, aren't you?"

"I'm not. It's just . . . I didn't know. . . ."

"Tuck had been chasing Mitch since the show opened," said David. "He finally caught him one night a few months ago. I don't know what happened except that Mitch is a shit. Tuck spent the next week in tears. He's a lot more sensitive than he pretends to be, and he's terrified of getting old. Say, you didn't really think that we were really the people you saw on stage did you?"

"No, of course not . . . I mean . . ."

"You did, didn't you? Is that why you think you don't like me? Because I'm the bastard who nailed poor Dr. Lewis?"

"That's not it at all," said Molly, feeling more naive, more out of place than ever.

"Then what is it?"

Before she could think of an answer, Tuck mercifully returned to the table, rubbing his hands together gleefully.

"It's all arranged," he chortled. "To keep busy in his retirement Bobby Prince has taken some kind of office job with Alexander Marinov, the producer, and I must say I am impressed. Marinov must be richer than Andrew Lloyd Webber by now. Every year, another hit musical. You see, my darling, the theater takes care of its own. Bobby says you can come out and see him tomorrow at work."

"That's wonderful," said Molly.

"Well, it's the least I could do for Margaret's granddaughters," said Tuck, bowing his head with theatrical modesty. "Bobby did seem a little put out that I'd awakened him, but still he promised to exert his influence with Marinov on my behalf. Every year

I audition, and every year I am cruelly rejected. I told Bobby if it happens once again I shall kill myself."

"Thanks, Tuck," said Molly.

"I've written down the address for you," said Tuck, presenting a marked-up napkin. "It's in some place in Queens called Long Island City. Bobby said Marinov needs a huge amount of space for their operation and apparently it would cost too much in Manhattan, even for him."

"Where is this Long Island City? How do we get there?"

"Well, I'm not sure exactly," said Tuck. "Anywhere beyond the East River is a foreign country as far as I'm concerned. Perhaps you can engage a limo."

"Long Island City is way the hell out there," said David Azaria, after trying to find one last sip in his empty glass. "Plus the neighborhoods can get dicey if you don't know where you're going. Hey, I'm not doing anything tomorrow. Why don't I take you?"

"I don't think—" began Molly, but Tuck cut her off.

"That's a splendid idea, David. Most generous. Everyone should have such a gallant and handsome bodyguard to help them survive the unknown wilds. I'd be tempted to journey there myself if I could find someone like you to take me."

Tuck batted his long lashes at David and sighed, theatrically.

"You're not my type," said David.

"Oh? Then who is, pray tell?"

"She is," he said, pointing with his ridiculous chin at Molly. "And if I'm lucky she'll give her sister the day off, so the two of us can enjoy a romantic subway ride to Queens alone."

Six

Molly sat in an uncomfortable armchair in the lobby of the Gotham Arms the next morning, trying to sort out why she was feeling so anxious.

Part of it was Taffy, of course. Molly had been calling the shop since eight o'clock this morning, and there had been no answer. Taffy hadn't even bothered to turn on the answering machine before deserting ship. Was she just out for breakfast for three hours? Could she still be asleep? Molly knew she hadn't gone home because there was no answer there, either. If Taffy had been off playing hooky when the Nicholsons had shown up to pick up their chest of drawers, Molly was going to kill her.

But Taffy being Taffy wasn't enough to tie Molly's stomach in knots like this. Nor was it lack of sleep—they hadn't gotten back to the hotel last night until after two o'clock.

That left David Azaria.

He was already half an hour late for their date this morning, and tardiness was one thing that drove Molly crazy. Not that this was a date, of course. David was just being a guide, that was all. Someone who could get them out to this remote Long Island City area. Though why shouldn't he ask her out on a date? It wasn't like she had two heads or anything, Molly thought, glancing at Nell, who smiled back dreamily. At least one of them had been able to sleep soundly last night.

Molly glanced at her watch again, which was working for a change. Eleven o'clock. That should give them more than enough time to find out what this Bobby Prince could tell them and still make the seven o'clock bus back to Pelletreau tonight. Molly had given the hotel bell captain two dollars to hold their suitcase. They would pick it up on their way to the station. There was no point in spending another night in New York. There was nothing else they could learn here.

Where was David? Molly wondered again, feeling the irritation welling up inside her. One half of her fully intended to tell him what an inconsiderate, arrogant jerk he was and that there wasn't a chance in hell that she was going to let him take them anywhere. The other half of her was looking forward to seeing him.

At that very moment David Azaria walked through the revolving lobby doors, looking gangly, menacing, and smug. He wore khaki slacks and a navy blue polo shirt. He hadn't shaved, which made his chin seem even squarer and the cleft in its center even deeper, like it had been created with a hatchet. Nell, a big smile on her face, popped out of her chair to meet him. Molly sat right where she was.

"I thought your sister was going to give you the day off," said David, kissing Nell lightly on the cheek. She blushed innocently and grinned. She liked him for some reason that Molly didn't understand, but then Nell's taste in people was hardly the most discriminating. After all, she liked Taffy, too.

David produced the single white rose, which he had been hiding behind his back, and handed it to Molly.

"What's this for?" she said, startled.

"Because it's Thursday."

"What's that supposed to mean?"

"It means I'm a romantic."

"Thanks," said Molly, feeling a good portion of her irritation abate, only to be replaced by something she had never felt before, a strange kind of nervous uncertainty. "Look, David, this was very nice of you and I'm touched, but I don't want you think . . ."

"Don't worry. I'm a realistic romantic. That's why I had the florist leave the thorns on your rose. Be careful."

Molly studied the flower in her hand, not knowing what to say. David reached into his pocket, unwrapped a bill from his money clip and held it out to Nell.

"Here's twenty bucks, kid," he said in a conspiratorial stage whisper. "Go play in Times Square."

Nell, beaming, took the proffered twenty and put it in her pocket, but made no move to leave.

"What? You want more?"

Nell nodded enthusiastically. David peeled off another twenty, which Nell also snatched, but still didn't budge.

"You know, you'd make a pretty good lawyer," he muttered, shaking his head.

"Can we get going?" said Molly, finding her voice and rising from the chair. "Or are you going to go through your whole net worth to prove the old saying about a fool and his money?"

"What's your hurry?"

"We have to be back in time to catch our bus. We're leaving for Pelletreau tonight."

"Don't worry, you'll probably make it. Unless we succumb

to the forces of darkness somewhere down there in the bowels of the subway system."

David turned to Nell.

"Did anyone ever tell your sister that she's quite a piece of strudel?"

Nell giggled soundlessly. Molly felt the blood rush to her face.

"I didn't think so," said David. "Probably you guys don't know from strudel, down there in the deep South, huh?"

Nell giggled again, then she entwined her arm in David's and playfully pulled him toward the door, leaving Molly to bring up the rear. They headed for a dark stairwell in the sidewalk two blocks away.

This was the first time Molly had experienced the New York City subway, and she was expecting something pretty frightening. She was surprised, therefore, to find a well-lit modern station neatly appointed in glazed red brick.

David passed something that looked like a credit card through a stainless steel turnstile three times to admit them. Normal-looking people bustled to and fro, without apparent trepidation. When a train arrived after a few minutes, the cars were sleek, aluminum-skinned and air-conditioned—nothing like the graffiti-covered horrors you always saw in the movies.

David showed Nell how to grab for support onto the metal rails attached to the ceiling, but Molly wasn't tall enough to hang comfortably from these. Instead, she wrapped herself around a metal pole in the center of the crowded car as the train lurched forward. When Molly stole a look at David she found to her discomfort that he was staring at her with the same intense inscrutable expression he had worn at the restaurant last night.

Molly quickly turned away and looked out the window, then

down at the rose he had given her. It was lovely, but already she had scratched herself on one of the thorns.

They passed through a few more stations that seemed as well maintained as the first. None of the other passengers seemed to notice the rose Molly was holding. They didn't even glance in her direction, though she couldn't help noticing them—businessmen and middle-class shoppers; a weary African American man with a lunchbox; a loud group of teenagers, all wearing the same expensive sneakers and turned-around baseball caps; a pregnant young woman who looked to be about Molly's age surrounded by three dirty-faced kids plus a baby in a battered stroller.

Suddenly the train broke out of underground darkness and began climbing into a huge metal structure, like some giant Erector set. Graffiti were everywhere here, like multicolored ivy gone wild. The tracks quickly leveled off in the upper reaches of the 59th Street Bridge, for this is what the structure was. As they reached land on the other side of the East River, Molly could see automobiles parked in the trash-strewn spaces between the supports far below, as well as the gleaming towers of Manhattan behind them.

The train slowed to a halt. The next thing Molly knew David was directing her and Nell out onto the dingy platform of a much older station than the ones they'd seen before. This one did look like a set from *Serpico* or *The French Connection,* with unwashed windows further opaqued with graffiti. It seemed like they had been traveling only a few minutes.

"Where are we?" asked Molly, blinking her eyes against the unexpected daylight.

"Long Island City," said David.

"I thought you said it was so far away!"

"Figuratively speaking, it is."

As he led them down a staircase, then across an open platform and down another ancient decaying staircase to the street, Molly saw what he meant.

The buildings here were as squat and dirty as Manhattan's were soaring and noble. The people were fewer, more ethnic and poorly dressed—worlds away from the high-energy pedestrians who swarmed the streets of Manhattan. Windows displayed signs in Spanish, Russian, and Hebrew. The tarry sidewalks steamed with summer heat. Above Molly's head loomed the steel structure of the enormous bridge, blocking the sun and plunging into gloom the traffic that inched along beneath its supports.

From the doorway of a restaurant that offered Hispanic-Chinese food a towering black man with dreadlocks and no shirt eyed them with an exceedingly unpleasant look in his yellowish eyes. For the first time Molly was glad that David was with them. At least she was glad until David smiled at the man and spoke.

"Excuse me, sir," he said, walking over and taking a napkin out of his pocket. "Do you have any idea where this is?"

It was the napkin on which Tuck had scrawled the address where they were supposed to go.

Molly feared for a moment that the man was going to spit in David's face, judging from his startled look. Instead he merely studied the address on the napkin and in soft, strangely accented English gave polite directions.

David thanked him and steered Molly and Nell down the street and around the corner. Within a few blocks the area changed from the relatively congested clamor of the subway station to a desolate section of lonely warehouses—not what Molly had been expecting at all for the offices of a big producer.

"This is it," said David abruptly, comparing the numbers on the napkin with the address on the metal door of a massive, four-story warehouse building with barred windows along one side.

It looked deserted, but name tags next to a row of buzzers suggested otherwise. There was no tag for the first floor but the second floor was occupied by the Flower Petal Dress Company. Next to the third buzzer was printed in small block letters, A. MARINOV STOCK & AMATEUR. The top floor's tenant was labeled only in Chinese.

David pressed the Marinov buzzer long and hard. When nothing happened, he opened the metal door. Inside was a dimly lit hallway full of litter and smelling of urine, beyond which a battleship gray stairwell led up into inky blackness. There was a sudden scratching sound that made Molly jump back, then silence.

"Probably mice," said David optimistically, closing the door. "Let's see if we can get someone to come down to meet us."

David pressed the doorbell again. After a few moments there was a sharp, faraway clank, followed by a mechanical grinding sound that went on for ten or twenty seconds. Then there was another clank that seemed to have come from close by.

David led them around the side of the building to a gaping, oil-stained loading bay. He stood pensively for a moment staring at the enormous upper and lower gray-painted doors that met inside the bay like a giant set of teeth. Then he jumped up on the landing, yanked open a metal handle that held the doors together, and with both hands pulled on a thick leather strap that protruded from within. The bay doors retracted into the floor and ceiling, revealing an open-sided elevator car large enough to accommodate an automobile.

"Come on," said David, holding out a hand to Nell and hoisting her up.

Molly stood where she was.

"Come on," repeated David, offering his hand to Molly. "They wouldn't have sent the elevator down for us if they didn't want to see us."

Feeling more than a little uncertain, Molly reached out her hands. Smiling broadly, David pulled her to the landing as if she weighed no more than the rose she was still holding.

As they got into the open carrier Molly looked up and could see a dirty skylight at the top of the elevator shaft. David studied the four unmarked buttons on the wall for a moment, then pushed the third one from the bottom. The elevator lurched up. Nell watched with fascination as the cinderblock walls of the open shaft passed leisurely by. Molly held her breath.

There was another lurch and a clank. The elevator had come to rest. David pulled down on the strap of another pair of upper and lower metal doors, and they walked out into an open area with an age-stained concrete floor. Light streamed into the room from floor-to-ceiling chicken-wired windows that looked like they hadn't been washed in decades.

At the right side of the room three men in jeans, T-shirts and no particular hurry were unpacking an enormous mound of cardboard boxes that were stacked directly in front of the elevator. Each box seemed to contain nothing but large books with sturdy brown covers. Behind the men, rows of steel shelving filled with the same kind of books stretched back as far as the eye could see.

By the grimy windows to the left was a bald man seated at a long table piled high with the volumes. He wore a long white lab technician's coat over his plaid shirt and black slacks. He seemed to be writing in one of the books with some kind of strange pen the size and shape of a bottle of Worcestershire sauce.

"We're here to see Bobby Prince," said David loudly in the direction of the box unpackers, his voice echoing faintly against the cinderblock walls.

"Bobby!" shouted one of them in reply.

"Yeah?" the man at the table shouted back.

"People here to see you."

When Bobby Prince made no move to get up, Molly walked across the room to him, Nell and David following.

"I'm Molly O'Hara and this is my sister Nell," she said quietly when she got to the table. "Tuck Wittington said you'd be kind enough to talk to us about our grandfather, Richard Jellinek—Richard Julian, I mean."

"Who's he?" the man said in a raspy voice, eyeing David suspiciously.

An ashen pallor accentuated the age spots that freckled Bobby Prince's bald head. His face was wrinkled like a raisin, except around the eyes where the skin was as smooth as a burn victim's, making Molly wonder whether he'd had his face lifted long ago. His nose was bulbous, his lips were cracked, and his scraggly eyebrows were the same orangish-brown color as his remaining fringe of hair. He looked to be about seventy years old. It was very hard to see how he could have once been as handsome as Tuck claimed.

"This is David Azaria," said Molly. "He's in the show with Tuck."

"Oh, yeah," said Prince, making a face at David that was halfway between a smile and a sneer. "I saw it in previews. Regional theater crap. What did you play?"

"I'm the mean prosecutor."

"Yeah, that's right. Well, maybe you'll have a career, maybe you won't. In the end they'll throw you away, like you were a piece of garbage. Save your money, kid, that's my advice. When you're young you think it's going to go on forever. Believe me it doesn't."

"About our grandfather, Mr. Prince . . ." said Molly, but Prince ignored her, fixing David with watery gray eyes.

"Fifty years in the theater and what do I get?" he said bitterly. "Nothing. Look at me. Look what I'm doing."

"What are you doing?" asked David in a quiet voice. "Are you writing music or something?"

The book on the table was open and Molly noticed for the first time that it was covered with staffs and musical notes.

"Ha!" snorted Prince. "That's rich. You know what this is?"

Prince held up the Worcestershire-bottle thing and pressed a button on its side, which caused it to buzz like a dentist's drill.

"It's an electric eraser," he said, answering his own question. "Marinov licenses the performance rights to all his shows. All those stupid dinner theaters and high schools got orchestras, and we rent them the music. They mark up their scores in rehearsal and when they send them back yours truly's got to clean them up. All day long, five days a week, I'm erasing music books. I'm *de*-composing, goddamnit. I'm decomposing and I ain't even dead. I can't even get an audition anymore."

"I'm sorry Mr. Prince, but about our grandfather . . ." said Molly again, weakly. "Richard Julian?"

"Yeah, what about him? Dick Julian was a schmuck. Like I told Tuck, New York is a better place without him. I don't know why you want to come way the hell out here and belabor the point."

"Weren't you a friend of his?" asked Molly, confused.

"Dick Julian? Are you kidding? The man would rob the baby teeth from a two-year-old. I hung out with him so he wouldn't be able to stab me in the back by surprise, and still he was always stealing parts from me. You know we got rats here? It's those sweatshops above and below us. We're workin' in a goddamned sweatshop sandwich."

"Please, Mr. Prince," said Molly. "I know this is an imposition, but we've come all the way from North Carolina."

"All right, all right," said Prince. "I told Tuck I'd talk to you and I'm talking, ain't I? What else do you want to know?"

"Did Richard Julian ever happen to mention to you where he had originally come from?" asked Molly. "A hometown?"

"No. And if he did, how the hell would I remember?"

"Did he ever talk about his wife? Margaret Jellinek? Maggie?"

"Never heard of her."

"He never mentioned the name Gale?"

"No."

Molly's face must have fallen because Prince's expression softened somewhat. He put down the electric eraser.

"Hey look, kid," he said in a somewhat kinder voice. "I know it's not your fault that you're related to an asshole. Dick Julian and I drank together, chased broads together, did a few of the same shows—but that was it. I just never knew much about him and didn't care to."

"I suppose you have no idea where he might be now," said Molly with a sigh.

"The last time I heard, he was in England."

"England!"

"Yeah," said Prince, wiping something unpleasant from the corners of his lips. "When work dried up for us in the early eighties, he married this rich English dame who'd been chasing him for years. Lady somebody or other."

"A lady?" said Molly, exchanging an amazed glance with Nell. "She was nobility?"

"Well, I don't know how noble she was," said Prince with a nasty chuckle. "When Julian and I did the revival of *Boys from Syracuse* together she used to sit in the front row of the theater and pop her tits out of her dress in the middle of his songs to rattle him. And boy was he ever rattled. There's not a lot a man can hide when he's wearing tights, if you know what I mean."

"Do you remember her name?" said Molly, swallowing hard. Anecdotes about her grandfather's erections weren't exactly what she had hoped to hear about today.

"Stacey," said Bobby Prince, flashing a smile that might have been rakish if his teeth had been in better shape. "Racy Stacey we used to call her."

"What about her last name?"

"Who knows? I never really paid any attention. Anyway, Poor Julian was scared to death of Racy Stacey. Every night she'd wait at the stage door for him with a magnum of champagne under one arm and a nightgown in the other. Once I had to smuggle him out of the theater in a laundry cart to get past her. Another time he painted red spots on his face and we pretended he had measles. I couldn't believe it when he actually married the broad, but I guess he wasn't so stupid, huh? Now he's in England being big Lord Fauntleroy, while I gotta run an electric eraser to supplement my social security."

"Where in England? Do you know where they live?"

Bobby made a sour face, clearly feeling sorry for himself.

"It's not like I was ever invited over for tea and crumpets," he said.

"Please try to remember."

"What remember? Stacey lived in England, that's all I ever knew."

"Did she ever mention people? Places? What did she talk about?"

"Well, besides sex, all Racy Stacey ever talked about was dogs and dog shows, if that's what you mean. Who took best of breed in 1928, that sort of shit. I guess that's why she appreciated a hound like Dick Julian, huh? I'm sure they're making each other miserable. My God, she was a bore. Anything else you want to know?"

"I guess that's about it," said Molly, discouraged. That Richard Julian/aka Jellinek had married a sex-crazed lady dog fancier somewhere in England wasn't much of a clue to his present whereabouts, if he were even still alive. "It was very nice of you to take the time to see us."

"Well, not that many women bring me flowers anymore," said Bobby Prince, pointing snidely at the rose in Molly's hand.

Molly looked over to David, who made a face, then shrugged his shoulders.

"I'll put it in water for you," she said.

"Hey, I was just kidding."

"No, I appreciate your help, and it will brighten up the place," said Molly. "Do you have something I could use as a vase?"

"There's some empty Coke bottles in the bathroom," said Prince, nonplussed. "Hey, you really don't have to . . ."

"It's my pleasure," said Molly. "Where do I go?"

Prince got up and led her to an unmarked door on the other side of the room, knocking loudly to make sure it was empty.

"Woman in the bathroom," he yelled in the direction of the men still unpacking boxes of music scores. They didn't look up as Molly closed the door behind her.

The bathroom was small and predictably dirty. Alexander Marinov might have been as rich as Andrew Lloyd Webber, but he obviously wasn't sharing his good fortune with his employees. Molly was surprised somehow. Had she expected rich people in the theater to be different than rich people in other businesses?

There was a cracked mirror behind the sink, a clean bar of soap, and plenty of paper towels. Molly rinsed out one of the old Coke bottles she found in the corner of the room and filled it with water. Then she washed her hands.

When she emerged David and Nell were waiting for her by the elevator. Bobby Prince was back at his table, staring out the window with an unutterably sad expression.

"Thanks again, Mr. Prince," Molly said, walking over and placing David's rose in its Coke bottle vase in front of him. "We really appreciate your help."

"I'm an actor, you know," he said. "I don't really belong out here. I'm not really like this."

"I know."

As she walked across the room to join the others Bobby Prince held up the buzzing eraser.

"Tell Tuck I meant what I said," he called out, a sarcastic smile returning to his ruined face. "I can get him that job with Marinov anytime he's ready. Provided he can learn to run one of these."

Molly didn't speak until the elevator had made it successfully back to the ground and they were safely outside in the sunlight.

"Well, that was certainly depressing," she said with a sigh.

Nell wrinkled her nose and scratched her head.

"What time does your bus leave?" said David.

"Seven," said Molly, checking her watch. It was barely twelve-thirty.

"You've got plenty of time," said David, holding up his hand toward a lonely yellow cab that seemed just as lost as they were on the empty streets. "There's one more place I'd like to take you before we have to say good-bye."

"You mean we don't have to take the subway back?"

"We didn't have to take the subway here," said David as the cab screeched across three lanes and pulled up at the curb beside them.

"Then why did we?"

"I didn't want to deprive you of a New York experience."

"Thanks a lot!" said Molly as Nell got into the cab beside her, sandwiching her against David. "So where are we going?"

"The marriage license bureau," he said.

"I'll bet you fifty dollars that they got married in New York," said David an hour later, as they exited the big ugly Municipal Building across from City Hall back in Manhattan.

Molly didn't answer. She still felt like a fool for making such a fuss when he had first suggested going to the marriage license bureau.

"I have no intention of getting married to anyone, thank you very much," she had screeched.

Molly winced, remembering the look on David's face. Part of her remained convinced that it had been a trap, that he had known she would jump to all the wrong conclusions and embarrass herself. To her horror another part of her was disappointed that all he'd had in mind was to check the license records in case Margaret and Richard Jellinek had gotten married in New York City when they'd first arrived. A license would include Grandma's place of birth and next of kin.

After long waits, endless forms to fill out, and a stiff fee, the upshot was that six weeks from now a copy of any marriage license that the search turned up would be mailed to Molly in North Carolina.

"Fifty bucks says they find your grandparents' marriage license," repeated David. "What do you say?"

"I say, a fool and his money," said Molly. The whole thing was beginning to look hopeless.

"We should be getting back," said Molly. "Our bus . . ."

"You still have plenty of time," said David. "Aren't you getting a little hungry?"

"We've imposed on you long enough," she said, trying to be polite. It was now nearing two o'clock and they hadn't eaten anything since an overpriced continental breakfast at the hotel coffee shop. Molly was starving, and she knew Nell must be, too.

"Don't worry," said David. "I'm not proposing to pay for your lunch or anything. Your rich sister over there can treat us. Come on."

The next thing Molly knew, he was leading them up behind the Criminal Court buildings into the maze of Chinatown.

It was as if they had suddenly been transported to a different continent. One minute they were standing on wide sidewalks, dwarfed by towering buildings; the next they were in a crowded rabbit warren of narrow, noisy streets filled to bursting with bustling Asians, goggle-eyed tourists, and strange sights and smells. The stores were full of kung-fu tchotchkes and sandals. Roasted ducks hung by their necks in every other window. Displays of fruits and vegetables, familiar and unfamiliar, filled the crowded sidewalks in between open storefronts full of baskets of fish so fresh they moved.

When Molly was thoroughly disoriented, David took them through a narrow doorway into a nondescript building and up a long escalator crowded with Chinese people. At the top was an enormous room that housed the largest restaurant Molly had ever seen.

The walls were red satin where there weren't mirrors, the ceiling was low, the noise level was thunderous. Hundreds of people, virtually all of them Chinese, were eating at dozens of large round tables underneath the watchful gaze of dragons and buddhas slathered with gold radiator paint. In the narrow aisles between tables, Chinese women pushed wheeled carts filled with assorted covered bowls.

"Dim sum," said David, as a host spoke musical Chinese into a walkie-talkie and found them three empty places at a table in the middle of the room, in between a trio of lunching women and a pair of businessmen.

"Dim sum?" said Molly, overwhelmed.

"Sort of appetizers. Small portions of lots of different things. Just point at the dishes that look good to you, and don't worry if you get something you don't like. Everything's remarkably cheap, and nobody's going to be upset if you don't finish something. Just remember that the Chinese have different tastes than we do. We like things crunchy, they like things gooey. The women with the carts don't speak much English, which is just as well. I figure it's better not to know exactly what we're eating."

Molly gulped bravely, as David pointed to something on the first cart that wheeled by. It was some kind of fish dumplings that they all shared—Molly and Nell having considerably more difficulty than David working their chopsticks (no silverware was evident anywhere in the room). Surprisingly the dumplings were not only edible but tasty.

The spell broken, they began ordering in earnest, avoiding the dishes that looked too odd (like the ones featuring clearly identifiable feet from unidentifiable animals). Some things were delicious, others merely strange. After twenty-five minutes they were all laughing and full and had the table to themselves—the other diners having finished their meals and left.

"We sure don't have anything like this back in Pelletreau," said Molly, regretting the words even before they were out of her mouth. She sounded like a hick again.

Nell stood up, focusing on a pair of pictograph signs an acre away that indicated where the bathrooms were located. Molly stood, too, but Nell shook her finger, then bounced off through the crowded room, looking back over her shoulder once, clearly pleased with herself.

"Ah," said David, taking a sip of steaming green tea that had been provided by a roving team devoted solely to that purpose. "Alone at last."

"What's that supposed to mean?" said Molly uncomfortably.

"It means that we're never going to get anywhere with a chaperon always on top of us."

"Look, I told you last night . . ."

"You love your sister, yada-yada-yada" said David. "Obviously she loves you, too. That's why she's giving us a little time together. She wants you to have a life, just like I do."

Molly took a deep breath and blew it out again.

"Look. David. You've been very nice about everything. I appreciated your taking us to see Bobby Prince this morning. And to the marriage license bureau. And this lunch was a lot of fun, too, I really enjoyed it—and so did Nell, obviously. But I'm not good at flirting. I never got any practice, I'm afraid. I don't understand what you want from me."

"I want to be your friend. I want to get to know you better."

"There's nothing to know," said Molly, flustered, running nervous fingers through her short hair. "I'm not educated. I'm not beautiful. I have a very small antique shop on a country road in a tired city in North Carolina."

"And a sister to take care of."

"And a sister to take care of, that's right. Besides, we're leaving tonight."

"Let me respond to your points, one by one," said David, sitting back in his chair. "Having prosecuted more than one person with graduate degrees on felony charges, I'm not very impressed by a person's education. I admire you for running your own business; I think it's admirable that you love and want to protect your sister; and as for appearance, I happen to think you're adorable, but then I'm a sucker for the well-scrubbed tomboy look."

"Well, I happen to think you're nuts. We have nothing in common. And we're still leaving tonight."

"There's a synchronicity in the universe that supplies people

like us with common ground, Molly," said David, staring his inscrutable stare.

"What do you mean, people like us?"

"People who like one another. I like you, you know. And you
like me."

"Not even a little bit."

"Yes, you do."

"I do not," said Molly, blushing angrily.

"Neither of us cares for the subway. We both like Chinese
food. If we spend some time together we'll find all kinds of con-
nections between us. We've probably been to some of the same
places, maybe even know some of the same people."

"I doubt it," said Molly, thinking of the unexceptional people
she knew and the few places she'd been.

"We both know Tuck, don't we? And I actually was in North
Carolina once. I took a deposition in Winston-Salem for a grand
larceny case."

"I hardly think that gives us a basis for a . . . whatever. And
living six hundred miles apart I don't see any practical way for us
to get to know one another better."

"Would you like to?"

"Would I like to what?"

"Get to know me better?"

"I don't know how to get through to you," said Molly. "Don't
you see it's impossible? That it just doesn't make any sense?"

"You didn't answer my question. Would you like to get to
know me better?"

Molly squirmed in her chair.

"Please, David," she said quietly. "I think I bruise easily. I'm
not even sure of that. No practice, remember? I think it would
make more sense if we just went back to our respective corners of
the planet and got on with our very different lives."

"You're very logical, you know that?"

"I suppose," said Molly miserably.

"I used to be logical," said David. "I would look down the road, and if I couldn't see my destination I wouldn't take a single step. From where I stood in the District Attorney's office in Stamford I could look forward and see my entire career stretched out before me, just the way my father saw it for me before I was born."

"Is your father a lawyer, too?"

David nodded.

"He was a founder of one of the biggest firms in Boston. He's now a federal judge. Dad sent me off to the same private school where he had gone and then I went to Yale, just as he had. He even gave me a clear vision of the type of girl I should marry. When I looked down the road I could see her clearly, an old-money debutante, socially well connected and comfortable in the world, but one who wouldn't commit suicide like my mother did."

"I'm sorry," said Molly. "How old were you?"

"Fifteen. It confounded my father when I turned thirty-five last year and still hadn't married. He didn't understand why I wasn't looking ahead. But I was looking ahead. I could see the problems of living down every path I looked, so I never took any of them, never got involved with anyone, never formed relationships. I was just as paralyzed by logic as you are."

"I'm not paralyzed by anything."

"Yes, you are. Oh, it's very intelligent not to make a move unless you can see exactly where you're going. The only problem is that you stop living. From where I stood in my courtroom, I could look out and see myself thirty years down the road, as successful and respected as my father is. The only thing I couldn't see was the mess and madness and elation that constitutes a life. Where are you going to be in thirty years, Molly?"

Molly looked down the road she was on and she could see

very clearly where she would be. She would be in a little antique shop on the outskirts of Pelletreau with her sister. Suddenly she was afraid.

"Anyway," said David, "since I've been doing *Bank Street Story* I look out and I can't see what I'll be doing six months from now, let alone in thirty years. There's just a mist of possibilities. When I took the part in the play, my father thought I had lost my mind. I suppose I had, but I'm happier for it. I've become an actor in more than one sense of the word. I'm doing things, not fantasizing them; I'm living my life, not thinking it."

"You could just as easily say you were gambling," said Molly. "Aren't you afraid that you'll end up like Bobby Prince?"

"Sometimes," said David. "But I believe that we have to risk, to strive into the unknown without a guaranteed outcome, and learn from our mistakes or else why bother? And you do, too, or you wouldn't be here in New York. You think you're looking for your grandmother's family, but you're really looking for yourself. And you have no guarantees that you'll like what you find, either."

"David . . ."

"It may not be practical or logical or even smart for me to want to get to know you better, Molly O'Hara," he said quietly, almost in a whisper, "but if I wanted to be practical or logical or smart in the way the world defines those things, I would be in a courtroom in Stamford today—and miserable for it. I hope you'll throw out your logic, too, and just see where things go between us."

Before Molly could think of anything to say, Nell returned. She looked pleased with herself as she watched the shy, hopeful, frightened glances that passed between Molly and David. When Nell paid for the lunch with the money David had given her, leaving a generous tip, she still came out almost twenty dollars ahead.

The three of them walked all the way back to the hotel, an impossibly long walk that passed by far too quickly. David pointed out the sights from Soho to Greenwich Village to the Empire State Building and finally Times Square. Molly asked questions, and tried not to look too impressed when he knew all the answers.

David carried their bag to the Port Authority bus terminal, then waited with them, while Molly tried Taffy again with no results. He told them funny stories about the theater and New York and sad stories about the court system. As the bus for Pelletreau finally began to board, Molly and David exchanged addresses and phone numbers. They promised to be in touch soon—even though it made no logical sense.

Molly's thoughts were still with him as the bus fought its way through New Jersey and into a sunset made beautiful by all the pollutants in the atmosphere. David's words were in her mind when she closed her eyes and fell easily into sleep. She dreamed of him as they sped through the night, and though she couldn't remember the dreams when she awoke, she woke up smiling.

When the bus pulled into the Pelletreau bus station the next morning, Molly felt the world was a wonderful place. She wasn't even angry when she called Taffy from a pay phone to come and pick them up and found there was still no answer at the shop. Molly just shrugged her shoulders and shook her head as she bundled herself and Nell into a taxi for the expensive ride out to Porcupine Road. She would simply take the full amount of the cab, plus a generous tip, out of what she owed Taffy.

As the taxi drove the last mile of U.S. 29 through the lush, familiar trees of Pelletreau, Nell kept stealing smug glances at her sister. The whole way from the bus station, Molly didn't blush once. She felt alive and warm and happy and wanted, and thought that nothing in the world could ever change the way she felt.

There was still a smile on her face when they pulled into their driveway. But her expression turned to one of horror as she stared at the lot where their little white house with its cozy porch and black shutters had stood.

There was nothing there now but a fieldstone foundation and a pile of charred rubble with a few blacked spars of timber protruding from the ashes. The burned-out shell of what had once been a white van sat underneath the collapsed carport. Molly blinked her eyes again and again, but the impossible picture wouldn't change.

Enchanted Cottage Antiques was gone.

Seven

"Blown to smithereens," said Stanley Hupperman, shaking his head and causing the great wattles of flesh beneath his chins to flap together audibly. "Poor little Taffy. She's singing with the Heavenly Choir now. She's singing to Jesus."

Molly nodded soberly. Taffy had been like a force of nature. As much as Molly didn't want to admit it, she had been their best friend. It was still hard to believe she was dead.

"And this office is going to miss Alice Markham, too, let me tell you," Mr. Hupperman went on, repeating what he had said endlessly at the funeral on Sunday. "She wasn't just another pretty face, you know. Alice was smart as whip. She went to classes every night after work, studying for her CPA. And she was quite a dancer, I understand."

Though Mr. Hupperman resembled Taffy in terms of size and shape, his voice was nothing like hers. It was deep and soft and sibilant, like the hiss of a steam radiator or bacon frying on a griddle. Sitting in a leather armchair behind his big desk, he looked like a walrus in a shirt and tie.

"I remember how pleased Mrs. Hupperman and I were when the two of them became friends," he went on, his eyes watery. "Alice was such a live wire. We really thought she could help poor Taffy come out of her shell, maybe meet a nice fella and settle down. Taffy was always such a shy, sensitive little thing, God rest her soul."

Molly nodded again. Mr. Hupperman had never had any idea who his daughter was. There was no point in shattering his illusions now.

Molly glanced over at her sister, but couldn't catch her eye. Nell was curled up in the second chair in Taffy's father's private office at Hupperman Insurance, staring out the window. Since they had returned to Pelletreau and found Enchanted Cottage Antiques in ashes, Nell had retreated further into her own silent world. The lively vivacious young woman who had danced the night away with the Broadway gypsies was gone, replaced by a zombie. It made Molly sick inside every time she saw her.

The past five days still seemed like some kind of surreal nightmare.

After the shock of finding their home and business destroyed, Molly had spent endless, excruciating hours with police officers and functionaries, answering questions and going over and over details.

She remembered that Nell had cleared the books out of their ancient gas stove and heated up a casserole before they had gone to see Clyde and their father last Tuesday (had they left for New York City only a week ago? Molly wondered—it seemed like a lifetime had passed since then).

Molly was certain that they had turned off the gas, but somehow there had been a leak. Exactly what had caused it would never be known since the explosion and the ensuing fire had destroyed everything. Molly was also convinced that they would have left some windows open before going out—it had been a hot day, she remembered—but apparently they hadn't.

The final link in the deadly chain of events had been a faulty light switch, according to the police. After Taffy had dropped Molly and Nell off at the bus station, she had driven directly to Enchanted Cottage Antiques with Alice Markham, opened the back door, and flipped on the lights. The light switch had sparked, igniting the built-up gas fumes, and everything had been blown to smithereens as Mr. Hupperman had so eloquently put it.

That was why Taffy hadn't answered the phone when Molly had called the shop from New York before going off with David last Thursday morning. There had been no phone left to answer after Tuesday night. There had been no shop. There had been no Taffy.

The police had naturally assumed that the fragments of two female bodies, found in the charred remains of Enchanted Cottage Antiques, were Molly and Nell. Taffy had been about Nell's height, and Alice Markham had resembled Molly in stature. The O'Hara sisters' deaths had made the front page of the newspaper. They had even printed Molly's high school yearbook picture. Perky young antique dealers weren't blown to smithereens every day in Pelletreau.

The police had been surprisingly sensitive, going through their questions without pressure, bringing Molly coffee, keeping their distance from Nell so as not to upset her more. One detective still remembered their mother's unsolved murder, having worked on the case.

Sergeant Arlo Couvertie had listened respectfully when Molly told him about the red-haired man with the mustache who had been at the nursing home before Margaret Jellinek died, and who had reappeared at the funeral and driven by their shop.

"He was going to kill us, just like he killed Grandma," Molly had said calmly. "We had been inside since Grandma's funeral. He must have been waiting for us to leave the house. When we did, he broke in, fiddled with the switch, closed the windows, and turned on the gas."

"I'm afraid there's no evidence of that, Miss O'Hara," Couvertie had replied. "There's no evidence that this man even existed. I called the nursing home like you said. The receptionist on duty, a Mrs. Springer, doesn't recall any such male visitor to Mrs. Jellinek before her death. Of course, she didn't remember you and your sister, either."

"He killed Grandma. I know it. And he was going to kill us. We were the ones who were supposed to die when the house blew up."

Molly had not even felt frightened when she said it, though the fear had grown over the past few days. She had merely felt sure.

"Why would someone want to kill you, Miss O'Hara?" Couvertie had asked. "Why would someone want to kill your grandmother?"

"Because . . ." Molly had begun, ready to tell him about the emerald ring. She had stopped in midsentence.

If the redheaded man had smothered Margaret Jellinek to get her ring, why would he rig an explosion for Molly and Nell? If he believed they were now in possession of the emerald, why blow them up and risk losing it entirely if they happened to have it with them? Or what if they had hidden it in the shop? As a motive for murder, the ring made no sense.

Besides, Molly still didn't know where her grandmother had gotten the emerald. She couldn't believe the ring was stolen, but telling the police about it was a can of worms that was better left unopened. Her dealer's instinct for secrecy took over. She shook her head.

"I don't know why anyone would want to kill us," Molly had said honestly.

"If you like, we can get a court order and have your grandmother's body exhumed," Sergeant Couvertie had offered. "It's not going to be easy for the coroner to confirm a cause of death on an embalmed body, but we'll try if that's what you want."

Molly couldn't bear the thought.

Instead she just had the sergeant call Oscar Winnick and let him know what had happened so the shock wouldn't be great when Molly got on the phone and asked if the old jeweler could put them up until they could get resettled. They had no other place to stay.

"So, what can we do for you, Mr. Hupperman?" said Molly wearily, snapping back to the present.

"Beg pardon?" said Stanley Hupperman, lost in thoughts of his own as he gazed at the framed photo on his desk of a six-year-old Taffy in a pink crinoline dress licking a lollipop.

Molly still felt guilty and horrible that Taffy had died in an "accident" that rightly should have killed Molly and Nell, but Mr. Hupperman had been incredibly decent about everything, not blaming anyone, just babbling on about his dear sweet little girl. Mrs. Hupperman had been just as nice, though she said after the funeral that she'd had premonitions of explosions ever since they had bought little Taffy her first chemistry set twenty years ago.

"You called and asked us to come over," said Molly. "Is there something we can do for you?"

"Oh, no, no, no," said Stanley Hupperman, shaking his jowls. "I asked you to come over here because there's something I wanted to do for you."

"For us?"

He opened the top drawer of his desk and took out a cashier's check that he passed across the desk. It was made out to Molly O'Hara for more money than she had ever seen in her life.

"I don't understand," she stammered. "What is this?"

"It's your settlement, Molly. The team here at Hupperman Insurance prides itself on facilitating benefit distribution in times of crisis. Your carrier, Mason-Dixon American Casualty, the Friendly Southern Neighbor, could hardly argue that what we have here is a total loss situation. I took personal charge of expediting the matter myself, felt I owed it to Taffy. The best way to cope with grief is to put on that harness, Molly. Start rebuilding right away is my advice to you."

"I don't know what to say, Mr. Hupperman," said Molly, staring at the check. "Thank you."

"I got something else for you, too," the big man went on. "At the house on Sunday after the funeral, you were saying about how you had gone to New York, looking for your grandfather and all. All you knew was that he'd moved to England and married a Lady Stacey somebody, who was a dog fancier. You wanted to find him, but didn't think you ever could."

"Yes, that's right."

"Well, that got me to thinking. I needed something to take my mind off . . . you know. Anyways, it's a whole new world out there with that Internet thing. You can do everything from ordering a truckload of gravel to reading the want ads in today's *Times Picayune*. So I asked our computer genius to go out and see what he could find for you. Five minutes later he comes back with a name on the membership roster of the Chinese Pug Association of Somerset, Great Britain, UK. Lady Stacey Farfel-Julian. Julian, that was what you said your grandpa changed his name to, right? So we called up international information and got the phone number."

He handed Molly a Hupperman Insurance notepad with a neatly printed telephone number beginning with the 011 44 dialing code for England.

Molly looked at the number and laughed.

"What's funny?" said Stanley Hupperman, smiling, too, eager to be let in on the joke.

"It's just . . ." Molly shook her head. "We go all the way to New York and come away with a blank. I didn't know if it even made sense to keep looking, and now, after everything that's happened, this just drops right into my lap."

Mr. Hupperman stood up from behind his desk. With one hand he unwrapped his sport coat from the back of his chair. With the other he pushed his telephone across the desk to Molly.

"You're welcome to use the phone if you want to give them a call," he said. "You'll have all the privacy you could want here. I got to take a meetin'."

"It's long distance to England. It'll cost a fortune."

"Now I don't think we're gonna worry about that, Molly," said Hupperman with a tired smile. "Taffy loved you and Nell like sisters, you know. Poor sweet little thing."

He closed the door behind him.

"Can you believe this?" Molly said, shaking her head.

Nell didn't answer.

"What do you think? Should we call him?"

Nell didn't answer again. She didn't even look around, just stared out the window as she had been doing since they had arrived.

Molly went over and knelt by her sister's chair.

"This could be Richard Jellinek's phone number. Grandma's husband. Our grandfather, the actor, who changed his name to Richard Julian. We can just call him up."

Nell stared out the window, showing no sign that she understood. Molly stroked her arm.

"I'm not wrecking your life, am I, honey? David thought maybe I was holding you back. You know, I would never want to do that. If you don't want us to be together, you'll tell me, won't you?"

Nell still didn't respond. Sergeant Couvertie had thought Nell was in shock when he first saw her after the explosion and wanted to have the police department psychologist take a look at her. Molly had refused adamantly, and he hadn't pressed the matter. Psychologists had gotten hold of Nell after Evangeline O'Hara Cole had been murdered. All they could think to do was shoot her full of chemicals and offer to fry her brain with electroshock. Even Clyde had been smart enough to stop them before they could do real damage. Molly wasn't going to let them get their hands on her again. Nell would come out of this on her own. She always had before.

Molly nervously picked up the phone and punched out the number that was written on the notepad. After several rings a male voice answered with a syrupy British accent.

"Telephone of Mr. Richard Julian and Lady Stacey Farfel-Julian."

"Is this Richard Julian?" asked Molly, holding her breath.

"This is his residence. He is not here at present."

"When do you expect him?"

"Her ladyship and Mr. Julian are traveling. They are not expected back until April."

"April!" exclaimed Molly. "Where have they gone?"

"Who is calling, please?" said the voice, polite but firm.

"My name is Molly O'Hara. I'm a relative of Mr. Jellinek's, I mean Mr. Julian's and . . . and . . . there's been a death in the family. I need to speak with him personally. I'm calling from the United States."

"One extends one's condolences, madam. Mr. Julian and her ladyship left yesterday for the Bedlingham dog show. They are staying with friends for whom we do not have an address. After Bedlingham, madam and sir are scheduled to leave for the first leg of their trip. They'll be staying in New Zealand beginning in September. I can forward a message to them there if you so desire."

"How long are they going to be at this dog show?" said Molly.

"They depart Bedlingham on Friday," said the voice. "The aeroplane leaves the following day."

"Can you tell me where it's being held? The Bedlingham dog show?"

"Why, in Bedlingham, of course. Will there be a message, madam?"

"No, no message. But thank you. I'll try to reach him some other way."

Molly said good-bye and hung up the phone. Then she sat staring out the window for a long time, lost in thought. A series of pictures paraded through her mind. Her mother with the bullet hole in her forehead. Margaret Jellinek's lifeless body, the pillow on her chest. Clyde. Daddy. The red-haired man behind the wheel of the white Mercury Sable. Taffy. Alice Markham. David Azaria, looking dark and intense, his intelligent eyes blazing.

She felt a hand on her arm and looked up. Nell was standing next to her, trying to smile and not succeeding very well.

"Welcome back," said Molly softly, taking her hand. "Are you okay?"

Nell nodded.

"Do you understand what happened, honey? About the shop? About Taffy?"

Nell nodded again. Her face was pale but her eyes were alive again. Molly wanted to take her home and protect her, keep her safe. But their home was gone. And Molly felt like they would never be safe again.

"Look, Nell," Molly said soberly. "I need to be honest with you. I don't want you to be frightened, but I think the explosion at the shop may not have been an accident. Someone might have done it deliberately."

Nell tilted her head questioningly.

"No, I don't know why. I don't even know if I'm right. But there were those stories in the paper over the past few days, about how it wasn't us who died. I'm worried about that red-haired man. Or maybe it's somebody else I should be worried about. Or maybe I'm imagining the whole thing. All I know is that if there's really someone out there who doesn't like us, he might try again to hurt us, now that the news is out that we're still alive. Do you understand?"

Nell nodded once more. Molly smiled and patted her sister's hand.

"The only problem is," she said grimly, "what are we going to do about it?"

—∘-∘-∘-∘

Oscar had lent them his car for the morning, a cozy old Volvo. When they returned from Stanley Hupperman's office, the old jeweler was watering his vegetables with a garden hose.

Molly stood next to a neat row of onions and told him about the insurance check, about her fears for their safety, about Richard Julian and how he would soon be unreachable for months. Oscar listened with his usual quiet calmness, but the concern was evident on his face.

"So what do you think?" Molly asked when she had finished.

Oscar stood in straight-backed silence for a moment and gave the tomatoes a final drink.

"Let me ask you a question, Molly," he said as he turned off the hose and sat down on the porch steps. "Why are the two of you sticking around in Pelletreau like sitting ducks?"

"That's what I've been wondering myself," said Molly. "There's not much to keep us here anymore, is there? We've got no home, no business. None of our family ever cared about us except Grandma, and she's gone now. Taffy . . . ."

Molly let her voice taper off.

"Is the insurance settlement enough to get you out from under the mortgage for your shop?" asked Oscar.

Molly nodded.

"Would you have enough left over to make a fresh start somewhere else? Maybe with that family of your Grandma's up North you've been wondering about?"

"I think so."

"So what's the problem?"

"The problem," said Molly, taking a deep breath, "is doing the right thing, being decent human beings. How can we just run away when somebody may have murdered Taffy? Maybe murdered Grandma, too."

"But the police don't think anybody was murdered, do they?"

"No," said Molly miserably.

"And you and your sister may be in real danger."

Molly looked at the ground and didn't answer. Oscar stared at her for a minute, then smiled a kind, knowing smile.

"I think you've already decided what you're going to do," he said finally in a gentle voice. "I think you're just looking for some wise older party to give you permission, aren't you?"

"We know Richard Julian will be at the Bedlingham dog show through Thursday," said Molly, looking up. "That gives us only two days, not counting today, to get there and talk to him. If we don't do it now, we won't be able to reach him for months and months."

"Then it seems to me you've got too much to do to stand

around gabbing with an old man," said Oscar, rising to his feet. "You've got passports?"

"In our safe-deposit box at the bank," said Molly, nodding. "We were planning to take a trip to Mexico one day. Can we really just leave, Oscar? Just walk away from this whole mess?"

"Not if you don't have plane tickets, you can't," said Oscar, leading them to the back door. "You phone the airport and see if you can get a flight or this will all be academic. I'll call Evelyn. She'll be able to settle things for you here, take care of loose ends."

Evelyn Winnick Trice was Oscar's daughter, an attorney with a Camp Avenue law firm.

"I've never run away from my problems before," said Molly, shaking her head. "I don't feel very brave about doing this."

"You're just looking out for your own interests," said Oscar, glancing at his watch. "And your sister's. The police can handle the rest. It's their job, not yours. Now come on, let's get going. It's past eleven already and you've got a lot to do if you're going to get out of here today."

Oscar called his daughter and told her he was on his way over, while Molly and Nell went upstairs to gather up their few belongings from Oscar's spare room. Then Molly called the airport. All the planes to London from Raleigh-Durham were sold out, but she was able to book two seats on an 8:00 P.M. flight out of New York City. They needed to get to the Pelletreau airport by four to make their connection.

Oscar drove the car himself to the bank, where Molly retrieved Margaret Jellinek's ring, the few important papers they had, and their passports and closed out the safe-deposit box. She also deposited the check from Mason-Dixon American Casualty into their account, taking enough money in traveler's checks to keep them going for a while. All the while she could hear Taffy's voice booming in her mind that she was being an impulsive nitwit.

But Taffy was dead. And whoever had blown her to bits had meant it for Molly and Nell.

"What about clothes?" said Oscar as they pulled out of the bank's parking lot. "Everything you owned was blown up with your store. What are you going to do about clothes for the rest of your life?"

"I guess we'll have to buy some."

"Well, I'm glad one of us is still thinking."

They stopped at the Wellers Square Mall, which was on the way to Evelyn's office. Molly and Nell augmented their wardrobe with enough extra clothing and necessities until they could shop more leisurely. They also bought two good suitcases, large enough to live out of for a while, and a small brown leather shoulder bag where Molly could put their money, passports, and family papers.

When they left Evelyn an hour later, Oscar's daughter had power of attorney to wind up all Molly and Nell's legal and financial affairs in Pelletreau. Evelyn would settle their mortgage with the bank, pay whatever credit card bills came in, and take care of their other obligations like tracking down the Nicholsons and refunding their four-hundred-dollar deposit on the chest of drawers that had been blown to smithereens along with Enchanted Cottage Antiques. Oscar's daughter would also sell the Porcupine Road property and wire the proceeds to Molly when she and Nell got settled.

There was one more stop Oscar insisted on making before driving them to the airport. At his son's jewelry store the old man picked out a thick gold chain for which he refused any payment.

"We're the ones who should be giving you a present, Oscar," said Molly. "For all you've done today. For putting us up when we really needed help. And for putting up with us."

"Oh, hush, Molly," said Oscar, opening the chain's clasp and stringing Margaret Jellinek's ring on it. "None of my friends have ever returned from the dead before. Just knowing you're still around, driving people crazy is present enough for me."

"Thanks, Oscar."

"I don't much like you traipsing around the world with this emerald, though. Why don't you let my son keep it here for you in his safe? You could always come back for it when you need it."

"My grandmother traipsed around for fifty years with this ring, and she was fine," said Molly, letting him put the chain with the ring on it over her head. She then slipped the ensemble beneath her blouse to conceal it. She did not say what she knew was in Oscar's mind as well as her own. She was not coming back. She was never coming back to Pelletreau.

At the airport Molly kissed him on one cheek, Nell kissed him on the other. It had all happened so quickly that Molly hadn't even had time to think of a fancy good-bye speech. Neither had Oscar, which was probably just as well. If they said any more, somebody was going to cry. The old jeweler watched in silence as their plane sped down the runway and ascended into the sky.

Three hours later Molly and Nell had checked their luggage through to Heathrow and were in the international departures terminal at Kennedy airport, waiting for their flight to board.

"Wait here and don't talk to any strangers," said Molly. "I have to make a call."

Nell pulled the New York Yankees baseball cap that they had bought at the gift shop down over her eyes and made a big show of pretending to be asleep.

Molly walked over to one of the nearby phones, took out the slip of paper on which David Azaria had written, and punched in his phone number.

"This isn't *exactly* David Azaria," answered David's voice after a ring, "but it can be if you leave your name and number after the beep, and he'll get back to you."

Molly was disappointed but not surprised. Of course she would get David's machine at this hour. He had a performance tonight. He was probably at the theater already.

"Hi, David," she said, feeling awkward saying his name aloud. It sounded more familiar in her head where it had been repeating itself endlessly since she had last seen him. "This is Molly. Molly O'Hara. I'm sorry I miss you. Missed you."

Oh God, she thought, I sound like an idiot.

"We're at Kennedy airport, which is why I'm calling," Molly rattled on, suddenly manic. "Look, that address and phone number I gave you for us in North Carolina, they aren't good anymore. I didn't want you to worry if you called and didn't get an answer. Not that you would worry probably. . . . I mean, not that I expected you to call or anything. I just thought . . . I just thought I'd let you know."

Molly wasn't usually tongue-tied. She hated answering machines. She wished she could start her message over, but it was too late.

"Anyway, it's too complicated to go into now, but we've left Pelletreau for good. We've got a line on Richard Jellinek and we're on our way to England to see if we can talk to him. I'm not sure where we're headed after that. I'll call when we're settled. Just to let you know where we are so you won't worry. Not that I expect you to worry, there's nothing to worry about, I think . . . I mean I don't think . . . I mean . . ."

Molly tried to think of what else to say. Nothing intelligent came to mind.

"I mean I'm sorry I missed you," she said again. "Nell says hello. Bye."

Nell had turned the baseball cap backward and had a big smile on her face when Molly returned. Her eyes darted back and forth, watching the promenade of travelers on their way to foreign places. The minute the plane had taken off from the Pelletreau airport, she had come alive again.

Molly felt different, too. It was more than just relief at being away from Pelletreau with its sad memories and the danger that may or may not still stalk them there. By walking away from all she had ever known it was like she was letting herself be reborn. There could be a new Molly: a Molly without the terrible burden of the past; a Molly with infinite possibilities; a Molly who could live her life, not just think it—just as David had said.

She had worried that she would feel like a coward, running away. But she didn't. She felt safe. And more important, Nell was safe, too. That was the whole point of burning your bridges behind you, wasn't it? No one could use them to come after you.

"David wasn't there," Molly said to Nell as an attendant announced over the loudspeaker that their flight was ready to board. "I left a message."

Nell nodded happily, picked up their carry-on bag full of guidebooks to Great Britain, magazines, and sundries they had purchased for the trip, and led her sister once again into the unknown, this time for keeps.

Local time was eight-fifteen when the plane landed in a very rainy London the next morning. The actual flight had taken only six hours, and Molly had gotten little sleep.

Between fitful naps over the Atlantic she had thought about David Azaria and had read about England in her guidebooks. The England of Chaucer, Shakespeare, and Dickens. The England of kings and queens and Ascot. The England of the Clews transferware platter that had once graced the mantlepiece of Enchanted Cottage Antiques and which was now blue-and-white earthenware dust.

Heathrow airport was hardly the quaint England of guidebooks, however. It was a hectic, modern place, which bore about as much resemblance to the land of Robin Hood and Thomas Chippendale as tin did to tintinnabulation. Businesswomen sat on plastic furniture typing on laptop computers. Men jabbered with their stockbrokers from tiny handheld cellular phones. Slick advertisements bombarded travelers from every wall. Aside from the customs officers speaking in British accents, Molly and Nell might have still been in New York.

"Any suggestions on what we do now?" said Molly to her sister as they made their way through the crowds.

Nell made hopeful motions of a fork bringing things into her mouth.

"You just had a croissant on the plane," Molly said, rolling her eyes. "You're turning into a human eating machine, do you know that?"

Nell grinned and nodded.

Molly hadn't worked out any brilliant plan about how to find their grandfather, Richard Julian, beyond just getting to the Bedlingham dog show and asking around for him. Bedlingham, she knew from a map in one of the guidebooks, was up in the northeast of England, near York. Problem number one was how to get there from here.

Happily there was someone who might be able to help. He sat in an information kiosk not far from the baggage claim, a man as thin as a yardstick whose Adam's apple protruded nearly as far as his nose.

"We'd like to go to Bedlingham," Molly said politely, approaching his desk.

"You are Yanks?"

"Yes."

"And you desire to go to Bedlingham?"

"That's right."

"Good Lord, a miracle."

"Is there some problem about going to Bedlingham?" asked Molly, concerned. The man had placed his hands together as if in prayer and was smiling beatifically at the ceiling.

"No, not at all," he said, craning his long neck back from heaven. "I'm just deeply moved to have an American with a sensible request. Yesterday I had eleven of your people who wished to have tea with a member of the royal family, four with messages for rock stars, and one poor woman from Beverly Hills, California, who insisted on being told Richard Burton's phone number."

"But Richard Burton is dead," said Molly.

The man nodded sadly.

"You see why I am presently in night school studying chiropractic. Soon I shall be no longer Mr. Tourist Information, knows all, tells all; I shall be *Doctor* Tourist Information, readjusts your spine. You are interested in dogs."

"Pardon me?"

"Dogs. If you wish to go to Bedlingham this time of year it must be for the dog show."

"Yes, that's right," said Molly. "I didn't know it was so famous."

"Oh, yes," said Mr. Tourist Information, tapping the tips of his long fingers together. "The Bedlingham Dog Show is *the* major event of the British canine world. I know this, you see, because my aunt Edwina is a positive fiend for schnauzers. She's actually begun to look like one, poor dear."

"So what's the best way for us to get to Bedlingham from here?" asked Molly again.

"Do you drive?" asked the man, then held up his hands in mock horror. "No. Silly question. Of course you drive. All Americans drive. It's a wonder you're not born with your fingers attached to tiny steering wheels, and little hooters in your heads."

"Hooters?" said Molly, incredulous.

"That's British for horns, you know. Klaxons. I expect you'll want to rent a car, won't you?"

"How long of a drive is it?"

"Four or five hours. Of course, that's four or five hours in a car that has the steering wheel on what would be the passenger's side in your country. And you'll be driving on the wrong side of the road for you. In a strange country. In the rain. Is there some reason why you don't wish to take the aeroplane, hmmm?"

"Maybe because we didn't know there was one."

"Yes, of course, there's a plane," said the man with a sigh indicative of long suffering. "A commuter flight to Leeds at let's see. . . ." He closed his eyes momentarily, consulted some inner airline schedule and blinked triumphantly. "Departs at two-fifty, gate forty-four *F* as in Ferdinand the Bull. You can rent a car at Leeds and from there it is only a short drive to Bedlingham and your famous dog show."

Molly proffered her thanks. Mr. Tourist Information bowed slightly from the waist, then turned his pained attention to a man with a Texas accent who wanted to know how he could take that James Bond fella out for a drink.

After changing a few hundred dollars of traveler's checks into British pounds and booking seats on the flight to Leeds, Molly and Nell had an inedible second breakfast of sticky buns and dishwater coffee at an airport coffee shop. They then wandered around exploring duty-free stores and newsstands until they came to rest at one of the less hectic seating areas. Here Molly read guidebooks and tried without success to nap until their departure, hours away.

Nell, who could sleep as comfortably on planes as she did on buses and who had gotten a good night's rest on the trip over, amused herself by watching people and nibbling candy bars, which she could do endlessly without gaining weight.

Finally they were in the air again, landing this time at a more picturesque location—if picturesque meant old-fashioned and a bit run-down. Leeds itself, which they passed over on the flight in, was just a gray blob they could barely make out, since it was raining here, too, though not as hard as it had been in London.

The airport car rental lot emptied out directly onto an anonymous modern highway that would not have seemed out of place in New Jersey. Molly pretended to be confident as she drove the little car, which indeed had its steering wheel on the passenger's side, through traffic that sped along on the wrong side of the road.

It was only when they got off at the exit designated on the rental agency map, did England begin to look a little more like it was supposed to—a quiet landscape of stone houses, sleepy villages, and ancient-looking forests—though TV antennas, telephone wires, and traffic signs still fought with Molly's illusions of what the country should be.

The rain had slowed to a drizzle when they finally reached their destination a little before five o'clock. It was too late to make it to the dog show, which must have been a very wet affair if it had gone on today at all, considering the rain. Fortunately the show had another day to run. The Julians would not be leaving for New Zealand until Friday, the day after tomorrow.

Bedlingham was technically a city, but it seemed not much bigger than most of the towns through which they had passed. According to one of the guidebooks it had been an important center as early as the fourteenth century, and there were Tudor buildings on the square. One of these was a pub called the Ploughman's Lunch, which reminded Molly how hungry she was, having had only one candy bar all afternoon to Nell's six.

It was a relief to get off the road and into the dark old pub. A crackling fire took all the chill out of the air that the rain had put in. Molly and Nell made their way through a crowd of jovial, ruddy-faced men drinking dark ale at the bar, to a quiet table in the back of the room.

As Molly squinted at the menu scrawled on a blackboard, she knew for the first time how far from home she was. They didn't serve bangers and mash in Pelletreau, North Carolina. Or cock-a-leekie soup. Or chip butties. It made her almost homesick for a plate of good old-fashioned American fried calamari.

A middle-aged woman dressed in slacks and a colorful top approached their table after a few moments, her hands on her hips, a disarming smile on her kind, open face.

"Aftanoon, ladies" she said. "Wha' canna gutcha, then?"

It was English, Molly knew, though the accent was strange and guttural—almost as if she was trying to swallow her words before they emerged.

"I'll have the ploughman's lunch," said Molly, figuring the pub's signature dish couldn't be too horrible if the place had been in business for as long as the oak tavern table they were sitting at seemed to indicate. From its patina and pegged construction Molly knew the table had not been made this century, and perhaps not in the last either. If she had had a shop left and a cheap way to ship it home, Molly would have made them an offer.

"Ta," said the waitress. "An' you, miss?"

Nell counted down on the blackboard six items.

"One toad in the 'ole, and one ploughman's lunch it is," said the woman, nodding, and hustled back to the kitchen.

"*Toad in the hole?*" repeated Molly incredulously. "Are you out of your mind?"

Nell nodded happily.

When their lunches arrived, however, it was clear that it was Nell who had gotten the better deal. Molly couldn't decide whether it was beginner's luck or whether her sister actually knew something. The ploughman's lunch was simply a chunk of cheese, a piece of crusty brown bread, and a pickled onion, accompanied by a tall glass of warm dark ale. Toad in the hole, on the other hand turned out to be hearty sausages cooked in some kind of batter, and served with several well-boiled vegetables.

When Nell had finished the last of the ale—it was too warm for Molly's taste—the waitress came back and asked in her strangulated dialect whether there would be anything else.

"Is there some place where we can find a room for the night?" said Molly.

"Na, miss. Na this time o' year. The dog show, y'see? Everythin' is ta'en moonths in advance."

"Oh, dear," said Molly.

"I ca' telephone around, if ye like."

"That would be very kind of you."

"It's na trouble," said the waitress. "We don't get many foreigners in these parts."

The woman disappeared through a doorway behind the bar and returned after a few minutes.

"I found you a place at the inn in Manxton," she announced with evident pride. "S'only a few miles from here, but I best draw you a map."

It was another half hour of hard driving on dark, rain-swept roads before Molly finally found the Dainty Shepherds Inn in Manxton. Settled in their room at last, Nell happily played hide-and-seek in the room's two enormous armoires. Molly collapsed into a overstuffed chair big and soft enough to live in, and waited for the color to return to her knuckles. Clearly she had made the right decision about not driving up all the way from London.

"Things are going to be different from now on, Nell," said Molly after a while, staring out across the room to the leaded windows and into the night. "No more Pelletreau, no more dead ends. We're going to make a whole new start, a whole new life. Everything is possible, just like David said. Can you believe we're actually here in England?"

But even if Molly's sister had been able to speak there would have been no answer. Nell was already asleep in the big bed.

The next morning was blissfully sunny and warm enough to feel like August again, which it was. Molly had slept soundly and felt rested and more relaxed than she had been in days. The nightmares of the past few weeks seemed like a distant memory.

After a big English breakfast that included red orange juice, eggs, kippered herring, and strange-looking bacon, they drove the fifteen minutes back to Bedlingham (it was much closer in the daylight apparently), and followed the signs to the dog show.

Even from a distance the Bedlingham dog show was as impressive as Mr. Tourist Information had implied. It was set up in a grassy field outside of Bedlingham that appeared larger in area than the city itself. Cars were backed up from the entrance on the narrow road as far as the eye could see.

It took a good twenty minutes before Molly and Nell moved to the front of the queue and were able to park. During that whole time Molly didn't stop talking. If all her hopes had surfaced last night, this morning it was all her doubts and insecurities.

"Oh, God, don't let me blow it," Molly chattered compulsively. "What will I say? Will he listen? You know there's a chance we won't even find this Richard Julian person. That would be pretty hysterical, wouldn't it, after coming all this way? Not that I'm really so eager to meet the guy. I mean, I'm not angry at him or anything. After all, he was never part of our lives. And Grandma got over him years ago, I'm sure. She never even mentioned his name, so she couldn't exactly have been pining, know what I mean?"

Nell nodded. She actually seemed to be listening for a change, but her eyes were worried. She kept smoothing her hair with a nervous hand.

"Our actual grandfather," Molly went on. "We're walking around with his genes. What do you say to someone like that? I mean, we can't just barge up and say, 'See, here, fella, why did you walk out on Grandma and where will we find the Gales?' But he'll know, Nell. He'll know."

Nell nodded again. Molly didn't feel any more confident, however, as she finally parked the car as directed by an attendant, next to a long line of other vehicles on the scrubby grass of a vast field.

The layout of the Bedlingham dog show resembled many of the county fairs that Molly and Nell had attended over the years. A series of colorful tents surrounded a large central lawn on which several different events were taking place simultaneously.

The people, however, bore little resemblance to the farmers and 4-H Club kids that Molly was used to seeing at big outdoor events in America. Here they dressed in silk and tweeds and spoke primarily in the clipped accents of the upper class, though Molly could also make out an occasional hard-boiled Cockney and soft Scottish burr. The men sported ties and carried walking sticks; the women wore expensive jewelry and sensible shoes. If the rain yesterday had inconvenienced anyone, it didn't show.

Molly had had no idea that a dog show would be so dressy. Both she and Nell had put on shorts that morning, and Nell had put on a tank top that did little to conceal her figure. The man who took their entrance fee at the gate gave them a curious stare. When Molly explained they were Americans, however, he ah-ed and nodded sympathetically.

The grounds were packed with tents of different colors. Under each one were benches on which dogs in various states of patience were being groomed by owners in various states of excitement. Each tent was devoted to a different breed. Scores of poodles yapped in one, dozens of bloodhounds snoozed in another.

As they walked from tent to tent, Nell, wide-eyed with happiness, accepted licks and nuzzles from dalmatians and Yorkies, collies and Airedales, as well as numerous breeds the identity of which Molly didn't have a clue.

After ten minutes or so they finally came to the Chinese pug tent, which was what Molly had been looking for. A congregation of the little buff-colored, goggle-eyed creatures with smashed-in faces greeted them with a warm chorus of barks and wheezes.

"Cease that defeatist attitude instantaneously, Tinkerbell," ordered a stern-faced man to a panting pug who was drooling on his shoe. "To be a champion, one must think like a champion."

Other inspirational talk that Molly could overhear ranged from, "Do keep the upper lip a bit more stiffened, Lester, old bean," to "Izzy, Izzy, goo goo, yes."

"I'm looking for Richard Julian," said Molly to one of the more approachable-looking dog owners, a mild-mannered lady wearing a comfortable old sweater rather than the more fashionable togs that most of the others sported.

"Don't know where *he* is," she said, beaming at the pug in her arms as if it were a baby. "*She*'s over there."

The woman tilted her head toward the other side of the tent. The only *she* in that direction was a stout, Margaret Thatcheresque figure with sculpted, hard-looking hair and a caboose like something one might find on the Atchison, Topeka & Santa Fe. Lady Stacey Farfel-Julian wore a peach-colored suit, heavy gold drops on her droopy earlobes, and a noblesse oblige smile. She didn't look like the type who played much peekaboo with her bosoms anymore.

Molly approached cautiously.

"Lady Julian?" said Molly, hoping it was the right way to address her.

"Yazzz?" said the woman, looking down her long nose with narrowing gray eyes.

"I'm Molly O'Hara, and this is my sister Nell. We're looking for your husband."

"Why?"

"We're his granddaughters. From America."

"How veddy creative," sniffed Lady Farfel-Julian, her eyes slowing shifting from Molly to Nell and back again.

"Mr. Julian and our grandmother weren't married for very long," stammered Molly beneath her withering gaze. "It was many years ago. When his name was Jellinek. He doesn't even know we're alive probably."

"Oh, you needn't embellish, my dear. Your story is already quite amusing enough. Isn't it, Mr. Moto?"

The pug at her feet, a tawny creature with eyes that sparkled like diamonds, looked up inquiringly at the sound of its name.

"Well, don't just sit there, Mr. Moto," Lady Julian commanded. "Say hello to these very amusing young gels. What did you say your names were?"

"Molly and Nell O'Hara."

"And of course they are Irish, as well. Yes. Very amusing, indeed."

"I don't think you understand . . ." began Molly.

"Oh, but we understand perfectly, my dear. Don't we, Mr. Moto?"

Mr. Moto broke into an aria of denunciatory yaps. Lady Farfel-Julian picked up her dog and stroked its gnarled brow.

"So veddy pleased to have met you," she declared imperiously, shooting daggers from narrowed eyes. "I meet so very few of Richard's little . . . relatives . . . these days."

Then she turned smartly on her heel and marched off to the other side of the tent.

Molly stood quivering in a daze of confusion and indignation. Nell petted a more amiable pug and smiled like she was having

the best time in the world. Out of the corner of her eye Molly
detected movement. When she turned she saw a small man in a
tweed suit blinking at her like some kind of elderly traffic light
gone mad.

" 'E's over at the refreshment tent, luv," said the man in a
loud whisper, having gotten her attention.

"Who is?"

"Richard. And I say every man is entitled to 'ave as many
granddaughters as 'e can afford, if you catch my drift."

Molly stood for a moment, basking in the fellow's good-
natured leer and trying to decide whether to defend the O'Hara
honor with Lady Farfel-Julian. The latter was now performing a
maneuver on one of Mr. Moto's ears that resembled French-kissing.
Molly decided that retreat was the more mature course of action.

"Come on," she said, pushing Nell off in the direction that
the leering man had blinked in.

"Can you believe that woman?" Molly said angrily as they
made their way across the grass. "Who the hell does she think she
is?"

Nell waved her hand and shook her head, as if to say it wasn't
important, that it didn't matter. Molly was still fuming, however,
when they got to the refreshment tent, two aisles over.

This tent was fully ten times the size of all the others. Beneath
its shelter were rows of wooden picnic-type tables covered with red-
and-white-checkered plastic tablecloths. At the back of the tent a
long serving area featured sandwiches, beer, hot and cold drinks,
and various varieties of bagged junk foods, the prices of which were
enumerated on a large board behind the servers.

Only a few of the tables were occupied, it being too early for
lunch, but a crowd was hovering by the tea and coffee urns.

At the back of the tent a tall white-haired man in an elegantly
tailored suit stood with his hand propped against a pole. Leaning

with her back against the pole, under the shelter of his arm, was a smiling young woman wearing a black-and-white serving uniform that could not conceal an impressive figure. She seemed to be pleased with what the man was saying. So did he.

The moment of truth had arrived.

Molly didn't understand how she knew this was Richard Julian, but she was sure it was. Unlike Bobby Prince, their grandfather still looked every bit like a leading man, a Cary Grant type full of charm and sophistication, sexy even in his golden years and fully aware of it.

Molly stared at him, not knowing what to do. This was the man who had run off with Grandma when she was just a kid, who had acted with her on Broadway and fathered her child. This was the man who had known Tuck Wittington and had chased girls with Bobby Prince. Most important of all, this was the man who could direct her and Nell back to Grandma's family, back to the Gales.

Suddenly his silver head turned. As their eyes met, Molly felt something deep down inside her instantly relax. There was something in his face that seemed to say he recognized her, too, that he knew who she was and why she was here, that she was the most beautiful woman in the world and that he loved her deeply.

Molly shyly smiled back.

As she did so, Richard Julian's thin lips drew together into a kiss. He winked as he blew it to her.

Molly stood for a moment with her mouth open, not knowing what to do. Richard Julian had already turned his attention back to the serving girl. Molly had not flown a thousand miles across the ocean to wait around until he was free. She strode through the tent and right up to him. Nell followed at her side.

"Mr. Julian?"

Richard Julian turned and regarded Molly, his blue eyes full of curiosity and amusement. Up close he was still handsome, but it was apparent that his face was beginning to go to seed. Slight bags under the eyes. Broken capillaries in the nose. Puffy cheeks that would soon collapse to the twin adversaries of gravity and age.

"My sister and I would like to speak with you."

"By God, I'm a lucky bastard," Richard Julian said in a smooth confident baritone, giving another playful wink. "And I should like to speak with you, too, only Gwendoline, here, and I are just getting acquainted. Aren't we, my dear?"

Gwendoline giggled. Apparently Lady Julian wasn't imagining her husband's roving eye. Molly felt almost sorry for her, but couldn't afford to be distracted by side issues. If she was going to get this man's attention she was going to have to be blunt.

"We're your granddaughters, Mr. Julian. From America."

"Granddaughters?" he said with a choked laugh, his eyes darting from one of them to the other. "Is this some kind of joke?"

His accent was English, but his vowels drifted back toward the American pronunciations of his roots.

"Our mother was the baby that you had with Margaret Gale, back when your name was Jellinek."

"Now see here," said Julian, his face reddening.

"Perhaps I should see to my tea urn," mumbled Gwendoline, twisting out from beneath his arm. "I'll speak with you later, Richard?"

"Sure, love, sure."

Gwendoline escaped back into the serving area. Molly's grandfather frowned as he watched her go.

"Now what's this all about?" he said when she was out of earshot.

"I told you. We're your granddaughters. My name is Molly O'Hara. This is my sister, Nell. She doesn't talk."

"Why not?"

"It's a psychological problem," said Molly, wanting to keep things between them as simple as possible. "Our mother was your baby, Evangeline. She died when we were kids."

Julian started to speak but then put a finger to his lips.

"Maggie is your grandmother?" he said finally.

"Was," said Molly. "She died recently. That's why we're here. There was a lot about her life that we don't understand. We came to England hoping to ask you some questions."

Julian frowned again, then suddenly his eyes lit up and his lips pressed together into a disarming smile.

"I think I understand," he announced in a happier voice. "My wife put you up to this, didn't she?"

"I don't know what you mean," said Molly.

"Oh, come, come, my dear," he laughed. "It's the only thing that makes sense. I know Stacey's jealous, but really, this is too much. If she wants to divorce and spend the rest of her life making love to Moto, I'll bring her all the evidence she wants on a silver salver. She doesn't have to go through this ridiculous charade."

"I promise you, Mr. Julian," said Molly. "*That* woman didn't put us up to anything. We're your granddaughters. We just want to ask you some questions."

"Right. Yes. Ho, ho, ho."

"Please, Mr. Julian, we've come a long way."

"I'm sure you have, my dear," said Julian smoothly, "And you're very charming. So is your silent sister, which is a nice touch, it really is. But I'll now have to take my leave, unless, of course, you can actually prove that you are who you claim you are."

Molly hesitated for a minute, then unbuttoned the top of her blouse, and brought out the emerald ring. There was one person who had to know about Grandma's ring—the man who slept with her.

Julian stared at it for a moment, then let out a long breath.

"It's been a long time since I've seen that," he said in a sub-dued voice.

"Will you talk to us, Mr. Julian?"

"It's all true then, about Maggie and the baby being dead?"

"Yes."

Julian sighed deeply.

"Funny," he said in a quiet voice. "I don't remember the baby much at all, just that it cried and cried whenever I rehearsed my songs. But I think of Maggie now and then. Your sister looks a bit like her. Not you, though."

"Where did the two of you grow up, you and our grand-mother?" said Molly, holding her breath.

"Hold that thought," said Julian, raising a pink, perfectly manicured finger, his voice brightening. "I don't have much ex-perience with these things, but if this is to be a family reunion then it calls for at least a cup of tea. Sit down over there and I'll be right back."

He gestured to a table at the side of the tent, far away from the few occupied seats. Before Molly could stop him he had crossed back over to the catering area. There he reengaged Gwendoline in jocular conversation, some of which was apparently of a professional variety, because when he returned in a few moments he was carrying a box stocked with refreshments.

"In England we face all life's little celebrations and dilemmas over a nice cup of tea," he said, placing steaming paper cups in front of them. "Sugar is here. Milk is here. Help yourself to the pastries. Gwendoline promises me they are very tasty."

Nell already had the largest sweet roll in her mouth, and was nodding her head in agreement and licking her fingers as if she hadn't eaten for days. The girl was a bottomless pit.

"Cheers," said Julian, raising his tea. The flirtatious twinkle had returned to his eye. Apparently he had already recovered com-pletely from the news about the deaths of his daughter and ex-wife. As family Richard Julian ranked right up there with Clyde and Daddy.

"Thank you, Mr. Julian," said Molly, determined not to let her disappointment in him show.

"Call me Richard. I like it when pretty young things call me Richard. Do you suppose this comes from vanity or is it merely part of the natural aging process?"

"Where did you and Grandma grow up?"

"You are a rather direct person, aren't you, my dear?" said

Julian. "No small talk. No niceties. I suppose you take after Maggie in that. Didn't she ever tell you the story of our lost youth?"

Molly shook her head.

"Grandma never said a word about her life before she got to Pelletreau."

"Pelletreau?"

"North Carolina. That's where she settled."

"Yes, of course. She had a happy life?"

"Yes," Molly lied. There was no point in letting him into their lives any further than she had to. "We came here to talk to you because you're the only one left who can tell us about Grandma's family, the Gales. Is it true they were rich?"

"Oh, yes," said Richard Julian, drawing out the words. "They were rich, all right."

"Where did they live? What were they like? We want to know all about them. And about you and Grandma."

"Well, it isn't the nicest story in the world," he said, sitting back. "But if it's what you want, it's what you'll get—that's the least I can do for my granddaughters. My granddaughters. Certainly is strange, finding those words together in one's own mouth, isn't it?"

Molly didn't say anything. Julian sighed and shook his head.

"Well, just please stop me when you can't stand any more," he said. "I tend to rattle on. Old Jellinek trait. To answer your question, Maggie and I grew up on a little island in the Ashalaca River up above Montpelier, Vermont. Gale Island."

"The Gales owned their own island?"

Julian nodded.

"That's how rich they were," he said. "The family fortune had originally come from railroads. When I was a kid, Atherton Gale, Maggie's dad, ruled Gale Island like he was some kind of feudal lord. He was the eldest son and had inherited control of the family interests, which he'd expanded into newspapers and radio stations. He was an incredibly nasty son of a bitch, which of course, made him all the more successful in business."

Julian stretched back in his chair, took a sip of his tea, and remembered.

"Gale Island wasn't a very big place, of course. Population was never more than about sixty people. But it was a world unto itself. The Gales lived in this honest-to-God stone castle on the island's highest point. Gale Castle. Last time I talked to my sister she said there were still some of them living there, though Atherton's long dead, of course."

A shiver went down Molly's spine. So there were still Gales. Molly and Nell had a family on an island in the middle of Vermont. It was almost too good to be true.

"When Atherton's father was alive, the whole family lived in the castle," Julian went on happily, "but Atherton eventually chased them all away. Wouldn't let any of them into the business, of course. He was a real control freak, the sort of guy who was always revising his will in order to keep people in line."

"And you lived on Gale island, too."

"Yes," he said with a nod. "Like everybody else on the island, we serviced Atherton. Dad and his brother had a trucking business, running back and forth, once a week, to bring in what was needed. We were about as far beneath the Gales as you could get."

"How did you and Grandma meet?"

Julian smoothed his sideburn with a finger and smiled.

"All the island kids were bussed over to the public school in New Melford," he said. "Atherton had wanted to send Maggie to some snooty private school, but Maggie's mother, Felicity, didn't want her boarded off. It was probably the only argument she ever won with Atherton. Usually he just ground Felicity into dust. Felicity Gale was a tall, pale, elegant woman—very lovely and aristocratic. She always looked so sad, and it was no mystery to anyone on the island why. Atherton was as coarse and brutish as Felicity was beautiful. I think he married her just because he enjoyed having such a classy lady to humiliate."

Julian shook his head sadly, then spoke again.

"Anyway, I knew Maggie from practically the time I was born—the way a cook's kid knows the master's daughter, I suppose. I never paid much attention to her, though, until we were cast together in the New Melford High School play, a production of *Pirates of Penzance*. I was the Pirate King, of course. Maggie was Mabel. The rehearsals turned out to be the most fun either one of us had ever had. And everybody thought we were wonderful, which was a surprise since I'd just tried out as a lark. Same with Maggie, she never thought she'd get a part."

Molly took a sip of tea and tried to imagine Grandma as a rich man's daughter living in a castle. It was difficult. Richard Julian took a sip of his own tea and continued.

"We had been rehearsing for about a month when Atherton Gale got wind of what was up. Instead of being pleased, he ordered Maggie to drop out of the play, said that no daughter of his was going to display herself for a bunch of riffraff. When she tried to argue, he announced he was going to send her off to a boarding school, that he should have done so years ago.

"Maggie called me on the telephone in tears. She had to talk with someone, but didn't have any real friends—how could she when Atherton made it his business to keep her away from everyone? She didn't know what to do. We met that night in the moonlight under the oak trees at the south end of Gale island. One thing led to another, and being as stupid and crazy as all seventeen-year-olds are, Maggie and I decided to get married, run off to New York together and become professional actors. Then we sealed our love with a kiss. We thought it was the most damned romantic thing that had ever happened to two people in the history of the world."

Molly couldn't help but smile. It was a sweet story, and it was nice to picture Grandma as young and happy for a change after all those years of seeing her old and without hope.

"We went back to Gale Castle," continued Julian, "and I waited while Maggie packed a bag. Atherton had gone off to Boston on business, but Maggie's mother had heard us come in. Maggie told her what she was going to do and begged her not to try to stop us. Felicity said to wait a moment, and disappeared. She returned with all the cash she could find in the house—two hundred and sixty dollars, a lot of money in those days—which she gave to Maggie, along with her emerald ring. She said she wanted us to sell the ring and build ourselves a life together and never look back."

"So you went to New York."

"That's right," said Julian. "And promptly got cast together in a Broadway musical, which just proved to us how talented we were and how right our decision had been. All our dreams were coming true. Then, the day after opening night we returned to our apartment after the show and found Atherton Gale and three detectives waiting for us. They were looking for Felicity Gale's emerald ring and had pretty much turned the place upside down. Maggie's father's first words to her were, 'You stole your mother's ring, you little thief. I want it back.' "

Julian said the words with a theatrical snarl. Molly could see suddenly the actor in him. He continued, all but acting out the parts.

" 'I didn't steal it, she gave it to me,' said Maggie, but Atherton just started screaming at her, calling her a liar and a whore.

'Ask mother,' Maggie begged, but her father wouldn't listen. He said Felicity was a liar and a traitor, too, that everyone was trying to cheat him. 'Where is that ring?' Atherton demanded, over and over, while the detectives restrained me, which was fortunate because I would have beaten the old boy's brains out."

"But she wouldn't give it to them," said Molly.

"No, of course not," said Julian almost proudly. "Maggie had the ring around her neck on a chain, just as you do now, and they never thought to look for it there. Which was just as well because Maggie was a pretty strong girl and she would have put up a hell of a fight if they had tried. Atherton finally stormed out, but not before saying again that Maggie had stolen the ring and the proof would be when she tried to sell it. Then he would have all the evidence he needed that she was a thief, and he would prosecute—she could bet her life on that, he said. His own daughter, this was her wedding present."

"My God," said Molly, touching the chain around her neck that held the ring.

"Maggie was pretty shaken," Julian continued, "but she was also madder than hell. She said she would never sell the ring, would never give Atherton the satisfaction. And she kept her word, even later on when things had gotten rough for us."

"After *Without Reservations*," said Molly,

"You know about that?" asked Julian, arching one eyebrow in surprise.

Molly nodded.

"I hadn't realized how much of her identity Maggie had tied up in being an actress," he said. "But suddenly here were all these people saying she wasn't any kind of actress at all. But if she wasn't an actress, then what was she? It was the only identity she had, the only thing she'd been able to build for herself outside of Atherton's malignant influence. Maggie didn't know what to do. She just sat around the apartment for months and months totally shattered, afraid of everything and unable to work."

He let out a deep sigh.

"I continued to get shows," he went on, "but I wasn't playing leads yet. A chorus boy's salary doesn't go very far and pretty soon we needed money. Maggie was pregnant. I wanted her to sell the ring, but she wouldn't hear of it. She kept repeating what Atherton had said about how her selling the emerald would prove that she had stolen it."

"Couldn't Grandma's mother intercede?" asked Molly.

"Oh, I thought of that right away, but Maggie didn't want to get Felicity into trouble with Atherton. Finally, though, she broke down and wrote her several letters, not asking for help, just for advice. None of these letters was ever answered. After Angie was born things got even tighter for us, but Maggie still wouldn't sell the ring, though I begged her to."

"Is that why your marriage broke up?"

"Oh, it was a lot of things," said Julian absently, waving a hand. "Mainly, it was just that we had been too young to get married in the first place. It had all happened too fast, for all the wrong reasons. I certainly wasn't ready to settle down and support a family. And all the fun went out of Maggie after *Without Reservations* bombed so badly. As I told you, she became a different person from the sweet gutsy girl I ran off with. Withdrawn. Morose. Bitter."

"So you left her."

"Why do you say that?" Julian said angrily, looking up. "Do you think I would just walk out on Maggie in that condition?"

"I . . . That's what people told me."

"Well, people told you wrong. I didn't leave her. Maggie was the one who decided to leave me and go back to her family. She was going to do it for the baby's sake, she said."

Richard Julian paused and took a drink of his tea, then went on.

"It made me sick, but Maggie wrote Atherton Gale a letter, telling him about his granddaughter and saying again that she didn't steal the ring, that Felicity had given it to her. She humbled herself, told him that our marriage wasn't working out, and asked if she could come home. He wrote and said she could come back if and only if she admitted that she had stolen the ring.

"Maggie agonized for a few days, then wrote him that she would return the ring to him if that's what he wanted. She didn't steal it, she said again, Felicity gave it to her, but she had been wrong to accept it and was very sorry."

"It must have been very hard for her," said Molly. "Grandma was very proud."

"Yes," said Julian in a subdued voice. "It really broke what was left of her spirit. I could see her crumbling in front of my eyes. I couldn't stand it, but there was nothing I could do."

"What happened?"

"There was no immediate answer from Atherton. Then about two weeks later, Maggie got a letter from the Gale attorneys advising her to send no further correspondence. Since she refused to confess to stealing the ring, Atherton Gale had disowned her. The letter also informed Maggie of what her father hadn't bothered to mention, that her mother had died nearly two years before."

"What a horrible man!" said Molly.

"Your family, not mine," said Julian. "Anyway, about that time I got cast in the national tour of *Annie Get Your Gun*. When I got back to New York, Maggie was gone. A few years later a lawyer from somewhere down South—I guess it must have been that town in North Carolina you mentioned—contacted me about a divorce."

"Did you never want to see your daughter?"

"Well, I could lie to you and say I did," said Julian, looking Molly in the eye, "but the fact is that I was pretty much relieved to be free. I had a career and a world of beautiful women to pursue. As you can see, I wouldn't have made a very good father. But I never bore Maggie any ill-will and would have given her child support if she had asked. We had some good times together. We were just too young to get married, that's all. It just didn't work out."

Molly nodded. The final pieces of the puzzle had fallen into place. Molly could now see how Grandma had come to live the life she had in Pelletreau: heartbroken, shamed, abandoned by her family. Grandma wouldn't want Molly to tell Richard Julian what had happened to her.

"So," he said, his smile returning. "Is my story everything you hoped it would be?"

"No," answered Molly, rising.

As she stood, Nell got up, too. Molly couldn't tell if her sister had been listening, had understood. Nell's face was blank, her eyes far away.

"Thank you for your help, Mr. Julian."

"Richard. Please."

"Richard."

"Say," he said, flashing a debonair smile, "why don't the two of you stick around and let me get to know you, at least for the rest of the day? We're leaving on a little trip tomorrow. I've never had granddaughters before. Maybe we can have a few laughs together."

Molly hesitated for moment, wanting desperately to say yes, to have a grandfather, to have someone who cared about her and

Nell. But all Richard Julian had offered were a few laughs, not love, not caring. He wasn't their grandfather any more than he had been a father to Mom or a husband to Margaret Jellinek.

"Thanks," said Molly, "but we have to be getting back to the United States."

"Yes, of course," he said breezily. "It's rather too bad we didn't meet under better circumstances. I think we might have enjoyed knowing one another."

"Oh, one more thing, Mr. Julian?" said Molly.

"Hm?" he said, gazing off at Gwendoline across the tent.

"Where did you get married to Grandma? Where was the ceremony?"

"We waited until we got to New York City," he said with a fond smile. "There's a little chapel in one of the government buildings down by City Hall. We spent our honeymoon night at the Algonquin Hotel."

Molly smiled, too. She owed David Azaria fifty bucks.

ℓ ℓ ℓ ℓ

After leaving Richard Julian to find happiness with Gwendoline, Lady Stacey, and Mr. Moto, Molly drove back to Leeds and got herself and Nell on the afternoon commuter flight back to London.

As they waited to retrieve their bags at Heathrow, Molly felt more weary than she had ever felt before in her life. It was as if all the events of the last month had suddenly caught up with her. She sank into a molded plastic chair, resting her head on her hands.

At the baggage carousel Nell grabbed one of their suitcases, then the other. Then she lugged and pushed them across the slippery floor until she stood with an expectant look on her face right in front of Molly.

"So what now, you may ask?" said Molly, asking the question

for her sister. "Why aren't we bolting to the ticket counter and booking the next flight to Gale Island?"

Nell waited silently for the answer.

"Well, excuse me," said Molly with a sigh. "But suddenly I'm not as excited as I was about reestablishing contact with our long-lost family. Atherton Gale was a monster. Somehow I doubt that whatever Gales are still living in that castle are going to welcome us with open arms."

Nell stared at Molly with a quizzical expression.

"Oh, I know we'll have to go to meet them sooner or later, just so we can get on with our lives. I just wish there was somewhere we could go first and catch our breath. Have any suggestions?"

Nell nodded. Then she dug into their carryall and came out with one of the guidebooks to England, which she riffled through until she had come to the page she wanted and passed it to her sister.

Molly wearily took the book and stared at a picture of Trafalgar Square. Beneath it was a quote from Samuel Johnson, "When a man is tired of London, he is tired of life."

"You can be pretty smart, sometimes," said Molly feeling some of her energy returning. "You know that?"

Nell didn't answer. She had already picked up her suitcase and was headed for a door marked GROUND TRANSPORTATION, TAXIS TO LONDON.

Ten

After a long taxi ride into London Molly booked a room at a modest tourist hotel that one of the guidebooks had rated a best buy. It turned out to be more expensive than the Gotham Arms in New York, but she and Nell had never been out of the United States before and they certainly needed a vacation. Besides, for the first time they had money to spend and no mortgage payments to worry about.

Covent Garden, Leicester Square, the Strand, Mayfair, Harrod's department store—they saw them all. They stood outside of Charles Dickens's house, walked along the banks of the Thames and wandered in the footsteps of kings and prisoners in the Tower of London. Most exciting of all, Molly and Nell visited the legendary antique markets in Portobello Road and Camden Passage.

Molly's heart soared as she wandered through the crowded stalls bursting with furniture and silver and ceramics—five hundred years worth of stuff, the attic of an empire. Wherever they finally ended up, they'd have to make a living, and there was only one way Molly knew to do that. Buying and selling antiques.

They bought "smalls"—the kinds of portable antiques that could be displayed easily and sold anywhere: tiny Vienna bronze animals; rosewood whist markers; enameled snuff boxes and burlwood card cases; silver spoons, matchsafes, and vinaigrettes (which the Victorians carried to mask the unsavory smells that were all around them); miniature china tea sets; Scottish agate jewelry; Chinese scholar's objects.

By the time they returned to Heathrow airport four days later on Monday morning, Molly and Nell had spent several thousand dollars of their settlement. Their suitcases bulged with enough quality "fresh merch" to set up shop (albeit small shop) anywhere in America.

At the airline ticket counter, Molly was able to reroute their return without penalty to Boston's Logan airport instead of JFK. Part of her wanted to spend some time in New York and tell David Azaria all that had transpired, but she couldn't afford to get distracted now. Arriving at Boston would put her and Nell a lot closer to the place they had to go—a small island in the Ashalaca River up above Montpelier, Vermont.

Molly's chest started to tighten with anticipation even before their plane took off. It was a 10:00 A.M. flight, and this time the time difference worked in their favor. They arrived in Boston shortly after noon, though to them it felt closer to dinnertime.

It took an hour for them to collect their baggage and clear customs. Then Molly went to one of the rental companies and got a long-term rate on a car. An airport van took them to the parking lot where a bright little red rental Ford was waiting. Molly had almost forgotten what new cars smelled liked, it had been so long since she had been in one. It was fitting somehow, to have been given a new car. It was a new beginning.

"Let's get this over with," said Molly, starting the car. "We can make Vermont in a few hours, meet the Gales, and get on with our lives."

As Nell skeptically started measuring distances with her thumb, Molly set off on the interstate. Soon it veered off in the other direction, and Molly had to settle for an older highway.

After an hour the scrubby landscapes of Massachusetts had given way to the granite hills of New Hampshire, and New England enveloped them. More hours passed as Molly navigated her way through thick forests, rolling mountains, and crystal streams. Only when they got into Vermont were they finally able to find a map at a gas station that included the tiny flyspeck that was Gale Island.

As they wended their way on twisting roads that snaked through the lush canopies of trees, closer and closer to the place where their grandmother had been born, Molly was nearly overwhelmed with intense feelings of loneliness and loss, fear and longing, and just the tiniest bit of hope.

Finally, after several wrong turns and getting lost on back roads, they were almost there. The Ashalaca River appeared beside them, widening as they drove west. The foliage all around seemed to become denser, lusher, more mysterious. A bruised signpost at the side of the road came into view: GALE ISLAND, ONE MILE.

"I can't believe we're here," said Molly, slowing the car to a stop. "Just a few weeks ago, there we were in Pelletreau, wondering why Grandma's picture was on that program. Now, after all that's happened, we're in Vermont a mile from where Grandma grew up. Where her family still is, maybe."

Molly felt Nell grab her arm and looked over to see her sister's eyes full of trepidation. Richard Julian's story had not been lost on her. Nell had understood every word.

Suddenly Molly felt her own nerve failing her. She was stiff and sore from the London flight and what had turned out to be a five-hour drive. It was nearly six-thirty by the clock on the car's dashboard—Molly's watch had stopped again. It had been too long of a day already.

"Maybe we shouldn't rush into this," she said. "We'll be more presentable after a good night's sleep."

Nell clearly wasn't going to offer any argument. Relieved, Molly turned the car around and drove to a weatherbeaten motel they had passed about ten miles back: The Yankee Clipper.

A thin old man who looked like he might still have his first nickel in a back pocket showed them to a small, dark room. Everything, including the night tables and the shower, was made of plastic. At least the sheets were clean, however, and there was plenty of room for both of them in the king-size bed.

The two of them spent the rest of the evening watching television, despite problematic reception. For once Molly didn't provide her usual running commentary, though she wasn't sure if this was from being nervous about meeting the Gales or simple weariness. They were still running on London time which was five hours ahead of Vermont's. When they turned out the light a little after nine o'clock it felt like two in the morning. They were both asleep in minutes.

—᠍᠍᠍᠍᠍᠍᠍᠍᠍ᦁ᠍᠍᠍ᦁ᠍ᦁᦁᦁᦁ—

When Molly awoke the next morning, Nell was gone.

At first Molly thought her sister was just in the bathroom. Molly lay in bed staring at the room's cinderblock walls, waking up slowly, waiting for Nell to come out. After fifteen minutes, she grew impatient.

"How long does it take for a person to shower and primp?" she yelled. "You're beautiful enough."

There was no answer.

Molly pulled herself up and opened the bathroom door. Nell was not there. Molly threw on her jeans and opened the room's outside door, thinking her sister had stepped out for some fresh country air. But Nell was not outside, either. And their car, which had been parked in one of the spaces directly in front of the room, was gone.

Fighting down panic Molly dashed back inside to the telephone. She wasn't clear whether she intended to call the front desk or the police. Only then did she notice a note on the pad next to the phone in Nell's careful hand: "I've gone out to get something. Don't worry. N."

But Molly did worry. She ran back outside and scrutinized the road that ran in front of the motel. An occasional car sped by on the road that led into the ubiquitous pine forest stretching out in both directions. There was no sign of Nell and their little red Ford.

"You idiot!" exclaimed Molly out loud. "What is going on in your confused little brain?"

She started to speak again, but stopped herself. It wasn't going to bring Nell back any faster. What time was it? Molly wondered, glancing at the useless watch on her wrist, which hadn't ticked for five consecutive minutes since they had left London. It felt late. She went back inside the room, turned on the TV and flipped through stations. A weatherman mentioned the time in passing: eleven thirty-five. They had slept for more than fourteen hours. Or rather, Molly had. There was no telling how long Nell had been gone.

Molly tried to stay calm. After all that had happened in the past few weeks the world no longer seemed like a safe place, if it ever had been. Where had Nell gone? What was she doing? At least Nell was a good driver, Molly consoled herself, though she hardly ever could be coaxed to take the wheel. The last time Nell had taken off by herself in their old van she had come back with a new dress and a hundred dollars worth of cosmetics, which she had never used. Thank goodness, she didn't have any money to spend this time. Or did she?

Molly ran over to her brown leather shoulder bag. Her wallet with their traveler's checks and all their cash was gone. If Nell had decided to go on a shopping spree with their nest egg, Molly was going to kill her.

It was already past the motel's checkout time, which was eleven o'clock according to the notice on the door. Molly had no intention of remaining in the drab little room another night, but she could hardly leave now, even if she had wanted to. Nell had the car, not to mention their means of paying. Molly picked up the telephone and dialed the front desk.

"Hi, this is Miss O'Hara in twenty-three," she said.

"Yep," answered a squeaky male voice that Molly recognized as belonging to the old man who had shown them to their room the night before.

"Is it possible to get a later checkout time?"

"Yep."

"What time would that be?" asked Molly.

"What time you want?"

"I'm not sure exactly. My sister went out, and I'm trying to figure out where she might have gone. Is there anything around here? A shopping mall, maybe?"

"Nope."

"No stores?"

"Ned Burny's general store down the road. Get yourself some nice Vermont cheese."

"What about clothing stores?"

"They're a few around, if you go lookin' for 'em. Buy mail order, myself."

How long would Nell be? There was no way to know. If she didn't come back in a few hours, maybe Molly would call the police.

"How about some time in the afternoon?" she asked.

"How about it?" came the answer.

"As a checkout."

"Stay as long as you like," said the voice. "I'll just prorate the room fee on an hourly basis."

"Gee, thanks a lot."

"Yep."

Molly hung up the phone, flopped back onto the bed, and tried to concentrate on a grainy old black-and-white movie. The hours passed with excruciating slowness. Finally, when Nell hadn't shown up at two o'clock, Molly began to panic in earnest. She turned off the set, and picked up the phone to ask the Yankee clipper at the desk how to call the police.

At that moment the door opened and Nell walked in.

"Where have you been?" demanded Molly, slamming down the telephone. "I've been worried sick! How could you run off like that and leave me here? Don't you know how frightening that would be for me? What's the matter with you?"

Nell hung her head, reached out and touched Molly's shoulder.

"Don't touch me," said Molly, squirming away, refusing to let her anger die down easily. "I'm furious."

Nell nodded. Her face brightened. For the first time Molly noticed that her sister was holding something in her left hand, a small box wrapped in red paper and tied with a ribbon.

"Is that what you went out for? What is it?"

Nell handed the package to Molly and indicated for her to open it. Angrily, Molly pulled off the ribbon and tore off the paper. Inside the box was a small silver wristwatch.

"What is this?" asked Molly. "Where did you have to go to get this? Back to Boston? Do you really think this was the greatest time in the world to buy yourself a watch?"

Nell pointed at little window below twelve o'clock on the watch's face. Inside was a tiny number five. It was the fifth. August fifth. It was Molly's birthday.

"This is for me?"

Nell nodded, then bent down and gave her a kiss.

"You crazy nut," Molly murmured. "I was worried sick."

Nell took her sister's hand and turned it until the old cheap watch that Grandma had given Molly was face up. Then she undid the strap and set the poor dead timepiece down in an ashtray.

"What is this, real silver?" said Molly, as Nell slipped the new watch onto Molly's wrist. "It probably cost a fortune. You shouldn't have spent our money that way."

Nell punched her in the arm. Hard.

"Ow," said Molly, rubbing the spot. She didn't know what to say. All kinds of emotions rushed through her, pushing out the fear and worry that had occupied her for the past hours. Molly wasn't used to anyone taking care of her; she only gave, didn't receive—as David Azaria had made her painfully aware of. She was supposed to be the caregiver, but now Nell had turned the tables. Molly shook her head. What were you supposed to do in a situation like this?

"Thanks," she said in a very quiet voice. "I love you, too."

Nell beamed.

"So, why are you standing there with that idiotic expression?

What do you say we get out of this rat hole and find something to eat? I'm starving."

After a postcheckout consultation with the dry little man at the motel desk, Molly and Nell headed for the Green Mountain Diner, where they ate satisfactory chicken sandwiches and drank lemonades. By the time they finished dawdling over pieces of birthday carrot cake, it was exactly 4:13 according to Molly's new timepiece.

"Well, I guess we can't put it off forever," said Molly as they got into the car. "Are you ready to meet the family?"

Nell looked up alarmed.

"Come on. We'll just do it, and it will be behind us."

Nell didn't answer, but she got into the car.

They followed the broad river next to the road for only a few more minutes. Another signpost appeared, but neither Molly nor Nell needed it to tell them that the looming black landmass ahead of them was Gale Island. The stone castle high atop the island's rocky high point spoke volumes about riches and isolation and unhappiness.

A one-lane bridge spanned the gray-looking waters of the Ashalaca. Molly crossed over the narrow expanse and followed the road, which circled around the island's perimeter, past a small community of perhaps twenty houses, then began to climb. Other houses, most of them small and made of stone, were visible from the road. Driveways off the road led back to other dwellings concealed behind the trees, leading Molly to believe that probably two or three times more people now lived here than had in Richard Jellinek's day.

In her mind Molly had pictured Gale Island as a tiny place that you could throw a stone across, totally surrounded by water. In fact it was quite large, like a mountain that had grown out of the river to match the rolling green Vermont mountains on the mainland. From most places as they circled the island, climbing up toward the top, Molly couldn't even see the river, just the lush trees and wildflowers that grew everywhere.

As they got closer to the island's peak the evidence of other houses diminished. The final approach to the top was marked with ancient conifers, stone walls, and a granite gate hewn with the single word GALE.

Finally they were at the top. The road leveled off and they drove through another pair of gates, these equipped with iron bars, into the circular driveway at the base of Gale Castle. Molly pulled into an open area, sheltered by a stand of massive pine trees, where several other vehicles were parked.

It was now four-thirty by Molly's new watch—as good a time as any for a meeting, she told herself. It was no accident that Nell had given her this present today. Like the new rental car it seemed symbolic. Time had started again for both of them.

Molly turned off the car's engine, ran a comb through her hair, and made Nell follow suit. Then she took a deep breath and got out of the car. Nell sat where she was.

"Come on, it's okay. There's nothing to be frightened of."

Nell bit her lip and didn't move.

"Look, I'm nervous, too, but there's really no reason. Grandma left here half a century ago. Atherton Gale is long gone. Probably no one will even know who we are. Come on."

Slowly, reluctantly Nell got out of the car, then followed Molly up the stone path that led to the enormous steel-banded oak doors of the castle.

There was a huge bronze knocker in the shape of a hideous face, but Molly simply pressed the doorbell. When nothing happened she pressed again. Finally the door swung open, revealing a tall, gaunt woman dressed in a nurse's white uniform. She had grizzled hair tied up in a tight bun on top of her head, thin, bloodless lips, and a hatchet face that was made more forbidding by the frown it wore.

"Yeah?" the woman snapped.

"Are you one of the Gales?"

"Close enough. What do you want?"

"Who is it, Mrs. McCormick?" asked a small female voice from inside.

"Don't know, ma'am. Strangers. You go back to your company, let me handle this."

But another woman had already come up behind the hatchet-faced Mrs. McCormick and now poked her head out of the door to see what was going on.

Being so short Molly wasn't used to looking down on anyone, but this elderly second woman who had appeared at the door was tiny, perhaps four foot six. She looked like the type of grandmother usually found only in fairy tales, with kind, milky blue eyes and a delicate pink dress that would have been old-fashioned in nineteen fifty-eight. She had a soft, primly powdered round face, gold-rimmed glasses, and curly hair as white as snow.

"We're Margaret Gales's granddaughters," Molly blurted in a nervous voice, wondering if either of these two women would even recognize Grandma's name. "Molly and Nell O'Hara."

But they did know the name.

Mrs. McCormick's bloodshot eyes widened visibly at the sound of it, but it was the old lady's reaction that was more startling. She covered her prim little mouth with a hand and let out a gasp. Molly could actually see the tears welling up in her eyes. As she fled back into the house, Molly could hear sounds of weeping.

Mrs. McCormick shot a furious look and dashed into the house after the tiny old woman.

Before Molly could decide what to do, three men appeared at

the door. The first looked to be in his sixties, a tall sallow man with an enormous nose. He was dressed in a black suit and looked like an undertaker. The second man was also probably in his sixties, but his complexion was reddish bordering on florid. He was portly and bald and wore plaid pants and a navy blazer. The last man was of Asian descent, younger than the others, and dressed more casually in chinos and a polo shirt.

The undertaker glared at Molly for only an instant before turning on his heel and rushing back into the house after the two women.

"What's going on here?" demanded the red-faced bald man angrily.

The younger third man—he was perhaps of Vietnamese or Cambodian extraction, Molly guessed from his delicate features— spoke in a more quiet tone.

"Is she all right?"

Molly turned around to where the man was staring. Nell stood there behind her. Her hands covered her face and her mouth was open in a silent scream. She was trembling like a leaf in a thunderstorm.

Eleven

"Is she all right?" the Asian man asked again. As before, his voice was gentle. His large dark eyes were full of concern.

"She's fine," said Molly, rubbing the back of her sister's neck. Nell had calmed down a little but still trembled. She didn't look up from the floor.

"Has this happened before?"

"A few times. It's nothing to worry about."

What had prompted Nell's episode this time, Molly wondered. The shock of seeing the little old lady run off in tears? The men, the way they had all clamored to the door? The hatchet-faced woman, Mrs. McCormick?

"Is it some kind of seizure?" the Asian man pressed.

"It looks worse than it really is," said Molly. "It's psychological. She'll be okay in a few minutes."

The Asian waited in thoughtful silence. He was slender and pleasant-looking with jet black hair and an unlined face that could have belonged to someone in his mid-thirties. There was something in the way he carried himself, however—a maturity, a presence—that convinced Molly that he was at least ten years older than that. She had not had much practice in Pelletreau reading Oriental faces.

Molly and her sister sat on a down-stuffed divan in the large living room off the castle's entrance hall where the Asian man had brought them. He stood in front of them, directly across from a pair of walnut armchairs that Molly had instantly recognized as period Queen Anne antiques, each worth in the low five figures. The room's other furnishings were equally impressive: Chippendale tables, Georgian silver candlesticks and salvers, antique Persian carpets. Elaborate tapestries with classical scenes covered the walls where there were not fine oil paintings. Eighteenth-century Kakiemon-style porcelain sat on the mantle above a fireplace large enough to set up house in.

"Who was that elderly woman?" said Molly after a moment, ashamed to be appraising the Gales' furniture, mortified at the fuss that she and Nell had caused by their arrival. "I don't know what we said that could have upset her like that."

"What did you say?"

"Nothing," said Molly, trying to catch Nell's eye. "We just introduced ourselves. Our name is O'Hara. I'm Molly. This is my sister Nell."

Nell seemed to be somewhat calmer now. The trembling had stopped. It must just be the shock of it all, Molly reflected. So much had happened in the last few days, so many changes. It was almost too intense for Molly, too.

"George Gale," said the Asian man, extending his hand, which Molly took. His hand was soft. His grip was cool and firm. "The woman you frightened was my mother, Mrs. Atherton Gale."

"Mrs. Atherton Gale!" exclaimed Molly, unable to conceal her surprise.

George Gale flashed a modest, self-effacing smile.

"Okay, I realize there's not much family resemblance," he said. "I was adopted, of course. Atherton died years ago. Mother is ninety-three."

"But she can't be Felicity Gale."

"No, she's Dora Gale, Atherton's second wife," said George, raising an eyebrow. "How do you know about Felicity? I thought only genealogy freaks like me remember Felicity."

"Felicity and Atherton Gale were our grandmother's parents," said Molly, repeating what she had recently learned from Richard Julian.

George Gale's eyes widened.

"Felicity and Atherton were your grandmother's parents?" he said. "What was your grandmother's name?"

"Margaret Jellinek," replied Molly, squeezing Nell's shoulder. "But before she married, her name was Gale. Margaret Gale."

"And that's what you told Dora?"

"We said we were Margaret Gale's granddaughters, yes. Why?"

George Gale gave a low whistle.

"Well, that certainly explains Mother's reaction," he said soberly. "It's been a pretty rough few weeks for all of us, but especially for her."

Before George Gale could explain himself further, Molly heard footsteps on the marble staircase in the hall that led to the upstairs of the castle. In a moment the fat bald man whom she had seen at the front door entered the vast living room.

Molly had never met anyone who wore plaid pants before. The man's belly protruded out above them in a manner that suggested that he had recently swallowed a basketball. His bald head bore a striking resemblance to an energy-saver lightbulb.

"Dora's locked herself in her room, won't let anyone in," he announced without ceremony, crossing to a bar at the far side of the room. "Henry's parked outside like some kind of Yankee vulture wondering who to sue, and McCormick is screeching the Twenty-third Psalm at the hall ceiling. Not a pretty sight, believe you me. Anybody else need a drink?"

Molly wanted to raise her hand, but restrained herself. What kind of madhouse was this?

"I think you should go up there, George," the bald man said, fishing for ice cubes in a refrigerator concealed behind the bar.

"Why?" asked George Gale.

"Didn't you hear what I said? Didn't you see how agitated Mama was? She could be having a heart attack for all we know."

"Do I break down the door?"

"Why are you asking me? You're the doctor."

Molly stared at George Gale, who smiled back.

"Sometimes you don't have to perform an examination to understand what's wrong," he said quietly. "I think maybe Mother just needs to be alone for a while."

"I still don't understand what set her off like that," said the bald fat man, constructing himself a scotch and soda. "What did these gals say to her? McCormick wouldn't give me a straight answer. Who are they, anyway?"

"Forgive me for not making introductions," said George Gale in a polite voice. "Molly, I'd like you to meet Russell Bowslater. Russell's my stepbrother. He was Dora's son by her first husband."

The red-faced bald man raised his glass and rattled his ice cubes perfunctorily in Molly's direction.

"Russell, may I present Molly O'Hara and her sister, Nell. Molly and Nell are the granddaughters of Atherton and Felicity's daughter, Margaret."

"Jesus Christ almighty," said Russell Bowslater in a choked voice, nearly dropping his drink.

Molly rose to her feet, feeling the room closing in around her.

This was not what she wanted, not the way it was supposed to be. Even after all she had learned over the past weeks, Molly still had a fantasy of what would happen today, a fantasy that had probably been brewing all her life. One day she would meet her real family. They would all be beautiful and kind. They would know her and Nell instantly and welcome them with open arms. There would be tears and hugs. There would be laughter.

"Look, I think we've made a mistake," said Molly. Suddenly all she wanted to do was get out, to run away and find somewhere to hide.

"Jesus Christ," repeated Russell Bowslater after taking a stiff slug of his drink. "Now I'm the one having the heart attack. Just when you think it's all over, another damned Gale shows up. Two of them, for crissakes."

"We just happened to be passing through the area and thought we'd look up our grandmother's family, that's all," Molly stammered. "We certainly didn't want to make trouble for anybody, but that's all we've seemed to have done. I think it would be better if we were just on our way. It was very nice to have made your acquaintances, thank you very much. Come on, Nell."

Molly pulled on her sister's arm, but Nell stared straight ahead and didn't budge from the divan on which she'd been sitting.

"Please bear with us, Molly," said George Gale in a soft voice. "Russell works down in Washington, D.C., so he's naturally hysterical, but for once there are good reasons for his behavior. Something terrible happened here a month ago, and I'm afraid you and your sister are involved in the whole complicated mess, whether you want to be or not."

"Look, I told you," protested Molly. "We're just distant relatives passing through. The last thing we want to do is interfere with your family, Mr. Gale. Dr. Gale."

"George," he corrected her. "And you're not distant relatives.

As Atherton's sons—adopted and step though we may be—Russell and I are technically Margaret Gale's brothers, which makes us your uncles. Or great-uncles, I guess I should say. Russell, why don't you pour our grandniece Nell a brandy?"

"And God only knows how many more of Margaret's line are going to turn up now," moaned Bowslater, shaking his head. "How many children did your grandmother have . . . what did you say her name was, George?"

"Molly."

"How many children did Margaret have, Molly? How many children did her kids have? How many do you and your sister have for that matter?"

"There's nobody but us," said Molly. "There was only our mother and Grandma, and they're both dead."

"About that brandy, Russell?"

Russell fiddled with a bottle of Courvoisier and brought a short snifter over to Nell, who made no motion to take it.

"I think it might help if your sister drank that," said George Gale in a gentle voice.

Molly nodded, taking the glass from Bowslater. She held the brandy up to Nell's lips, fighting back the impulse to take a sip first, herself. What was going on here? Why was everybody so upset?

Nell drank automatically, then broke out coughing.

George Gale came over and knelt down on one knee beside her to be at eye level.

"Are you okay now?" he asked.

Nell's eyes darted up for only an instant. She nodded, then stared back at the floor.

"Tell me how you feel."

"She doesn't talk," said Molly.

"Not at all?" asked George.

"No. But she's all right. She just gets this way sometimes."

"Why doesn't she talk?" asked Bowslater.

"It's a long story," murmured Molly.

George Gale put his hand on Nell's back, stroking it gently in small circles. Then he checked her pulse against his wristwatch. Nell didn't seem to mind. Or notice.

"Now, wait a second," said Russell. "How do we even know these kids are who they say they are? You know Henry's going to want to see some proof. Frankly so do I."

"Can you prove you're Margaret Gale's granddaughters, Molly?" asked George Gale.

"Why do we have to prove anything? I told you, we're just passing through, just stopping to say hello. And good-bye."

"See?" said Russell with a sneer. "They're probably con artists. I swear, George, you're as gullible as a Democrat congresswoman."

Molly felt the blood rush to her cheeks, but fought down the impulse to say something defensive. Why shouldn't these people want to be sure of Molly and Nell's identities? You didn't just let strangers into your life, especially when you had the kind of money that the Gales obviously did. Not that Molly intended to stay here any longer than it took to make sure the old woman was all right.

"We've been traveling, so I happen to have a lot of identification right here with me," said Molly reaching into the brown leather bag that she had gotten into the habit of bringing with her everywhere automatically. "Here are our passports, copies of our birth certificates and our mother's marriage license. I know there's a record in New York City of Margaret Gale's marriage to Richard Jellinek. They can send you a copy. It will take four to six weeks."

George Gale took the proffered documents and glanced them over.

"Thanks, Molly," he said, passing everything to Russell

Bowslater. "We have to be sure, you understand. Considering the circumstances. It all looks pretty good to me, Russell."

"Henry will want to verify everything, he's such an old woman," said Russell, studying the documents.

"Henry Troutwig is Mother's attorney," said George. "He's the man who's still upstairs with her."

"Well, I guess it's a whole new ballgame," said Russell with a sigh, passing the identification back to Molly. "Welcome to the family, girls. Don't forget to wear your batting helmets at all times. They throw bean balls around here."

He raised his glass and finished what was left of his drink.

"Look, I'd really like to know what's going on," said Molly turning to George. "You said before that something terrible happened here a month ago and that we were involved. Is that what this is all about?"

"Might as well tell her, George," said Russell, heading back to the bar. "Tell her about the reunion. She's got to be told sooner or later."

George Gale nodded.

"About a month ago Dora hosted a family reunion, here at Gale Castle," he said, looking calmly into Molly's eyes. "Mother's in pretty good shape for a woman her age, but she has certain health problems and is aware that she won't be around forever. She wanted to meet her heirs."

"Atherton left all his money to a trust that takes care of all of Mama's expenses," explained Russell. "That's the whole problem: that bastard Atherton, still trying to control everyone from the grave. When Mama dies, the trust is going to be split up in equal portions among all the Gales."

"Then this doesn't affect us at all," said Molly. "Our grandmother was disinherited years ago."

"Well, she was reinherited," said Russell, freshening his drink. "Atherton's will named all bloodline Gales as beneficiaries. The trust will be split among all Atherton's natural descendants and all the natural descendants of his sister and three brothers. I've been over the language with my lawyer a hundred times, so believe me, I know."

Molly took a deep breath. Could it be true? The thought that Grandma might have really been forgiven almost brought tears to Molly's eyes. If only she had lived. To be vindicated for the emerald ring would have made her so happy, Molly knew. And any money she inherited, no matter how little, would have made a real difference in her life.

"The family had all gone their separate ways years ago," explained George. "Of Atherton's siblings only Barnaby had stayed on Gale Island. He'd married one of the island girls when he was in his sixties and had Jimmy. Grant went to South America. Melville and his family moved to California. Louise, the youngest, married a Texan and settled in Corpus Christi."

"They were the knob kings," said Russell wistfully. "Had the biggest knob factory in the Southwest. If you've ever turned on a toaster oven, you've probably twisted one of Louise's knobs."

"Mother contacted everyone and flew them all up here first-class," continued George. "Of the original siblings only Louise was still alive, but everyone else's descendants came, along with their wives, children, grandchildren, even Melville's two great-great-grandkids. For three days, all the living Gales were together for the first time, here on Gale island."

"All except Margaret and her line," said Russell. "Mama tried to find her but couldn't. Henry even put some private detective on the case, who turned up a record of Margaret's marriage in New York City fifty years ago like you said, but lost her shortly after that. We all figured she must be dead. Why else wouldn't there be any driver's license, credit cards, or telephone number for her anywhere in the United States?"

Molly felt the blood rush to her face. Margaret Jellinek was dead, but Molly still felt protective of her. And proud. How could she explain to these people that her grandmother was too poor to have a car or credit or even a phone in her own name?

"It was a lovely reunion," said George Gale, getting back to his story. "Good food, good talk—most of the folks didn't know much about their heritage at all."

"George is the unofficial family historian," said Russell, "so he was the one who had to explain to everyone how they were related to Atherton and to one another, if you can appreciate the irony in that."

"At the end of the three days we ended with a luncheon set out in Dora's rose garden in the back," said George, pointedly ignoring his stepbrother's comment. "Mother gave a little speech about the responsibilities of wealth, about how she hoped that everyone would find the same satisfaction in giving that she had. Giving is very dear to Mother's heart. She's on the board of directors of three national charities—including the one Russell works for— and does volunteer work up here for a dozen others. She wanted to exert as much influence as she could to see that the Gale fortune does some good in years to come, after she's gone."

"Not that there was going to be much left for everyone to inherit once the taxes and attorney fees were paid and the trust was divvied up twenty-two ways," said Russell.

"It would still have come to at least a few million dollars per person, the way I figure," said George. "Maybe more."

"A few million dollars!" exclaimed Molly.

Russell waved the air contemptuously.

"Like I said, not a lot of money. What's it going to yield you these days after taxes? Barely enough to make ends meet down in my neck of the woods, let alone get you started in philanthropy."

"Better than a poke in the eye with a sharp stick," said George.

"You mean you're finally admitting that you don't like being paid in roosters and promises?" said Russell with a sneer.

George didn't answer.

"You see, dear grandniece, George pretends he doesn't care about money, but really he's just as unhappy as I am that Atherton cut the two of us out of the will."

"I thought you said all of Atherton's descendants participated," said Molly.

"All bloodline descendants, all naturally born Gales," said Russell. "I was an embarrassing reminder that Mama had had a life before she met Atherton and was elevated to Galedom. And old George here was bought and paid for as a baby. Atherton had expected him to be a big strong man and go into the family business, not waste his life healing ordinary sick people. Your grandmother, I'll bet, could tell you something about the price of disloyalty in this family."

Molly found that she was clenching the sides of the sofa so hard her knuckles hurt. So money was what all this was about— lots and lots of money. And if what George and Russell were saying was true, then Molly and Nell might be entitled to inherit a few millions dollars apiece. That might not seem much to Russell, but to Molly it was a fortune.

"Anyway," said George, pointedly raising his voice, "the reunion was over. Limousines arrived to take everyone over to the airport in Montpelier. Mother had chartered a special plane to take everyone to Boston from where they could catch their connecting flights back home. Not much flies out of here direct. Fifteen minutes after takeoff, the charter went down over the mountains, killing everyone on board."

"Oh, my God," whispered Molly, involuntarily raising her hand to her chest. "What happened?"

"There were thunderstorms in the area that day," said George. "The investigators' preliminary report says that the plane was probably struck by lightning."

"The federal aviation people were all over the place," said Russell, chewing on an ice cube. "The FBI got involved, too—you can't assume anything these days, what with terrorists and all. The plane's wreckage was strewn over a square mile. If you ask me, they're never going to be able to say for sure what happened."

"Just days after bringing them all together," said George, "Mother had to bury practically her entire family—at least what they could find of them. Twenty-one Gales, ranging in age from Louise at eighty-nine to Melville's granddaughter's three-month-old baby. In fact, every Gale who had come in for the reunion was suddenly dead."

"All except Jimmy," said Russell.

"Jimmy Gale is Barnaby's only son," explained George. "He still lives here on the Island, which is why he wasn't on the plane."

"My God," said Molly again, her mind reeling.

She had thought that she and Nell were safe. She had thought they had left death behind them in Pelletreau. Now twenty-one more bodies had been added to the count. Twenty-one heirs to the Gale Trust had died in a plane crash. Another had died with a pillow on her chest in a nursing home. And two more would have died if Molly and Nell had been in Pelletreau to flip on the lights at their house. Had the evil that lay behind everything been here in Vermont all along? Had they walked right into the monster's lair?

"That was why Mother was so upset when you told her who you were," George went on. "For reasons painfully fresh in her mind, Mother just wasn't expecting to meet any more Gales in this lifetime."

"Jimmy's going to be pretty upset, too, I'll bet," said Russell, with an unpleasant chuckle. "You'll meet him tonight. You know he'll be here for dinner, George?"

"What a treat for us all."

"Still hate him, don't you?"

"I don't hate anybody," said George Gale.

"You see, Molly," snickered Russell, "Jimmy used to call George a faggot gook and beat the crap out of him when they were kids, so George actually has good reason to hate Jimmy. The rest of us just hate him on general principle."

George Gale frowned at his stepbrother but didn't speak.

"Since the funerals Jimmy's been pretty damned pleased with himself," chuckled Russell. "Thought he was going to be the sole heir to the Gale trust. Thought he was going to get the whole boodle. Now he's going to have to share all that lovely money with you two girls."

"Shut up, Russell," George finally said in a soft voice.

"Why should I shut up, George? It's the truth. It's not like we're going to get a nickel. And frankly I could use some of that money just as much as you. I'm the one with the three ex-wives to support, remember?"

"We've done pretty well for ourselves over the years. You know we've got nothing to complain about."

"Well, I suppose that's true," conceded Russell. "I just hope Mama's going to be okay about having two new Gales to worry about all of a sudden. Who knows what she's going to do?"

"She's going to love them," said a little voice from the doorway to the room. There stood Dora Gale, her lip quivering, her eyes huge and watery behind her thick glasses. In back of her, looking thoroughly unhappy, were the woman called McCormick and Henry Troutwig, the tall, gray-faced lawyer.

Molly rose to her feet automatically, as did Russell and George. Nell sat where she was, regarding the scene with an opaque expression.

"Mrs. Gale—" began Molly, but Dora Gale cut her off by walking over and enveloping Molly to the extent she could with her childlike arms.

"Welcome to your family, girls," the old lady said in a hushed little voice, reaching out and taking Nell's hand in her own. "Welcome home."

"Anybody want more quail?" barked Mrs. McCormick, rising from the table, a mahogany three-pedestal George III antique.

"No more for me," said Russell, licking his fork and taking a final sip of wine. A chorus of additional no-thank-yous ran around the room.

"I'll tell Ruby and Mrs. Prin to set up dessert and coffee in the library," said McCormick, heading for the kitchen door. "If it's all right with you, ma'am."

"That would be very kind of you, Mrs. McCormick," said Dora Gale in her childlike little voice. "And please thank them for a lovely dinner."

"Yep," said McCormick, exiting.

Setting an additional two places for Molly and Nell at tonight's dinner had presented no apparent problem. Perhaps the Gale kitchen always kept extra coquilles St. Jacques, braces of quail, and associated side dishes on hand in case unexpected guests dropped by.

The food had been beautiful to look at and plentiful, but Molly had barely tasted anything. Too many questions raced through her mind. Were they really the heirs to a fortune? Could it be a coincidence that practically the entire Gale family had died in a plane crash a week before Margaret Jellinek had died, too? And what about the deadly explosion at Enchanted Cottage Antiques? How could these events not be related? What was going on?

There was no time to sort out any answers, however, amid the flurry of dinner conversation and the visual stimulation of the table.

Everything in sight was something to make an antique dealer salivate, from the Coalport china to the French silver salts to the Dutch floral paintings on the damasked walls of the dining room. Even the flatware was stunning. Molly had never had to cope with so many expensive spoons, knives and forks during an actual meal (the capital letter *M* beneath the maker's mark on the reverse of each Tiffany "Japanese" pattern spoon and fork told Molly that the set had been made between 1869 and 1891). And when a maid brought out crystal finger bowls, Molly almost let out a squeal. She had sold such things over the years in her shop, but had never dreamed she would actually have occasion to use one. The pride Molly had taken in their suitcases full of smalls suddenly seemed silly.

The family gathering into which Molly and Nell had stumbled was in honor of Russell Bowslater, who was returning to Washington, D.C., on Wednesday. Russell had flown in for the ill-fated family reunion a month ago and had rearranged his summer plans so that he could stay on with Dora after the plane carrying the Gales had crashed. Congress would soon resume, however, and Russell had to be getting back.

Tonight was the first time George Gale had returned to Gale Castle since the funerals. He was something of a workaholic, according to the others—which was why this dinner was on a Tuesday. The other six days a week George was on call at the hospital in Hadawoken, New Hampshire, where he lived alone (he had never been married) and practiced pediatric medicine. Though Hadawoken was only about an hour's drive away, apparently George's visits to his former home were few and far between.

Henry Troutwig, on the other hand, was a frequent guest at Gale Castle. The morticianlike attorney had been spending even more time with Dora since the tragedy, lending "moral support."

James "Jimmy" Gale, the cousin George had told them about, who lived on the island and who, apart from Molly and Nell, was now the sole surviving Gale heir, had not shown up. His absence hadn't appeared to upset anybody very much, however. In addition to being disliked by everyone except Dora (who seemed to be one step behind Mother Teresa in her acceptance of others), Jimmy Gale was notoriously unreliable.

The dinner conversation had begun politely with the weather, wandered to the problems of squeezing contributions out of healthy people for dread diseases (the charity Russell worked for was Cancer Answer and the answer apparently was money) before finally settling onto the questions in which everyone was most interested. What had happened to Margaret Gale? How had Evangeline O'Hara Cole died? What work did Molly and Nell do and what had brought them to Vermont?

The best course of action, Molly decided, was just to play along until she could figure out what to do. She had tried to put the best face on everything, speaking proudly of her grandmother's Broadway career and just saying that Margaret Jellinek had tired of the stage and had chosen to lead a quiet life in Pelletreau. As for themselves, they recently had decided to relocate and were taking advantage of this buying trip to scout locations for a new antique shop (which was in fact true).

There was no way to minimize what had happened to their mother. Molly simply said that it had been an unsolved murder, and that Nell had seen everything, resulting in her condition. The table had fallen silent. Dora put a prim hand to her lips. Russell and George exchanged surprised glances. Only Mrs. McCormick, Dora Gale's nurse and companion, had been unimpressed.

"Is she dangerous?" McCormick had asked bluntly.

"Of course not," Molly had replied.

"There was that boy in Titcomb who didn't talk, either. Killed his parents with a meat ax last spring."

"Nell is perfectly all right, except for not being able to talk," said Molly, glancing at her sister.

Nell had recovered from her earlier episode but was very subdued. Still, her natural grace showed through her timidity and seemed to touch everyone. George Gale had smiled at Nell often throughout the meal and even the garrulous Russell Bowslater had taken pains to try to include her in his endless anecdotes.

Dora Gale presided at her table with an old-fashioned graciousness that had made Molly feel more comfortable than she would have imagined possible considering the circumstances. No one had said anything about the plane crash and the deaths of all the Gales, and Dora gave no evidence of any self-pity or unhappiness.

Molly kept wanting to rush over and give the old woman a big hug, she was so adorable, so prim and proper and cute. Atherton Gale's second wife had a funny little voice and the kind of manners that are usually only exhibited by good little girls at imaginary tea parties. Her faded blue eyes still twinkled despite her age and all that had recently befallen her.

Dora, like the others, had seemed fascinated by Molly's silent sister. She was continually tossing questions and tidbits of conversation Nell's way, trying to draw her out the way one does with a shy child. Nell had returned the interest, often staring at Dora with a puzzled expression of unconcealed curiosity, but then her gaze would wander off, and she would be lost to the conversation again.

Henry Troutwig, the forbidding old attorney, had been cold and uncommunicative throughout the dinner that had now concluded.

"You really mustn't mind Mrs. McCormick," said Dora, after the hawk-faced nurse had disappeared into the kitchen to arrange for dessert. "She has a prickly manner, I know, but it conceals a gentle soul. Mrs. McCormick took care of Atherton during his final illness. She was such a help that I asked her to stay on after his death. She has been wonderful to me, and we have a lot in common. She's a widow, too. Her own husband died many years ago."

Dora rose from her chair. Standing, she was no taller than she had been seated.

"Shall we retire to the library?" she said.

"I really should be getting along, Mother," said George, who had come over to hold Dora's chair when she stood. "I'm six miles behind on my paperwork."

"Oh, please stay a little while longer, George," Dora implored, taking his arm. "I hardly ever get to see you anymore. And it's not every day that you get to meet two beautiful young women."

"All right," said George, smiling at Molly. "I guess I can stay a bit longer."

"Thank you, dear," said Dora. "It's so nice to have us all together. I don't know how many more occasions like this I'll be around to enjoy."

"Don't say such things, Dora," said Henry Troutwig, who had barely uttered two words in the past hour. "You'll be with us for a long, long time."

"Thank you, Henry," said Dora. "We'll see."

The library was on the other side of the living room and almost as big. A fireplace occupied one wall, the other three were lined with brass grilled bookcases full of leather bound volumes, hundreds of them. "Bindings," as such books were called in the trade, were cheap enough to be sold by the yard to decorators. These, however, looked to Molly like actual first editions.

Coffee and an assortment of pies, cakes, and chocolates were set up and waiting for them when they arrived, along with the surly Mrs. McCormick. They served themselves and found places in comfortable old (as in English Regency) library furniture. Dora situated herself between Molly and Nell on a leatherbound sofa.

"I'm so happy our girls have come home," she said, giving them each a gentle pat on the knee.

"Good pie," said Russell, shoveling a piece into his face. "I'm surely going to miss all this when I get back to Washington and resume my bachelor ways. Fund-raising dinners always leave you feeling wanting. You should come down and visit me sometime, George. Two single men, out on the town—we could have a hell of a good time."

"I'll think about that, Russell," said George in a voice that indicated that he wouldn't.

"How long do you and your sister plan to be in the area?" asked Henry Troutwig in his flat New England dialect, looking down his huge nose at Molly like some kind of gigantic owl.

"We're really just passing through."

"Wouldn't you consider staying for a while?" asked Dora. "You said at dinner that you didn't have any immediate plans. It's going to be terribly lonely here again when Russell leaves."

"No, we couldn't possibly."

"I know you're polite girls and don't want to impose," Dora went on in an intense, earnest voice, "but at my age I'm allowed to be selfish and ask for what I want. I really wish you both would stay here at Gale Castle with me awhile. Please, my dear?"

"Well we'd like to, of course, but . . ."

"Then it's settled, and I won't hear another word. You can have your own room in the west wing. You'll have all the privacy you could want and there's plenty to do—gardening, there's the badminton net and the pool in back. We can even surf the Internet on the new computer that Russell bought me. You're determined to make me into a techno-babe, aren't you, Russell?"

"Aw, Mama," said Russell, his bald head blushing beet red.

"Mrs. McCormick, will you be kind enough to have Ruby make up one of the big rooms in the west wing before she leaves for the evening?"

"Can't I at least finish my damn piece of pie?" said McCormick, her fork in midair.

"Oh, I'm terribly sorry," said Dora, raising a hand to her mouth. "Of course finish your pie. Where are my manners?"

"Very neatly done," said Henry Troutwig to Molly in a voice as dry as dust.

"Excuse me?" said Molly.

"The way you've already insinuated your way into the family. A few hours ago nobody even knew you existed. Now you've arranged for a bedroom."

"Henry, please," said Dora, her kind round face registering dismay. "Molly and Nell are my family. They are my guests."

"I'm sorry, Dora, but this is all just a little too pat for me. These two showing up from nowhere like this. Now, when you're most vulnerable. And when the payoff is the largest."

"See, I told you so," said Russell to George. "We saw their credentials, Henry. Everything looked pretty good."

"Not good enough for me," said the attorney. "I intend to

put my investigator, Mr. Puttridge, on the case by the morning. We'll see what he has to say."

"Henry, I forbid you to make trouble for these girls."

"Please, Mrs. Gale," said Molly. "Please don't get upset again. There's nothing anyone will find about us but the truth."

"Thank you, Molly," said Dora, reaching over and taking Molly's hand, a pained smile returning to her face. "I appreciate your concern. But I won't have you embarrassed in my home. And let's not have any more of this 'Mrs. Gale' business. I'm just plain Dora."

"Even if they are who they say they are, Dora," said Troutwig, making a sniffing sound, "remember the kind of people they're coming from. It was no secret that Atherton's daughter Margaret was a tramp and a common thief."

"That's not true," said Molly, rising from her seat.

"She stole a valuable ring from her mother so she could run off with some nobody. I've heard the story from a dozen people who knew Atherton well."

"Well, I have news for you, Henry Troutwig," said Dora, before Molly could respond. "Felicity Gale was my best friend and she told me the whole story of that ring the year before she died. Felicity gave it to Margaret along with her blessing. When Atherton and I started seeing each other after Felicity's death, he told me that Felicity had lied about Margaret, about him, about a lot of things. I believed Atherton, but it wasn't long before I learned who the real liar was. If I had trusted Felicity I could have saved myself many years of unhappiness."

"Well, I only know what I've heard," declared Troutwig. "And until it's proven to the contrary, I will continue to believe what everyone else believes: that Margaret stole her own mother's ring and sold it to support her selfish ways."

"Then this must be the proof you're looking for," said Molly.

Everyone in the room turned to look at Molly. She took the chain from around her neck and held it out. The dangling emerald caught the light of the fireplace and sparkled with an eerie green glow.

"My grandmother didn't sell this ring because she didn't steal it. It was a gift from her mother, just as Dora said."

No one spoke. For a moment Molly didn't know what to do next. Then suddenly everything became clear.

"This ring has caused so much grief for so many people over the years," Molly went on, breaking the silence. "I think our grandmother would want some good to come from it. You're involved with a lot of charities, Dora. Would you help us arrange to donate it to a worthy cause? That is, if it's okay with you, Nell."

Everyone turned to look at Nell, who surprised everyone by breaking into a big smile and nodding her head vigorously.

"Thank you, girls," said Dora, taking the proffered ring, her pale old eyes again moist with tears. "I think that Felicity would be very proud of you. I know I am."

"Game, set, and match," said McCormick, rising to her feet. "Guess I'll go have that room made up."

Henry Troutwig stiffened and made a noise that sounded like "harrumph."

"Well, I really must be running along," he declared. "Thank you for a lovely dinner, Dora, as always. George, a pleasure. Russell, I'll probably see you again before you leave. I enjoyed meeting you and your sister, Miss O'Hara. I'm sure we'll have occasion to speak again."

"So long, Troutwig, been good to know you," said Mrs. McCormick heading back to the kitchen.

Troutwig scratched his cheek.

"I'm sorry if I embarrassed you, Dora my dear, but you know that I have an obligation to look out for your interests. I'm also very fond of you as a person and I don't wish to see you hurt again after all you've just gone through."

"I appreciate that, Henry," said Dora, primly. "I won't stay mad at you for long, but I will not have you coming between me and my family."

"Very well, then. Good night."

"Good night, Henry."

The lawyer turned on his heel and marched out of the room.

"Thanks," said Molly in a soft voice. She wasn't used to having anyone stick up for her.

"Oh, Henry's harmless," said Dora. "Everybody's been so very protective of me lately. You see, Molly, a terrible thing happened here last month. I haven't been exactly sure how to tell you this, but . . ."

"We already know. George and Russell told us all about it."

"About the reunion? About the terrible plane crash?"

"Yes."

"I'm so sorry, my dears," said Dora, reaching out and taking Molly's and Nell's hands. "I'm just a Gale by marriage. After hearing about how alone in the world you've been, I understand what it must have meant to you to find your way here to Gale Island. Now the rest of your family is gone before you ever got a chance to meet them."

"We still have you." said Molly. "And George and Russell."

Dora gave her hand a little squeeze.

"Thank you, Molly. That means a lot to me. Russell, say thank you to your cousin."

"Aw, Mama," said Bowslater. "I'm eating my pie."

"Our grandniece," said George, correcting Dora. "We're all happy to have you here, Molly."

"Thanks," whispered Molly.

The library's magnificent old tall case clock chimed ten times.

Molly found herself yawning. She was suddenly immensely tired, and no wonder. Only yesterday they had been on another continent. What they learned over the past few hours had placed them in a different world.

"George, please hand me that photo album from our reunion," said Dora. "It's right there on the bottom shelf of the cabinet next to you."

"Are you sure you want to, Mother?"

"They're just pictures, George, and I know Molly and Nell would like to see them. I wish everyone would please stop treating me like I am made of glass. I am a resilient person and an adult."

George brought over a large photo album bound in red leather. Dora opened it on her lap and began flipping through the pages. There, in four-by-six color photographs, were the Gales, laughing with one another, eating outdoors, posing with Dora, Russell, and George.

As Dora turned the pages she named each relative and said a little something about him or her, always nice. Beverly Gale, Grant's daughter, had the most beautiful clothes. Little eight-year-old Winston Gale had just won a prize for his clarinet playing. Melville's grandson, Louis, was a doctor.

George and Russell came over behind the couch, adding their often humorous perceptions. Lolly Gale had had so many face-lifts that she looked like a snare drum. Alesandro Gale and his wife Marta had come in from Buenos Aires but all they wanted to talk about was their new Mercedes. Louise Gale Sockelberry wanted to know if everyone liked her knobs.

Nell looked and listened and nodded like she was having the best time in the world. Molly smiled and tried not to yawn too obviously. She wasn't ready to go to bed yet. Despite the deaths of the Gales and her fears about what had happened in Pelletreau, it was easy to be with these people, it was as if she had known them forever. Molly felt full and happy, like she and Nell really were part of a family for the first time.

When they finished one album, Dora brought out another and kept turning the pages until Molly found herself looking at the last photograph. Unlike most of the others, this one had only one person in it.

"And here is your cousin James, Barnaby's son," said Dora sweetly. "He's never been very sociable and wasn't too keen on having his picture taken with the group."

"Where was Jimmy tonight, anyway?" asked Russell. "I thought he was supposed to come for dinner."

"I called him on the telephone twice this afternoon to remind him," said Dora, "but there was no answer. Lord knows what that boy gets up to."

Molly stared at the photograph. All the cozy warm feelings she had been reveling in vanished. Molly suddenly felt cold and frightened, yet strangely unsurprised. From the minute she learned about the Gale trust and Atherton's will, she had expected something like this, but hoped against hope that it wouldn't be true. At last everything was beginning to fit together, however. At last the puzzle was beginning to make sense.

The man in the photograph had a glass of iced tea in his hand and an annoyed expression on his face. Jimmy Gale also had rust-colored hair and a bushy mustache.

Molly was being attacked by giant bumblebees. They cascaded from the sky like black-and-yellow dive bombers. She ducked as one missed her head by inches, buzzing angrily. Buzzzzzbuzzzzzz. Buzzzzbuzzzzz. She awoke with a start.

She was lying in an impossibly comfortable bed in a strange room. Nell was asleep in a bed that was the twin of Molly's. Light poured through a lacy curtain and made elegant patterns on the pale yellow wallpaper.

Buzzzzzzzzzzzzz, droned the sound again.

For a moment Molly thought the bumblebees of her dream had pursued her here, but then she noticed an intercom next to the room's polished rosewood door. The buzz was coming from there.

Suddenly it all came back. The Gales. Dinner. The photograph of the man with the red hair and mustache—their cousin, Jimmy Gale.

After Molly and Nell had finished looking through the albums from the ill-fated family reunion, Dora had brought them to this lovely room with its own adjoining bath, its own telephone line, and its own John Singer Sargent watercolor. They had crawled into bed without further ado. There was no point trying to decide what to do next until they had gotten a good night's sleep.

Buzzzzzzzzzzzzzzzzzz.

Molly pulled herself out of the bed and scurried over to the intercom in her bare feet, shivering. The room's wide-plank floor was uncovered save for a small Turkish rug, and she was wearing one of the skimpy white cotton nightgowns that she had bought at the mall in Pelletreau with Oscar just a few days ago. Despite its still being the dead of summer, the morning here was cold enough for flannel.

"Hello?" Molly said, picking up the handset.

"Someone here to see you," snapped a curt voice that Molly recognized as that of Mrs. McCormick.

"To see us?" Molly asked. Who knew they were even on Gale Island?

"It's the law," said McCormick, answering the unspoken question. "The New Melford sheriff. Gale Island comes under his jurisdiction."

"We'll be down in a few minutes," said Molly, amazed. The police were the first people she had intended to call this morning. The New Melford sheriff must be some kind of a mind reader.

"Take your time," rasped McCormick. "I'll fix him a waffle. Can't hurt to make friends with the cops is my motto. Never know when you might get busted."

Molly hung up the receiver and walked back to the beds. Nell had pulled a pillow over her head to block out the noise and light. According to the gilt brass mantle clock over the room's dormant fireplace and Molly's new silver wristwatch it was nine thirty-five.

"Come on," said Molly, giving her sister a push. "We've got to get dressed."

It took a few more pushes, but finally Nell emerged from beneath her pillow. It was another ten minutes before they had brushed their teeth, washed their faces and rummaged through their suitcases for something unwrinkled to wear. The law would have to settle for T-shirts and blue jeans.

They emerged from their room into a long, deserted hallway, filled with old master portraits, Brussels tapestries (she could tell from the monogrammed *B*s stitched into their bottom selvages) and suits of armor.

Molly had been too tired last night to appreciate fully the pains to which Atherton Gale had gone in creating his castle, but marveled now at the exquisite details that were everywhere—Renaissance bronzes of sea monsters and horses, intricately carved Flemish coffers, repoussé silver candle sconces. The whole place was like a museum. And it was huge.

The wing in which their room was located was to the west of the great central mahogany staircase. Dora's room and the others were on the other side in an even longer hallway. You could probably hold a rodeo on either side and not disturb the people on the other.

Molly and Nell descended the stairs together and made for the dining room where they had eaten last night. No one was there, but the aroma of frying bacon was coming from beyond the rear doorway.

Molly led her sister through the door into a dark passage lined with china cabinets that rose to the high ceiling. This opened into a huge, light-filled kitchen as cozy as the rest of the house was ornate and formal. Big old-fashioned ovens dominated one wall, long metal sinks another. The floor was checkered with black-and-white tiles. A rear door led out to a drive alongside a wall of conifers that circled the castle.

A man in a *Smokey Bear* hat and tan shirt with a gold badge over his breast pocket sat at a long rustic pine table by the windows. With one hand he sopped up maple syrup with a forkful of waffle. With the other he held a piece of bacon and nibbled blissfully.

"You two want breakfast?" she barked, seeing Molly and Nell. "This is Prin's day off, so you'll have to trust me not to poison you."

Nell nodded enthusiastically and plopped herself down at the table across from the man.

"Where's Mrs. Gale?" Molly asked, sitting uncertainly, wondering why he was here.

"Russell took her over to the hospice in Newbyville," said McCormick. "She's got a woman on her last legs over there who she visits on Wednesdays."

The sheriff had now finished the last piece of bacon on his plate and was wiping his fingers with a linen napkin.

"I'm Molly O'Hara," said Molly, taking the initiative. "This is my sister, Nell."

"Dan Glickman," he replied, reaching across the table to shake her hand.

The New Melford sheriff was a handsome man in his early fifties. Though he was seated Molly could tell he was tall. He had a pleasant open face with tired blue eyes, short graying hair, a straight nose, and perfect white teeth. He put everything to good advantage in a sad, but friendly smile.

"What was it you wanted to see us about, Sheriff?" asked Molly, taking a sip from the stoneware mug in front of her. Mrs. McCormick's coffee was strong enough to kill a cat.

"Here's your waffles," said McCormick, depositing plates in front of Molly and Nell. With her face well scrubbed and her sleeves rolled up, the hatchet-faced nurse looked almost human in the morning light.

"Troutwig the lawyer thinks you're mass murderers though I'm not supposed to tell anybody he said so," said Glickman, rising to his feet with his mug. "Any more of that coffee, Mrs. M.?"

"You just sit yourself right down, Sheriff," said McCormick, going over for the coffee on the stove. "I never let men with guns serve themselves."

"We are not mass murderers!" exclaimed Molly. Nell buttered her waffle.

"Then you're opportunistic impostors, according to Troutwig," said the sheriff. "He gave me a choice."

"That's ridiculous," said Molly. "We're the ones who are in danger. In fact it's ironic that you're here. I was going to call you this morning."

"In danger from who?" said McCormick, pouring more coffee into Sheriff Glickman's cup. "I mean whom. Interrogations always make me forget my grammar."

Molly started to answer, but Glickman put his hand up and stopped her.

"I think we'd better have a little privacy at this point, if you don't mind, Mrs. M.," he said with a sigh. "I'm beginning to come back to my senses, thanks to your fine cooking. This is official business."

"Oh, come on, Sheriff. Things are just getting interesting."

"If they turn out to be killers, I promise to let you know before they get you, too."

"Slim consolation," McCormick said, her face screwing up in a frown. "Henry Troutwig strikes me more the mass murderer type than these kids. Not that I'm afraid of anybody, mind you. I sleep with a ball-peen hammer. And don't make any cracks."

"I never wise off to a beautiful woman," said the sheriff. "Thanks for breakfast, gorgeous."

"In a pig's eye," muttered McCormick. "No pun intended."

Then she wiped her hands on a dish towel and left the room in a huff.

"So what's this about your being in danger?" asked Glickman when she had gone.

"If anyone is a mass murderer," said Molly, "it's Jimmy Gale. He's Mrs. Gale's nephew, I think. I haven't got the family straight in my head yet."

"Don't worry about that. I've been here for a long, long time. Believe me, I know Jimmy."

"You mean he's been in trouble before?"

"My introduction to Jimmy Gale, twenty-five years ago," said Glickman, "was when I chased him halfway across the state. He was drunk out of his mind. Ended up smashing through some poor lady's picture window. His uncle Atherton hired an expensive lawyer who got the charges dismissed on a technicality. Then they shuffled him off to the army. That was the only time Jimmy hasn't been in trouble around here. I still run him in as regular as clockwork, mostly for fighting in bars."

A shiver ran down Molly's spine.

"Is he a suspect in the plane crash that killed all the Gales?"

"You only have suspects when there's a crime, Miss O'Hara. The crash you're talking about was an accident. The National Transit Safety Board is saying that the plane was struck by lightning."

"It didn't bother anybody that Jimmy Gale was suddenly the sole beneficiary to the Gale Trust?" Molly asked, incredulous.

Glickman took a sip of coffee without taking his eyes off Molly.

"I gather from Troutwig that the two of you will inherit as well," he said in a quiet voice.

"But don't you see?" Molly exclaimed. "That's why Jimmy killed our grandmother and tried to kill us!"

"Whoa," said Glickman, holding up a big callused hand. "Jimmy killed somebody?"

Molly proceeded to describe Margaret Jellinek's death, the explosion of the Enchanted Cottage and the various sightings of the man with rust-colored hair and mustache. The sheriff listened, making occasional notes in a small notepad he took from his breast pocket.

"You say she was murdered, your grandmother," he said when she had finished.

"By the time we figured everything out it was too late to do an autopsy," said Molly. "But the police know what happened. She was suffocated with her pillow by her last visitor—the man who was following us, waiting for us to leave our house so he could booby-trap it."

Glickman rubbed his jaw.

"And when you saw Jimmy's picture in Dora Gale's album last night, you recognized him as this man whom you had seen back in North Carolina."

"Well, not exactly."

Glickman raised an eyebrow.

"What do you mean, not exactly?"

"I only saw the man in North Carolina from a distance," said Molly. "He was sitting in a car at my grandmother's funeral. Then I saw him a few times driving past our house. He was always wearing sunglasses and I never really got a good look at him, beyond noticing that he had red hair and a mustache. Just like Jimmy Gale. Just like my grandmother's last visitor at the nursing home."

"Just like probably a million other guys in the world," said Glickman.

"But this is too much of a coincidence," said Molly. "I don't believe in coincidences. And as a law enforcement professional, neither should you."

"Could you swear that the man you saw was Jimmy Gale, Miss O'Hara?"

"I . . ."

"Could you swear?"

"No," Molly had to admit.

"What about your sister?" Glickman indicated Nell, who had polished off her waffle and was eying Molly's. "Can she positively ID. Jimmy?"

"Actually, I don't think Nell saw him."

"Just as well," said Glickman with a sigh. "Her testimony probably wouldn't be worth much in court anyway."

"Why not?" demanded Molly.

"Troutwig mentioned to me about her . . . difficulties."

"There's nothing wrong with my sister," said Molly between clenched teeth, transferring her untouched waffle to Nell's plate and passing her the maple syrup. Nell smiled at Glickman and dug in.

"No," said the sheriff. "I'm sure there isn't. But you can see why I have to be a little skeptical of all this. Even if you had videotaped your sightings of Jimmy in North Carolina, what would it prove? That he attended a funeral? That he drove by your house?"

"A man who blows up a whole planeload of people so he won't have to split his inheritance isn't going to stop at killing a few more," said Molly, trying to keep in control.

"But like I said, Miss O'Hara, the plane was apparently struck by lightning. No evidence of explosives or tampering was found. Don't you think maybe you're being a little paranoid here?"

"For God's sakes, Sheriff," Molly exploded. "Our grandmother is dead. Our best friend is dead. Our house and business is blown to smithereens. All within the span of a couple weeks. If I'm paranoid it's because I'm scared to death. Won't you please help us?"

Nell had stopped eating. She looked at Molly, then at the sheriff, then back again, clearly unhappy to see her sister so upset.

"All right, all right," said Glickman. "Calm down. I guess I can send a picture of Jimmy to that detective you spoke to in North Carolina . . . what was his name again?"

"Sergeant Arlo Couvertie," said Molly.

"Sergeant Arlo Couvertie," repeated Glickman, jotting down the name. "We'll see if one of the people who saw this red-haired man at the nursing home can identify Jimmy."

Nell rose from her place and collected the dishes and went to rinse them off in the sink.

"Actually that's a problem," said Molly. "No one at the nursing home remembers seeing the red-haired man."

"Wait a second," said Glickman, ruffling through the chicken scratches in his notebook. "Didn't you say that's how you learned in the first place that a red-haired man with a mustache was your grandmother's last visitor? From the receptionist at the nursing home?"

"That's what happened," said Molly, "but then later when the police asked her, she didn't remember seeing him or telling us."

Glickman rolled his eyes.

"What about the bombing of your house? Were there any witnesses to that? Do the police have any physical evidence?"

"Not really," Molly admitted. "They can't prove it wasn't an accident. But you said Jimmy Gale was in the army. Wouldn't he have learned all about explosives and booby traps there?"

"I'm getting a headache," said Glickman, massaging the bridge of his nose. "God is finally punishing me for not going into medicine."

"Talk to Sergeant Couvertie."

"I'll do that, Miss O'Hara. I'll even go by and talk to Jimmy. But now I want you to answer some questions for me."

"Like what?" said Molly.

"Like where were you the week of July fourteenth?"

"I . . . we were mostly at our antique shop, I suppose. In North Carolina."

"Can anyone corroborate that you didn't leave town that week?" Glickman asked.

"I don't know. We lived by ourselves and didn't exactly have a big social circle in Pelletreau. Why?"

"That was the week that the plane carrying Dora Gale's guests went down."

Molly involuntarily put her hand to her chest.

"You couldn't possibly think that we . . ."

"Please, Miss O'Hara," said Glickman, shaking his head. "I've spent the last month smack in the middle of a federal investigation. I thought it was winding down, but you can bet that if Troutwig contacted me, he's also talked with the federal boys."

"So what?" said Molly, crossing her arms in front of her. "Aren't they the ones who are saying the plane crash was an accident?"

"The case isn't officially closed yet," said Glickman. "And you can't imagine what pains in the ass the FBI can be if you don't have the answers they want to hear. Now, I'd like to know what made you decide to come to Gale Island just now."

"I told you," said Molly, wondering why she was the one who had to defend herself. "Somebody blew up our house and killed our grandmother. A man with red hair and a mustache. There was nothing left for us in Pelletreau and we were frightened. We wanted to make a new start somewhere, and we had just learned about the Gales."

"Just learned about them?"

Molly tried to explain.

"You mean," Glickman said finally, "that all these years you knew nothing about Dora Gale, nothing about Gale Island? It's pure coincidence that you just happened to show up now, just in time to inherit millions? Is that one of those coincidences that we law enforcement professionals aren't supposed to believe in?"

Nell returned from having done the dishes. Glickman flashed a weary grin.

"Listen, Miss O'Hara. Henry Troutwig's a schmuck, but I've got to do my job, you know? And let me tell you right now, the fact that I like you more than I like Jimmy doesn't mean that I'm automatically going to believe your version of things—even if I thought that there was anything sinister going on here, which I don't."

There was noise from the doorway. The three of them looked over simultaneously in time to see Russell Bowslater come in. Dora's bald potbellied son wasn't wearing plaid pants this morning, but his silk shirt was striped with practically every color of the rainbow.

"Oh, hi," he said, startled. "Didn't mean to interrupt anything. Just thought I'd make a little icebox raid—didn't get much breakfast. Prin's day off."

"You're Mr. Bowslater, right?" asked Glickman, rising to his feet. He was even taller than Molly had imagined and looked like a giant standing there beside her.

"Yes. And you are . . . ?"

"Glickman. New Melford sheriff. We talked after the funerals."

"That's right," said Russell with a big smile. "Nice to see you again, Officer. Morning, girls."

"Hi," said Molly for both of them.

"Mama said for you and your sister to make yourselves at

home," said Russell, crossing to the refrigerator and opening the door. "She's sorry she wasn't here when you woke up. She had to visit with this sick lady over in Newbyville, didn't have the heart to postpone it. Mama's an absolute nut about her charities. I'm going back in a hour or so to pick her up. You two can come along if you like."

"Thanks, Russell," said Molly. "Do you know if Jimmy Gale has been out of town recently?"

Glickman shot her an irritated look.

"Yeah, he has," answered Russell, too busy exploring the refrigerator to notice the exchange. "A couple weeks ago. He was gone five or six days I think. Said he was going hunting down South."

"Interesting coincidence," said Molly, firing a meaningful glance back at Glickman. Russell emerged from behind the refrigerator door with a piece of pie and a carton of cranberry juice.

"I talked to Jimmy on the phone right after he got back but haven't seen him since," he said. "In fact, Mama's been a mite worried about him, now that you mention it."

"Worried?" said Glickman. "Why worried?"

"Oh, we had this family dinner last night and Jimmy didn't show up. She had called yesterday to remind him. She called again today to see if he was okay. There was no answer either time, but when we drove by his place this morning his truck was in the driveway and all the lights in the house were lit up. Mama wanted to stop in and see if he was okay right then, but we were running late."

"Maybe I'll pay him a little visit," said Glickman.

"He's probably dead drunk on the floor, like he was after the funerals," said Russell, his mouth full of pie. "I had to go pick him up out of a puddle of his own vomit. Said he was celebrating. He does that a lot."

"I know, believe me," said Glickman, opening his little note-book. "Did you say he lives around here? We usually only meet in places with liquor licenses."

"He's just down the road," said Russell. "It's the only house on the way down the hill, you can't miss it. Say, would you mind if I came with you? I should probably try to get him sobered up. I know Mama's going to insist we pay him a visit when I pick her up later. I don't want her to have to see him like that."

"I'd like to come, too," said Molly.

"Miss O'Hara . . ." Glickman began in a stern voice, then just shook his head. "Oh, hell. I guess it doesn't matter. We can't put him in a lineup with what we've got."

"Lineup?" said Russell. "My cousin in trouble again, Sheriff?"

"No, no," said the sheriff. "I just want to talk with him, that's all. Introduce him to Miss O'Hara, here."

"Well, you'll certainly meet the real Jimmy," Russell said to Molly, chuckling. "Though I don't know why you'd want to."

Finishing up the remains of his pie, Russell led the way through the door at the rear of the kitchen and back around to the front of the castle. Glickman's four-wheel drive was parked in the circular parking area, alongside Molly's rented car.

Nell seemed pleased to be in a police cruiser. Molly tried to keep from looking as frightened as she felt. She'd have to meet Jimmy Gale sooner or later. Best to do so with a sheriff at her side and Russell there as a witness.

A plan had already formed in Molly's mind. It wasn't bril-liant, she knew, but it was certainly better than running away again and spending the rest of her life always looking back over her shoul-der, worrying that Jimmy Gale would find them.

She'd confront Jimmy face on. She'd let him know in no uncertain terms that they were all on to him, that everyone knew what he had done in Pelletreau, that if anything happened to her and Nell he would be the only suspect. It might not stop him, but at least it would slow him down, give him something to worry about. And in the meanwhile, Molly could find proof somehow of what he had done.

The road curled back down the mountain. After no more than a few minutes they came to a hidden drive—Molly hadn't even noticed it when she had driven up to Gale Castle yesterday. The house and Jimmy's car were visible from the road, but just barely. They had to drive in and get past a tall stand of firs before Molly noticed that there were lights on inside the house as Russell had said.

Sheriff Glickman pulled his vehicle up behind Jimmy's truck. Then they all got out and walked up the slate walk to the house, a stone cottage with blue-painted trim that would have been charming had it been better kept. Paint was peeling everywhere. The small lawn in front was overgrown.

"Guess not much of the Gale fortune stuck to Jimmy," said Glickman, pressing the doorbell.

"Yeah," said Russell. "He went through his father's money years ago. Not that Barnaby had much to begin with—Atherton pretty much kept everything for himself. It'll be a different story when Mama dies, though. It'll take Jimmy quite a while to go through that."

Glickman pressed the doorbell again. From outside they could hear it ring, but no one appeared. Molly thought she could hear the faint sounds of a television coming from inside. Russell knocked on the door with the heel of his fist and tried the handle. It was locked.

"That stupid son of a bitch," said Russell. "This is just what I was afraid of. Another floor full of vomit and me in my good pants. Come on. We'll try the back."

Clearly irritated, Russell led the way around the house to a back porch, where a big black gas grill looked to be the only well-maintained thing on the property. The small backyard was strewn with garbage and rusted tools. An old wheelbarrow was piled high with empty beer cans and bourbon bottles.

Russell rapped on the mullioned back door with his knuckle. Through the glass Molly could see a figure sitting at a dinette in the shadows. A small television set was on. Cans of beer and unwashed dishes were littered about the room.

"Jimmy," shouted Russell. "Open the goddamned door."

He tried the handle. It turned. The door opened easily. As Russell reached in and flipped on the kitchen overhead light, a foul smell rushed out and assaulted them all.

Molly gasped, then turned and pulled Nell away before she could see inside. A man with red hair and a mustache was seated in a straight-backed chair. Molly was close enough to notice that Jimmy Gale had blue eyes and bad teeth. He also had a neat little hole in the center of his forehead.

Fourteen

"Remember that time Jimmy pulled your arm out of its socket pushing you off the toolshed?" asked Russell Bowslater, munching on a canapé.

"One of the high points of my childhood," said George Gale.

Molly sat with Nell on a divan in the living room across from their two great-uncles, the only people in the room the sisters knew besides Dora and Henry Troutwig. About forty people had come back to Gale Castle after Jimmy Gale's funeral. Most were elderly neighbors from the island who were here out of respect for the Gale matriarch. Even the younger couples were Dora's friends, not Jimmy's. Apparently Jimmy had had no friends. Dora had many.

"What was that, thirty-five years ago?" Russell went on cheerfully, taking a sip of his scotch and soda. "You know, I don't think I ever told you this, George, but after Dora took you to the hospital that day Jimmy sidled up to me and tried to convince me that you had done it to yourself, throwing a punch at him. God, he was a shit—even as a kid."

"Atherton actually believed that story," said George in his soft voice.

"That you threw your arm out of the socket trying to punch Jimmy? You're kidding."

George shook his head.

"When we got home Atherton told me how proud he was of me. He even offered to take me to a Red Sox game in Boston if I could give Jimmy a black eye."

"I never heard this," chortled Russell. "Did you do it?"

"Of course not," said George as they watched Dora finally break free from Henry Troutwig's pompous condolences and make her way across the crowded room. "You know I hate sports."

"Hello, children," said Dora Gale upon arrival. "It's such a comfort to have you all here with me."

Dora looked prim and pretty in her flowered blue dress. At the funeral she had been the picture of cute dignity with her little patent leather purse, white gloves, and a hat that Mamie Eisenhower would have approved of.

"Sit down, Mama," said Russell, rising and offering his chair. From one moment to the next his jovial good cheer had been replaced with grave earnestness. "It's a sad day, sad day. You look tired."

"I'm fine," said Dora. "Oh, there's Zebulon Stanton and his wife. I didn't know they were here—I don't think I've seen him in twenty years, I really must go over and thank them for coming. How are you, Molly, dear? I'm sorry you had to go through all of this, but I don't know how I could have managed without you and Nell."

Molly nodded. She was glad there had been so much to do. Over the past few days Molly had fielded telephone calls and answered condolence notes from family friends, gone with Dora to see about the cemetery plot, the funeral, and the casket, and had helped out with the sheriff's questions, the obituary for the New Melford County paper and the arrangements for this obligatory postburial hospitality.

Still, there had been too much time left to think. With Jimmy dead, the O'Hara sisters were now the sole heiresses to the Gale Trust. Molly tried to imagine what it would be like to have millions and millions of dollars, but couldn't. Somehow, the money didn't seem real.

All the people who had died were real enough, however. Their ghosts kept intruding into Molly's mind with a solidity that was frightening: the dead Gales from the family album; Grandma with the pillow on her chest; Taffy smiling wryly and rolling her eyes; Jimmy Gale with the little hole in the center of his forehead.

At least Nell hadn't seen him, sitting there in his chair like that, Molly thought with a shudder. Every time she thought of it the horrible scene from her childhood flashed into Molly's mind—of coming home from the movies to find her mother dead on the floor with a similar wound, and a blank-faced, silent Nell sitting cross-legged by her side.

Oddly enough, in the midst of thoughts about death and the flurry of details that surrounded Jimmy's funeral, the question of who had killed their cousin and for what reason had begun to seem almost irrelevant. A man like Jimmy Gale must have made many enemies after a lifetime of bar fights, Molly told herself. She was ashamed to be relieved at his death.

"Poor old Jimmy," said Russell with a deep sigh. "It's really a shame he had to die without making anything of his life. So sad."

"Tragic," added George with a straight face.

"You know, my dears," said Dora, addressing them all, "I've seen much of life and death in my time. I know that death is something natural. It is nothing to fear, and I am very close to it. None of us know what exactly we are doing here, but I believe that every life has importance and its own meaning. I know that James wasn't well-liked, but he, too, was here for a reason."

"That's because you're a saint, Mama," said Russell. "An ever-lovin' saint."

"I just prefer to believe the best about people, Russell," answered Dora. "Oh, hello, Helen. So nice of you to have come. Will you all please excuse me?"

They murmured assent, and Dora went off with another elderly lady no bigger than she was.

"I hope you're giving her something, George," said Russell when she was out of earshot.

"Giving her something?"

"You know. Something to calm her down, help her sleep. Mama's keeping up a brave front, but this has got to be a lot harder on her than she lets on."

"Dora's fine," said George. "And even if she weren't, you don't start pumping barbiturates into a ninety-three-year-old woman in delicate health."

"You know I'm on that five-thirty plane tonight," said Russell, shaking his finger at his stepbrother. "I can't delay going back to Washington any longer. You know Mama's bound to start feeling depressed and lonely pretty soon. You've got to give her something."

"Molly and Nell will be here with her," said George. "You are staying awhile, aren't you?"

"I guess," said Molly uncomfortably. She hadn't given any thought to what they would do next, what they would do for the rest of their lives.

"How about that melatonin stuff?" asked Russell. "Totally natural hormone, knocks you right out with no side effects. I take it myself for jet lag."

"Are you a doctor, now, Russell?"

"I'm just thinking of Mama. If you don't like melatonin, then how about a good old-fashioned tranquilizer?"

"I told you . . ."

"Half the people in Congress and a hundred percent of the spouses take something, George. Pharmaceuticals are as American as apple pie. What kind of doctor are you if you don't realize . . ."

The two of them continued to bicker. As they did so, a subdued Mrs. McCormick came quietly up behind the sofa, bent down, and whispered into Molly's ear.

"Sheriff Glickman wants to talk to you. I've got him parked outside, didn't want him to come in and upset Mrs. Gale again. Can you come out to see him without making a fuss?"

Molly nodded. The only time Dora had broken into tears during the past week was when she came downstairs the day after Jimmy's death and overheard Glickman taking statements from everybody about where they were on Tuesday morning. Apparently Jimmy had been shot sometime before noon on the same day Molly and Nell had arrived at Gale Castle and met their family.

Molly waited until McCormick had disappeared into the crowd, then rose.

"I'll be right back," she said. "I'm going to get some air."

Russell and George barely acknowledged her and continued to argue. Nell glanced over quizzically for a moment, then turned her attention to a tray of finger sandwiches being offered around by one of the island girls who had been hired to help out for the day.

It was another cool morning, though the temperature would rise into the eighties by afternoon, Molly knew. The sky looked an unnaturally deep blue against the massive pine trees that stood like a fortress wall around Gale Castle. Sheriff Glickman was leaning back against his four-wheel drive, his arms folded in front of him, his eyes invisible behind sunglasses. As Molly approached he straightened to his full height, which had to be nearly six and a half feet.

"Morning," he said, touching the brim of his hat.

"Good morning," said Molly.

"Was it a nice funeral?"

"Yes, it was. Dora has a lot of very supportive friends."

"How's your great-grandmother doing?" asked Glickman.

Molly didn't know who he meant for a moment. She had come to think of Dora as a wise new friend in her life, but of course the sheriff was right. As Atherton Gale's wife, Dora was Molly's great-grandmother—at least by marriage. This was the first time anyone had made the relationship explicit.

"She's fine," whispered Molly.

"Listen, Miss O'Hara," he said after a moment, "there have been some developments that I need to discuss with you."

"Okay," said Molly and waited.

Glickman removed his hat for a moment, ran a hand through his short gray hair, then put his hat back on. He was obviously uncomfortable about something.

"First off," he said, "you were right about Jimmy Gale's being in North Carolina. We've now found airline and credit card records of his plane trip down. He arrived in Pelletreau the day before your grandmother's death, rented a car—a white Mercury Sable—and boarded a connecting flight back to Vermont about two hours after your house blew up."

"I knew it," said Molly, letting out a deep breath.

"We still have no physical evidence that Jimmy committed any crimes, but circumstances obviously suggest that he could indeed have had something to do with recent events. Unfortunately neither the Pelletreau police nor my department has the resources to spend time building a case against a dead man for what's officially considered one natural death and two accidental ones. But off the record, Miss O'Hara, I think you were right. The only reason for Jimmy Gale to be down in North Carolina was to do what you thought."

"Thank you, Sheriff," Molly said, wondering why his admission didn't make her feel any better. "I really appreciate that. Thanks for telling me. Thanks for coming."

"I'm not finished," said Glickman. He was silent for a moment, then began again.

"You know, I've been working with your Sergeant Arlo Couvertie on this. Pretty nice fellow. He told me the circumstances of your mother's murder."

"That was a long time ago," said Molly, stiffening. "I thought you were working on who killed Jimmy."

"I am," said Glickman. "It looks like there's a connection."

"Between my mother and Jimmy? What do you mean? What kind of connection could there be?"

"I'm sorry to have to spring this on you like this, Miss O'Hara," said the sheriff, slowly and carefully, "but ballistics on the bullet taken from Jimmy's brain indicate that it was fired from the same gun as the bullet that killed your mother."

"That's impossible!" exclaimed Molly. "My mother was killed seventeen years ago."

"I know."

"She didn't even know Jimmy existed," Molly continued, barely stopping to breathe. "Why would somebody murder her, then wait all this time and kill Jimmy?"

"That's the question," agreed Glickman. "Do you have any ideas?"

"No. This makes no sense at all."

Molly's legs suddenly felt like rubber. She sank down onto

one of the stone lions that guarded the driveway, feeling as if she had been punched in the stomach. After only a moment, however, she looked up.

"Wait a second," she said. "What you're saying is that if you find out who shot Jimmy, you'll also have found the person who murdered my mother."

"Not necessarily," answered Glickman.

"Yes, necessarily if they were shot with the same gun."

"Just because the same weapon was used, Miss O'Hara, doesn't mean it was fired by the same person."

Molly wondered what had happened to the nice fellow with whom they had had breakfast the other day. In front of her stood a policeman with his arms folded, his face a mask.

"Then what happened?" she asked.

"Sergeant Couvertie proposed one theory. I don't think you'll like it very much."

Molly stared at him, her jaw tightening. His expression was unreadable.

"Go ahead," she said when he didn't speak immediately.

"The Pelletreau police believed and still believe," Glickman began in a neutral, emotionless voice, "that your mother was killed in a random act of violence committed by an intruder unknown to her who panicked and fled. Unfortunately the murder weapon was never recovered. But let's suppose for a moment that someone did find it. Let's suppose the killer dropped the gun at the site, and it was picked up by a little girl who kept it all these years."

"Are you saying . . ."

"Just let me finish," said Glickman. "So now, seventeen years later you and your sister are in Vermont and you see Jimmy. Maybe it's just a coincidence—he's crossing the street or buying a pack of cigarettes, but there he is. We know that you believe that Jimmy Gale killed your grandmother, Miss O'Hara. You also think he blew up your house and killed your friends, and it's very possible that he did. Revenge is a powerful motive. It would be understandable if an angry young woman followed Jimmy home, aiming to confront him about what happened in North Carolina. Maybe he just laughed. And maybe the young woman in a fury took out the pistol she had kept all this time, pointed it at his head and pulled the trigger."

"I can't believe this," said Molly, angrily rising to her feet. "Are you actually accusing me of shooting Jimmy Gale?"

"I'm not accusing anyone of anything," said Glickman quietly. "This is Sergeant Couvertie's theory, not mine. But for the record, he wasn't talking about you, Miss O'Hara. He was talking about your sister."

"I . . . he . . . you . . ." sputtered Molly. "It's insane to think that Nell could have killed anybody. And stupid. And ridiculous. I thought Sergeant Couvertie was on our side."

Glickman removed his sunglasses and fixed Molly with his soft blue eyes.

"As I told you before, Miss O'Hara," he said carefully. "I can't automatically accept your version of things just because I happen to like you. I may not get much challenging crime up here, but I'm no dummy. I have to look at the facts, and as things stand now one fact keeps jumping out: You and your sister are the ones who will profit most from Jimmy's death. Profit to the tune of millions and millions of dollars—oh, I know all about the Gale Trust from investigating the plane crash, believe me. And in my book money is an even better motive for murder than revenge."

"So now we both did it so we could inherit? I suppose we bombed that plane, too?"

"I'm not accusing you of anything, Miss O'Hara," said Glickman. "You don't see me here with any warrants, do you? I'm just trying to figure things out. If you have any thoughts, I'd really like to hear them."

"Then what about this gun that Nell is supposed to have picked up when she was eight years old with our mother lying there dead on the floor?" said Molly, throwing her hands in the air. "I guess she hid it before she went into shock. Funny, but you'd think I would have stumbled upon it at some point over the last seventeen years with us living in the same room and half the time wearing each other's clothes."

"Are you saying that both of you would have had to be involved for Couvertie's theory to be right?"

"Of course I'm not," said Molly angrily. "I'm being sarcastic. And contemptuous. And what about airline security? I told you the other day, we were just in England. Aren't they supposed to be X-raying luggage these days? Wouldn't someone at one of the airports we passed through have noticed a gun in Nell's suitcase, even if I managed to miss it rummaging around for my hair dryer? Whoops, didn't mean to implicate myself again."

"I'm just presenting one theory that seems to fit all the facts," said the sheriff quietly. "Can you present another?"

"Give me a minute to think," said Molly. "I'm sure there are plenty of people around here who didn't like Jimmy Gale."

"Including yours truly," said Glickman. "But I wouldn't have had access to the gun that killed your mother and neither would any of the people we'd naturally suspect in a crime like this. I've got to thank you for that gun, Miss O'Hara, even though it seems to be pointing in your direction."

"Me?"

"Sure," said Glickman. "If you hadn't put me in touch with Couvertie and he hadn't had what frankly I thought was the pretty oddball idea of comparing ballistics, then Jimmy's death might have been a perfect crime. I'd have spent the next six months running down the alibis of half the lowlifes and drunks in Vermont, trying to find somebody who'd had a fight with Jimmy or owed him money or who had some other motive to kill him. We might have even decided it was just a botched burglary. But the gun changes everything. How do we explain the gun?"

"My God," said Molly with a gasp. "It must have been the guy who shot our mother. He must have followed us here from North Carolina."

"Yeah," said Glickman, nodding his head. "This is the crazed-serial-killer-who-specializes-in-Gales theory. One of my deputies who watches too much television has already suggested this one. Trouble is, it makes no sense. What, our serial killer waits seventeen years, then all of a sudden he follows you over to England, back to the States, up to Vermont, and then blows Jimmy away for no reason at all, except for those crazy reasons that make sense only to serial killers?"

"Maybe he felt guilty for our mother's death," said Molly, struggling to find some sense. "Maybe in his twisted brain, he wanted to do something to make up for things."

"Excuse me, Miss O'Hara, but you couldn't even sell that one to the networks."

"It makes as much sense as your theory."

"Couvertie's," said Glickman, holding up a correcting finger. "But it doesn't. Jimmy was a secretive, paranoid, combative man, the type who got into bar fights with guys who looked at him the wrong way. Even if your hypothetical serial-killer-with-a-conscience could find out where Jimmy lived, which is doubtful, why would Jimmy let him in, then just sit there in his chair and let the guy shoot him? Remember, there were no signs of a forced entry. No signs of a struggle. Jimmy was just sitting there in a chair, facing his killer. To me that indicates he wasn't afraid, which he probably wouldn't be if an attractive young woman like your sister came to his door."

"Or if it were somebody he knew. A good friend."

"Jimmy didn't have any good friends. Any friends at all."

"A family member then."

Molly immediately felt guilty. Everyone at Gale Castle had been so kind to her, to Nell. Now she was thanking them by pointing suspicion in their direction. She was unable to stop herself, however.

"Look," she raced on. "Jimmy was killed last Tuesday morning, right?"

"That's right."

"Well, before we went over to Gale Castle that afternoon nobody even knew we existed. They all thought Jimmy was the only heir to the Gale fortune. It seems to me that you should be looking at the person who believed he was next in line to inherit if Jimmy were dead."

"Sorry, Miss O'Hara," said Glickman, shaking his head. "If no bloodline Gales survive Dora, the Gale Trust will be divvied up among a dozen different charities. I'm afraid the American Medical Association, the Audubon Society, and the Salvation Army don't make very good suspects."

"Well, maybe there are other bloodline Gales," said Molly, thinking furiously. "Maybe somebody walked away from the plane crash. Russell said all the bodies weren't recovered."

"Yeah," said the sheriff. "This is the Agatha Christie theory, my wife's favorite. Except I saw the wreckage of that plane and the condition of the bodies, such as they were. Believe me, Ms. O'Hara, nobody survived that crash."

"Maybe someone didn't get on."

Glickman shook his head again.

"Sorry. The FBI has been investigating just that idea for the last month. They're certain that everyone who was supposed to have boarded actually did. Besides, you've got to consider the gun. How do you explain the gun being the same one that killed your mother? The gun is the key to this whole thing. As things stand now, only Couvertie's theory accounts for it."

Molly sat in silence for a moment, then held up her hand.

"Wait a minute," she said, trying to assemble the strands of thought that kept twisting through her mind. "What if it was Jimmy who killed our mother?"

"What do you mean?" asked Glickman, raising an eyebrow.

"Maybe Jimmy killed our mother all those years ago. He kept the gun, had it in his house. Then someone came over. An acquaintance, maybe—I don't know. But someone who hated him, had hated him for years, which could have been almost anybody from around here, according to you. Jimmy took out the gun to show off or something. Or maybe it was just lying there on the table, and this person saw his chance to commit the perfect crime. All his resentments came to the surface. He simply picked up the gun—that way there would be no struggle—and pulled the trigger."

Glickman rubbed his chin.

"Now that's interesting," he said. "Nobody's suggested that one before. It makes a strange kind of sense. Nobody up here could find your grandmother for that reunion, not even a private detective. So how did Jimmy come to show up there last month, unless he had been there before maybe, been there to kill your mother?"

"That's right," said Molly.

"But why would Jimmy have murdered your mother, Miss O'Hara? We know why he might have wanted you and your grandmother dead, but why your mother, way back then?"

Molly shook her head.

"I don't know."

"And I surely don't, either," said Glickman, fingering the

butt of his holstered automatic. "I don't understand practically anything about this case. Unfortunately, if Jimmy did kill your mother, it only strengthens Couvertie's theory."

"What do you mean?"

"Are you going to get mad at me again?" asked the sheriff in a wary voice.

"What are you going to say?" asked Molly, folding her arms in front of her. Glickman folded his arms, too.

"My problem with Couvertie's version of things rested on something you told me the first time we talked, Miss O'Hara. You said that you didn't think your sister ever saw the red-haired man with the mustache who you thought was following you around. You only saw him from a distance, so how could Nell have gotten a better look? And if she didn't get a good look at him in the first place, how could she have recognized him up here in Vermont? Even if Nell did think it was the same man, why would she have reacted so violently? You weren't really sure that this man you saw a few times in North Carolina had killed your grandmother and your friends, were you?"

"No," Molly admitted.

"Then your sister couldn't have been sure either. It's a bit much to swallow that she went chasing after the first red-haired, mustached man she saw, followed him to his house and shot him. How could she know it was the right man? And even if she were sure, how did she know he had really done those things back in your hometown?"

"That's right," said Molly. "How does Mr. Couvertie explain that?"

"He can't. His answer is that mentally ill people don't have to be totally logical."

"My sister isn't mentally ill," said Molly angrily.

"I believe that," said Glickman. "I can see there's someone smart and alive in there. Your sister had to block out the horror of what she saw as a little girl and in so doing, blocked out a certain portion of herself. It's a tragedy. But Nell saw your mother's killer, Miss O'Hara. His face must have been burned indelibly into her brain. If she had seen this man again, this murderer on a Vermont street corner, then that's something that might surely make her snap. The sight of him. The memory of what happened to your mother. Boom."

"No," said Molly.

"Yes," said Glickman. "Nell would have had a real reason to want to shoot Jimmy if she remembered seeing him shoot your mom, a much better reason than what Couvertie suggested, a much better reason than your hypothetical acquaintance ready to commit murder on the spur of the moment."

"But I was just making it up," said Molly frantically. "About Jimmy being our mother's killer. There's nothing that connects him to her death. It could have been anyone."

"Perhaps," said the sheriff with a sad smile. "But why would someone want your mother dead, Miss O'Hara? What was the motive? And why would that same person want to kill Jimmy? It's his death that we're investigating, after all, and right now we have only two theories that give us suspects with plausible motive, method, and opportunity. One, that you and your sister conspired to kill Jimmy for the Gale money. And two, Couvertie's theory that it was Nell, acting alone, out of revenge. Frankly, that's the leading contender, considering the fact that your sister doesn't have an alibi for the time Jimmy was shot last Tuesday morning."

"I told you last week," stammered Molly. "Nell was with me. At the motel."

"Well, I checked that story, Miss O'Hara. Eustace Cubby at

The Yankee Clipper says that you were in your room all morning, which frankly is why Couvertie and I didn't zero in on you. After all, it could just as easily have been you who picked up that gun when you were a child, then brought it to Vermont and killed Jimmy with it. But Eustace says your sister was off somewhere."

"She was just gone for a few minutes."

"I don't think so. Eustace says he saw your car drive off at ten o'clock, and thought the two of you might be skipping out. He came over, looked through the window and saw you still in bed. Then you called the desk at about eleven-thirty that morning and asked for a later checkout time. You said your sister had gone out, you didn't know where. She didn't come back with your car until after two o'clock."

"She was just out buying me this watch," said Molly, holding up her wrist. "It was my birthday."

"Mazel tov, but it doesn't take fours hours to buy a wrist-watch, Miss O'Hara. Look, I know your sister's been through a lot. If Couvertie turns out to be right I doubt that Nell would be held legally responsible, considering all that's happened to her. I'm sure that there are plenty of good lawyers who could—"

"My sister didn't kill anybody," insisted Molly, though her voice cracked and tears threatened to form in her eyes. "It had to be somebody else. Wasn't there anybody else who knew Jimmy and who didn't have an alibi?"

"Oh, I've got people without alibis coming out the wazoo," said Glickman. "Dr. George hated Jimmy from childhood. Tuesdays are his days off. Last week he was tooling around the White Mountains without any witnesses. Russell Bowslater didn't like Jimmy, either. He says he was off alone fishing somewhere that morning and of course didn't bring anything home to show for it. Mrs. McCormick, who is probably capable of anything, was out picking up some things for the dinner you all had that night, leaving poor Mrs. Gale alone in the house except for the cook. Even Troutwig the lawyer won't tell me who he was with that day, claims client-attorney confidence. Now all you have to do is tell me how any of these people stands to profit from Jimmy's death as much as you and your sister do, and we'll be in business."

They stood in silence for a moment. Fifty yards away the door of Gale Castle opened and an elderly couple came out, giving Molly and Sheriff Glickman a curious look before heading up the drive toward their car.

"I've got to go back inside," said Molly. "I appreciate how hard you've been working on this, Sheriff Glickman. Thank you."

Glickman's big hand went to the brim of his hat.

"You're welcome, Miss O'Hara. You are planning to stick around for a while, aren't you?"

"Do I have any choice?"

The tall sheriff shrugged, then reached into his breast pocket and produced a little white card with his phone number, which he handed to her.

"If anything occurs to you," he said, "if you hear anything or just want to talk, please give me a call."

"I will."

He stood by his car and watched Molly walk slowly back to the door of the castle.

It seemed dark inside after the summer sunshine. The living room was large enough not to seem crowded, but there were still a lot of people milling about. The noise of their laughter and conversation was irritating.

Molly suddenly felt trapped. A few days ago the future was a blank book. Now the Gale money, the Gale fortune, the Gale name were like weights strapped to her as she was drawn inexorably down into the whirlpool of Jimmy's murder.

Molly couldn't stop thinking about all Glickman had said.

There were too many threads, too much uncertainty to work it out logically. All the sheriff's theories and methodology meant nothing. You had to trust your instincts in a situation like this, and Molly's whole being told her that Nell couldn't have hidden a gun for seventeen years, much less used it; Nell was innocence itself.

If Nell didn't bring the gun from North Carolina, however, it could only mean that someone from here, from Gale Island, had come down to Pelletreau seventeen years ago, shot Molly's mother, and then returned home. Perhaps it had been Jimmy, but more likely it had been somebody else, somebody who last week had used the gun again.

It all meant that something connected Jimmy and Evangeline O'Hara Cole. But what?

Molly's instincts practically screamed the answer at her. The reason for both deaths was right here in this room—from the walnut Queen Anne chairs to the malachite table ornaments to the gigantic oil painting of strutting peacocks above the fireplace. It was about money. The Gale Money. The grasping fingers of Atherton Gale controlling all of them from the grave. Molly suddenly knew it as certainly as she knew the markings on the bottom of oyster plates.

Nell had gone over to the back window, and was gazing out into the rose garden behind the house. George had joined an elderly couple at the other side of the room, leaving Russell alone on the sofa. Molly walked over and joined him.

"Nice party," he said contentedly, putting down his empty glass and absently exploring his somewhat hairy ear with a somewhat hairy finger. "Jimmy would have gotten quite a laugh if he had known how many people would turn out to see him off."

"You didn't like him much, did you?" said Molly.

An image of her mother flashed into Molly's mind. A picture of her in the yard, smiling, happy for a change. And then someone had just reached out of nowhere and taken her life. Molly's life had stopped that day as surely as had Nell's. And the killer had gotten away with it. Was he here in this room now? Maybe even seated right beside her?

"Jimmy?" asked Russell. "Sure I liked Jimmy, pathetic thing that he was. Man, you should have heard him go on about how screwed up things are in Washington. I'm surprised he hadn't gone off to Idaho and joined one of those militia things or become a talk radio host. The boy was a kook, but funny as hell. Did an imitation of old Troutwig that would have you rolling on the floor."

"Who do you think killed him?"

"Hard to say," Russell declared, picking up his empty drink and examining the ice cubes. "Hard to say."

"Somebody told me that if we hadn't turned up, the Gale Trust would have gone to charity," said Molly.

"That's right."

"Would you have gotten any? Your charity, I mean."

"Cancer Answer? No, Atherton was too much of a bastard to let my little outfit get any. Not that we couldn't have used it, mind you. Can't have too much money for cancer, you know, millions of people depend on it. Doctors. Nurses. Hospitals. Insurance companies. Medical products people. Get-well-card manufacturers. If they ever find a cure for our friend the Big C, the unemployment rate will probably go up six points. Hey, I don't mind you and your sister inheriting, if that's what you're getting at. No skin off my nose. I wouldn't have gotten anything personally, no matter what happened."

"Yes, I remember you said last week that the will was pretty airtight."

"Man, it's like a steel drum," said Russell.

"I guess Mr. Troutwig's a good lawyer, then."

"Oh, Troutwig didn't do the Gale Trust. He did do a few

wills for Atherton over the years—Atherton was always proving what a big deal he was by disinheriting somebody or other. But I guess at the end Atherton decided he needed somebody more high-powered. He got the top lawyer at the top firm in Boston to write up the Gale Trust, make it unbreakable. The man's now a federal judge."

"A federal judge from Boston," repeated Molly. Why did that sound familiar?

"Yeah," pronounced Russell with a smile. "The guy was a goddamn legal wizard. Azaria was his name. Martin Azaria."

"That's wonderful," said the warm voice of David Azaria on the other end of the telephone. "Didn't I tell you we would find we had things in common?"

"You mean that it's a coincidence that your father wrote my great-grandfather's will?" exclaimed Molly.

"Sure. What else could it be? And not coincidence. Synchronicity. Just as I said when we first met: The universe is full of synchronicity for people like us."

Molly tried to picture him, sitting there in his apartment in New York where she had reached him, all earnestness and big brown eyes. She paced back and forth in front of the bed, tethered by the cord of the old black rotary telephone, hoping that no one downstairs would miss her.

"I'm sorry," Molly said. "I'm not as naive as you may think. I just don't believe it."

"What's not to believe?" asked David with a mild little laugh. "You say your great-grandfather was a millionaire living in the middle of Vermont. Well, my father was one of the most prominent lawyers in Boston, the nearest major city. Why is it so unbelievable that your great-grandfather might have come to him? If the guy had money and wanted the best, Dad was a logical choice."

"You don't understand," said Molly, feeling like she would explode. Her eyes filled with tears. She collapsed onto the bed.

"No, I don't understand. Tell me."

"They're all dead. Everyone's dead. And the same person who killed Jimmy killed our mother, and . . ."

"Wait a second, wait a second," said David. "Who's dead? What are you talking about?"

Molly fought down the panic that had welled up again inside her. She took a deep breath. Then, as calmly as she could, she told him for the first time about everything that had happened: the suspicious death of Margaret Jellinek; the explosion of their house and shop; the red-haired man; the reunion of the Gale family and the plane crash that killed them; seeing Jimmy Gale's picture, then finding him dead with a bullet hole in his head, shot with the same gun that had killed Evangeline O'Hara Cole; the sheriff's suspicions about Nell, and the fact that she and Molly would now inherit the Gale Trust.

"You poor kid," said David Azaria finally when Molly was finished. "I didn't understand the message you left me the other week. I thought you were just flustered because you liked me."

"I don't like you," declared Molly. "I don't even know you."

"Then why are you calling me for help?"

"I'm not calling you for help! I just want to know why your name keeps coming up in my life."

"Well, I didn't have anything to do with killing any of your relatives, if that's what you're getting at."

Molly didn't say anything. She didn't know what she thought anymore.

"Thanks for the vote of confidence," murmured David. "Am I really so awful?"

Suddenly all that Molly had been trying to hold in burst loose. Tears were running down her cheeks. She tried to stifle an audible sob, but couldn't. David let her cry.

"You've had a pretty tough time of it, haven't you?" he said gently after she had quieted down and blown her nose.

"I'm okay."

Neither of them spoke for another moment. Molly stared at the pale yellow wallpaper, dried her eyes and blew her nose again. Outside in Dora's garden, a bird was singing. Through the open window the fresh pine scent of Vermont wafted into the room.

"How's your sister holding up?" asked David.

"I don't know," answered Molly. "She knows what happened to Jimmy, but I'm not sure she understands what his death means for us. I'm always afraid that she'll have another one of her attacks. She had one when we first got here."

"Yeah. You mentioned she had fits. What set her off this time, do you think?"

"Maybe it was seeing Dora so upset," said Molly. "I don't know."

"Now, who's Dora again?"

"She married Atherton Gale, our great-grandfather, after our great-grandmother died. Dora's very old. Ninety-three. She was devastated to learn who we were. Everybody else was just angry."

Talking too fast again, Molly described the people who had also come to the door that first day. Russell Bowslater, Dora's child from her first marriage. Dr. George Gale, her adopted son. Mrs. McCormick, the nurse-companion. Henry Troutwig, Dora's attorney.

There was silence again on the other end of the phone. Molly listened for David's breathing but couldn't hear anything except a car alarm going off in the distance. Or was it an ambulance? A fire truck? The police? Whatever it was, it sounded like New York.

"This Gale Trust must somehow be involved in what's been going on," said David finally in a thoughtful voice. "Will any of the people you just mentioned get anything when Dora dies?"

"No, and you're going around in the same circles that the sheriff and I are going around in," Molly said wearily. "Nell and I are the only beneficiaries of the trust now that all the other natural-born descendants of Atherton Gale are dead. And if we weren't around it would all go to charity."

"Are you sure?"

"Yes," said Molly. "The sheriff told me."

"Have you seen the trust document yourself?"

"No, but—"

"Then you're assuming that this sheriff knew what he was talking about," said David, "Perhaps that's not such a good idea. He's not a lawyer. He may not have understood what he was reading. Or maybe whoever told him about the terms of Atherton Gale's will left something out."

"I suppose."

"Look," said David. "I'm going to give my father a call. Maybe he remembers something about all of this. Is there a number where I can reach you?"

Molly read him the number off the dial of the telephone in her room. She didn't want to give him the main number for Gale Castle, then have to explain to everyone who David was. She wasn't sure herself.

"Please call me back right away," she said. "I can't stay at this phone very long."

"Okay," said David. "Oh, by the way. Did I mention that you sound very pretty today?"

"No, I don't," said Molly.

"Yes, you do," he answered. Then he said good-bye and hung up.

Molly lay back on the bed and stared at the ceiling. For all she knew David's father had some sinister involvement in all this. Perhaps David was involved as well—it was impossible to know whom she could trust anymore. But if David were involved, what was kind of world was it? What was the point of anything? Why even bother to go on living? Did she really sound pretty? Or had he just said that to be nice?

The door of the room opened with a squeak. Molly jumped up in alarm, then fell back as she recognized Nell's familiar silhouette.

"Hi," Molly said. "I'm just lying down for a moment. I wasn't feeling well."

Nell came over and sat down next to Molly on the bed. Then she put her cool hand on Molly's forehead. Nell shook her head to indicate there was no fever, but her eyes were full of concern.

"No," said Molly. "I don't think I'm sick. It's just beginning to get to me, you know?"

Nell nodded.

"Nellie," said Molly, looking in her sister's deep green eyes. "When you went out to get me the watch for my birthday, why were you gone so long?"

Nell shrugged. She mimed holding a car wheel. She brought the flat of her hand to her brow, like she was searching for something.

"You had to look around to find a store with the right watch?"

Nell nodded.

"Of course you had to look around," said Molly, relieved. "We're in the middle of nowhere up here."

Nell grinned and motioned bringing a fork to her mouth.

"And naturally you got something to eat. I should have known."

Nell seemed calmer than she had been in a long time, almost serene. It was ironic: Now that the person who had been the biggest threat to them, Jimmy Gale, was dead, it was Molly who was falling to pieces.

Nell grabbed Molly's hand and gave it a tug.

"No," said Molly. "I think I need to be still for a bit. Maybe take a nap. I'll be fine. Will you cover for me downstairs? I don't want Dora to worry."

Nell nodded and rose. At the door she stopped and glanced back at her sister.

"I'm okay," said Molly. "You go. I'll be back down in a little while."

Nell left, shutting the door behind her. Molly closed her eyes and waited for the phone to ring, relieved that Nell had an explanation of why it had taken her so long to buy the watch last week. How could the sheriff possibly think that Nell might have had anything to do with Jimmy's death? It was absurd. Molly knew her sister. Nell was the gentlest soul on earth. She wouldn't hurt a bluebottle fly.

The phone was silent. Molly's thoughts turned again to David Azaria. She didn't know him at all, not really. Why then had it been so reassuring just to hear his voice? And why was he so interested in her? What had been David's father's relationship to Atherton Gale? How did any of it tie in to Evangeline O'Hara Cole?

The minutes dragged on for what seemed like forever. Molly worried that David wouldn't call back, that she would never hear from him again. Then she worried that he would call back—call back and tell her she was too short, too talkative, too much trouble.

Suddenly an old-fashioned bell jangled loudly enough to make her jump. It was the telephone. Molly grabbed it, worried that someone downstairs might have heard. Then she remembered how isolated this wing of Gale Castle was. You could probably shoot a cannon off here and no one would be the wiser.

"Sorry it took so long," said David's calm voice at the other end of the line. "I had to get him out of a hearing. Nobody ever does that. He wasn't happy."

"What did he say?" Molly asked, her palms moist, her stomach dancing with butterflies.

"Well, my father does remember your great-grandfather's trust," said David. "He didn't usually get involved with personal matters—corporations are his specialty—but Dad didn't build Azaria Klein Morthall & Nathan by turning away clients like Atherton Gale. You know, I didn't quite understand what you were telling me before. Millionaires are a dime a dozen these days. Apparently this Atherton Gale was in a different category entirely. You and your sister are going to be very wealthy women from what my father tells me."

"We don't want the money," said Molly, standing up and walking around the bedroom.

"Sure you do," answered David with a laugh. "Everyone wants money. But let's deal with that later, shall we? First I have some disturbing things to tell you."

"What disturbing things?"

David's voice suddenly became dry and professional.

"It turns out that my father set up not one, but two different trusts for Atherton Gale over a period of a few months," he said. "The will that went into effect divides everything among all living bloodline Gales upon Dora's death, as you said. But there was an earlier arrangement with much different terms. Before Atherton changed his mind and decided to include his whole family there was going to be only one ultimate beneficiary for the trust's principal."

"You mean that somebody thought he was going to get everything and then Atherton pulled the rug out from under him? My God, that must be it! That's the person with the motive! He would have been angry enough to kill all the Gales."

"I'm afraid you're jumping to the wrong conclusion, Molly," said David. "The sole beneficiary of the earlier will was to have been Atherton Gale's granddaughter."

"Granddaughter? What granddaughter?"

"The daughter of his only natural child, Margaret."

"But that was my mother," said Molly, then gasped. "Are you saying that Atherton Gale was going to leave everything to my mother?"

"That's right," answered David. "Atherton told Dad he had never met her and didn't want to. He said he ended up hating anybody he got to know, especially relatives. Apparently Atherton only knew about your mother because she had sent him some letters or something."

"He never answered," murmured Molly, sinking into one of the room's big overstuffed chairs, her mind reeling. "Mom thought that Grandma's family might help us, but she never heard anything back. We assumed that they just didn't care. But why did Atherton rewrite his will in the first place?"

"The stepson and adopted son who had previously been his heirs had done something that Atherton found intolerable," David replied. "Atherton wouldn't tell my father what it was, just that he was furious. The new will was going to be Atherton's punishment for them, leaving the entire Gale fortune to this young woman that nobody else even knew existed."

"But when we first got to Gale Castle nobody had ever heard

of my mother," said Molly, trying to understand. "How can that be if Atherton had named her in his will?"

"Probably because Atherton had come to my father in secret," David replied. "That's one of the reasons that Dad remembers this, it was all so odd. Nobody was supposed to learn about the new will until after Atherton was dead. And since Atherton relented a little and rewrote his will again three months later to include all of his natural relatives, the terms of the earlier document never came out."

Molly took a deep breath. At least some things were beginning to become clearer.

"So somebody must have killed Mom to prevent her from inheriting the Gale fortune," she said. "I knew this was about money. I just knew it."

"You would think so, yes," said David, "but that's the problem."

"What problem?"

"As far as my father can recall, nobody would have been better off with your mother dead. Under the earlier will, if your mother didn't survive the Atherton Gale Trust was to have been divided among various charities upon Dora's death."

"But then we're right back where we started from," exclaimed Molly, crumpling back into the soft chair. "If nobody profited from Mom's death, then why did somebody kill her? And why did somebody kill Jimmy now? Nobody profits from his death, either. Except Nell and me. It's crazy."

"I promise we'll get to the bottom of this, Molly," said David gently. "There must be something about Atherton's wills that Dad has forgotten or something so mundane that nobody's even considering it. When I was an assistant DA our office once prosecuted a maid for murdering her elderly employer. The maid didn't care about the woman's million-dollar estate. She just wanted the five thousand dollars she had been promised—big money to her. It could be something just as simple in this case."

Molly shuddered. There was something horrible about speculating why someone had killed a person you loved. If it had been about money—whatever the amount—that somehow made it worse.

"Dad's having someone from his old firm dig out both of Atherton Gale's wills and overnight them to me," David went on. "If there's anybody who could conceivably have gained something by your mother's death—or by Jimmy's—we'll know soon enough."

"In the meanwhile Nell is still the prime suspect in Jimmy's murder," said Molly, rising and beginning to pace back and forth again.

"Nell will be fine, you'll see," said David. "You need evidence to prove a case in court. Witnesses. From what you've told me, all your sheriff has against Nell is conjecture."

"But who knows what pressures he's under to do something?" said Molly angrily, all her frustrations boiling up to the surface. "Just because you were a lawyer doesn't mean that you can convince me that police never arrest innocent people. If Nell is the only suspect, they'll lock her up sooner or later. Or they'll turn her over to some shrink who doesn't know anything except how to fill people full of drugs. It would destroy her."

"Okay, okay," said David. "Calm down."

"Don't tell me what to do! I hate it when people tell me what to do."

"And I like a girl with a temper. It's nice that we're getting to know each other like this, don't you think?"

"No!"

"Look, I'm just trying to help," said David. "I think I could do that better if you were here."

"Where? New York?"

"That's right. It's going to be a lot harder for some back country sheriff to arrest your sister if she's in New York. If you leave now, you and Nell can probably be here in time for the show tonight."

"You're crazy," said Molly, sitting on the bed. "We can't leave."

"Sure you can. And you should. There's still a killer running around up there, remember?"

"It's nice of you to be concerned," said Molly, "but nobody has any reason to harm us."

"Molly, let me point something out to you," said David Azaria, his voice measured and concerned. "Your mother was the sole beneficiary of the Gale Trust and somebody killed her. Then everybody thought your cousin Jimmy was the only one left to inherit and somebody killed him, too. We may not yet understand what's going on, but you and Nell are now the sole beneficiaries of the Gale Trust. I'd really feel better if you were out of there."

"But we don't have the trust. We won't have anything as long as Dora is still alive." Molly stopped and put a hand up to her mouth. "My God, you don't think she's in any danger, do you?"

"Nobody's knocked her off so far, have they?" said David with what was obviously meant to be a reassuring laugh. Molly wasn't reassured.

"Look," he went on, "if you're really worried, you can bring her along, too. I like old ladies, and I've got one of those big old Westside apartments. Dora can have the extra bedroom. Nell can sleep on the couch in the living room. You can sleep in my room. I'll curl up on the floor at your feet and guard you from all evil. Nobody will know where you are."

"Nobody but you."

"Still don't trust me?"

Molly didn't answer. David let out a sigh.

"You're probably right," he said after a moment. "I don't know that I could trust myself. I'm pretty goofy about you, you know."

"Why? I wish you would tell me why."

"It's mostly physical at this stage, I think. But I'm optimistic that we'll find other things in common besides Atherton Gale to sustain us over the years. For starters, look how easy it is for us to talk to each other."

"I can talk to anybody on the face of the earth," muttered Molly. "Perfect strangers. Garbage men. Brick walls."

"You think about New York. I'll call you tomorrow. What's a good time?"

"It's not that I don't like you, too, David. I . . . I just can't leave Dora alone right now."

"How about three o'clock?" he replied. "That will give me enough time to get the wills and look them over."

"All right. I'll be at the phone at three. Thanks, David."

"See? Aren't you glad you came to me for help?"

"I didn't come to you for help."

"I like you, too," answered David. "Good-bye, Molly. Be careful."

"I will."

Molly hung up the phone, lay back on the bed and stared at the now-familiar ceiling.

She wanted more than anything just to leave everything behind and go to David, but that was impossible. Nell was the prime suspect in Jimmy Gale's murder. If they left now it would look like they were just running away. Besides, after the way Dora had welcomed them into the family, they couldn't just up and desert her.

It was all Atherton Gale's fault, Molly fumed. Him and his

filthy money. Molly didn't want any part of it. The Gale fortune was like some kind of poison. Everyone who had stood to benefit from it was dead. Everyone, that is, except her and Nell.

Molly closed her eyes and watched stars wander across the inside of her eyelids. Unsettling questions resumed their chase across her mind. Were she and Nell in danger now that they would inherit the Gale Trust? Who stood to gain if they, too, were suddenly out of the way? Was she just making excuses about why she couldn't go to New York? Was she more afraid of David and what going to him meant than of whoever it was that had killed Jimmy?

After several more minutes of tying her brain into knots, Molly breathed a deep sigh and forced herself to open her eyes and sit up. Only one thing was clear: Nothing was going to be resolved today. Today was a day for burying the dead.

The birds had stopped singing in the garden. A sharp breeze coming through the window made the lacy curtain dance. Molly rose to her feet and went over to breathe in the summer before going back down to the strange gathering downstairs, the remembrance of a man whom no one wanted to remember.

Dora's garden was still and perfect, alive with tiny explosions of color that were roses. The two figures sitting on the garden swing looked almost like dolls that had been placed there for effect by a gigantic child. They were even holding hands and shyly looking off in different directions like young lovers sometimes do. It was a charming picture, yet there seemed to be something wrong with it. It took Molly a moment to figure out what it was. When she did she almost fell over backward.

The two figures were Mrs. McCormick and Henry Troutwig.

Sixteen

"Please pass the ketchup," said Mrs. McCormick, rubbing her hands in front of her.

The ketchup bottle was sitting in a pierced silver holder that its English Victorian silversmith had undoubtedly meant to hold a bottle of claret. Molly pushed it to Nell who passed it along to McCormick who opened the bottle and drizzled the stuff over her hamburger with evident satisfaction.

"What a treat," declared Dora, cutting her burger into neat little quarters. Molly had cut her own into halves. Nell hadn't bothered to cut hers at all and was already halfway through it.

The last guest had finally gone home. The telephone had fallen silent. Mrs. Prin and the hired girls had cleaned up and left hours ago. Dora, Molly and Nell, and Mrs. McCormick were alone in the house for the night.

People in Vermont were as neighborly in the wake of death as they had been in North Carolina, and the refrigerator was full of cookies and homemade casseroles. Mrs. Prin had dutifully been serving up cookies and homemade casseroles every night, along with everything else she considered suitable for mourning: overcooked vegetables, dry biscuits, gray sauces. After four days of such treatment, Mrs. McCormick's hamburgers were a welcome change. The shoestring french fries she had engineered in the kitchen were practically a revelation.

"I hope Russell got back to Washington all right," said Dora, staring at a neat little wedge of hamburger, a worried expression on her face. "Planes make me so nervous since . . . since what happened."

Molly chewed fast in order not to reply with her mouth full. Gale Castle's elegant dining room and the gravity of events did wonders for one's table manners.

"I'm sure Russell's okay," she said at last.

"He promised to call when he got in."

Dora might be ninety-three, but she was clearly still a concerned mother. She had made George call, too. He had arrived at his New Hampshire hospital an hour ago.

"Den of iniquity, if you ask me," said McCormick, licking a finger. "I wouldn't give you a dollar for all the senators and congressmen in Washington. Less if you throw in the wives. You really have to wonder about gals like that. What woman in her right mind would intentionally marry a politician?"

They ate in silence. Dora looked tired after the long day. Nell didn't seem to be paying much attention to anybody, off in a world of her own. Mrs. McCormick chewed noisily as though she didn't have a care in the world.

What was going on between the surly nurse and the perpetually indignant attorney? Molly wondered again, as she had been doing ever since she had seen them together in the garden. Why were McCormick and Troutwig keeping their relationship a secret?

Molly was bursting to know but couldn't figure out how to broach the subject. Finally she couldn't stand it any longer.

"I actually saw Mr. Troutwig smile this afternoon," said Molly, taking the indirect approach. "I didn't know he could do that. You know, he's not altogether a bad-looking man, don't you think, Mrs. McCormick?"

"Henry Troutwig? I've seen better faces on grandfather clocks."

"Oh, I don't know," said Dora. "Henry isn't exactly a movie star, but he has a certain presence. He carries himself very confidently. He was quite handsome when he was younger."

"That old lunch pail?" snorted McCormick. "I've got bunions more attractive than him. And the man is as dim as grass. He's stubborn, opinionated, egotistical, intransigent, and an all-around pain-in-the-petunia."

"Why, Mrs. McCormick," said Dora with a smile, her wire-rim glasses magnifying her pale blue eyes into saucers. "If I didn't know better, I might think you were actually sweet on Henry."

McCormick's face turned nearly as red as the ketchup on her plate.

"Sweet on Troutwig? Sweet on that insufferable . . . that detestable . . . Why I'd sooner be hung up by my dainties above a boy scout campfire, or trapped in an elevator with a toothache and an insurance agent, or thrown into the Nile while a marine band—"

A loud telephone bell rang far off in the direction of the kitchen.

"Maybe that's Russell," said Dora hopefully, rising from the table and placing her napkin on her chair. "I'll get it. Please excuse me, ladies. I'll be right back."

She quickly disappeared through the archway to the kitchen.

Molly exchanged glances with Nell, who looked pensive. Mc-

Cormick took a huge bite of her hamburger, her eyes as bright as two nickels in a wishing well. If she didn't want to talk about Troutwig it didn't seem right to invade her privacy, Molly decided, but perhaps she could fill in some of the blanks about Atherton Gale.

"You took care of Atherton Gale during his final illness, didn't you?" Molly asked.

"Yep," said the grizzled housekeeper, her mouth still full.

"What kind of man was he?"

McCormick chewed for a while and swallowed before answering.

"He was a maniac," she announced unceremoniously. "He liked to tear off his clothes and make me chase him naked around the upstairs to give him his bath. Said he'd leave me a million dollars if I'd have sex with him. Doctor said it was probably the cancer going to his brain, but the man was serious as oatmeal, believe me."

Molly almost choked on the food in her mouth, remembering David's story of the murderous maid. She knew she was probably more than a little paranoid after all that had been happening, but could McCormick have been going around, murdering people, because Atherton Gale had left her some money? Molly drank half a glass of water before she was able to speak.

"Did Atherton end up mentioning you in any of his wills?" she asked conversationally. "I understand he changed them a lot."

"Well, I didn't sleep with him if that's what you're getting at."

"No, of course not," said Molly. "I certainly wasn't trying to suggest—"

"I have my standards," said McCormick, raising her nose into the air and making a little sniff. "Besides, you couldn't trust the old bastard to keep his word or I might have been tempted. A million bucks was real money back then, even to Atherton Gale. He haunts the place, you know."

Nell had finished the food on her plate a while back and had been staring off into space. Now she turned to Molly, her eyes wide.

"She's just kidding," Molly assured her. "Aren't you, Mrs. McCormick?"

"I've seen him plenty of times," said McCormick, poker-faced.

"No, she hasn't, Nellie," said Molly, placing her hand on her sister's. Nell had turned dead white.

"Have, too," McCormick pressed on. "I think he's still panting after yours truly."

"I thought you were already spoken for," snapped Molly.

McCormick's gray eyes narrowed into slits.

"What's that supposed to mean?" she said angrily.

"I saw you and Henry Troutwig in the garden this afternoon," Molly replied. To hell with McCormick's privacy if she was going to frighten Nell like this.

"What was there to see?"

"You were holding hands."

"No, we weren't."

"I saw you."

McCormick looked for a moment like she might explode. Then she relaxed, a sickly smile crossing her face.

"Oh, yeah," she said, snapping her fingers. "Now I remember. I was feeling a little light-headed and went into the garden for some air. Old Troutwig came out at one point and took my pulse. That's what you saw."

"Oh, really?"

Molly didn't say anything, just stared.

"Oh, all right. The old idiot and I are involved. So what?"

"Why are you keeping your relationship with Mr. Troutwig a secret?"

"Because I want to keep him, damn it," barked McCormick. Then her face softened. "Look, you don't know how it is for a woman like me. I was never a basket of looks, and I'm not young anymore. Even up here a man like Henry could do a lot better for himself. If word ever got out that Henry was seeing me, fraternizing with Dora Gale's help, he'd be a laughingstock. He'd have to dump me just to save face."

"I'm sure that's not true."

"Shows how little you know," said McCormick, waving a bony hand in the air. "The winters are awful long up here. And cold. I'm sick of being alone. Some women can take it, like Dora. Not me. You won't tell her about Henry, will you?"

Molly hesitated. Was that all there was to this? A lonely woman? Cold Vermont nights?

"It would kill her, I tell you," insisted McCormick. "Down she'd go like a little sack of potatoes. Thump. Sssh. Here she comes."

"Well, I'm very relieved," said Dora with a sweet smile, emerging from the kitchen. "Russell is home safe. And he's going to have lunch with the vice president's wife next Thursday."

She took her place at the table again.

Everybody murmured congratulations except for Nell. Molly took a handful of her french fries and put them on her sister's plate, but Nell ignored them.

"The back door in the kitchen was wide open," said Dora. "We have to remember to close and lock it, Mrs. McCormick, now that Russell is gone and we're alone in the house. You can't be too careful these days. Someone might sneak in and murder us all in our beds."

"Don't remind me," said McCormick. "Do you want me to heat up your burger in the microwave, Mrs. G?"

"Thank you, Mrs. McCormick, but I'm not very hungry," said Dora, regarding the remains of her now-cold supper. "I put up the kettle in the kitchen, though. Maybe you could bring us all a nice pot of tea?"

"Why not?" said the nurse. "Save any interesting gossip until I get back."

She gave Molly a meaningful look, then marched through the door to the kitchen.

Dora, Molly, and Nell sat in silence for a moment. Molly's thoughts began to turn from McCormick and Troutwig to her and David Azaria before she managed to push it all from her mind. How to clear Nell of the suspicion the sheriff had focused on her was the only thing she should be thinking about. Suddenly it seemed more important than ever to find out what had happened between Atherton Gale and his two sons seventeen years ago. What had set in motion the events that were still unfolding? If anyone knew the truth it was Dora.

"I'm glad Russell is okay," said Molly, trying to lead into the subject naturally. "You must be very proud of him."

"Oh, yes indeed," said Dora. "When Russell was younger I used to worry that he'd never find his place in the world, let alone become involved with such a wonderful charity. He went from job to job, never seemed to connect with anything. George was different. George always knew he wanted to be a doctor, to help people. Of course, Atherton hated that. He'd wanted George to come into the business with him, but George had other plans for his life."

"Why did Atherton cut them both out of his will?"

Dora shook her head and shrugged her shoulder.

"I don't suppose we'll ever know what went on in poor Atherton's mind. Atherton was always redoing things, changing his plans. He thrived on confusion and uncertainty. It was difficult to know where you stood with him from one day to the next."

"Even you?"

"Oh, yes, indeed."

An unhappy look passed across Dora's sweet open face. She took a nibble of her cold hamburger, chewed, and executed a dainty swallow before continuing.

"Atherton kept me so off balance for the first years of our marriage that I really didn't understand the kind of man he was. I was too busy trying to defend myself, please him, figure out what he wanted. Felicity had told me about some of the problems she'd had with Atherton, but the man who courted me seemed like a different individual—so kind and thoughtful, so charming and shy. It was only later that I began to see who he really was."

"He was cruel to you?"

"He was cruel to himself," said Dora. "Yes, Atherton often humiliated me verbally in front of what few visitors we had here. But it wasn't like he had singled me out; Atherton was horrid to everyone. He would fly into impossible rages from one moment to the next and everyone would have to scramble to figure out what they had done wrong. But it was all a distraction, Atherton's ploy to prevent people from looking at him and seeing the frightened, selfish, unhappy little man he really was. It was himself he hated, you see? All he had really was his money. That's why he kept accumulating more and more. He never saw that he couldn't buy the self-respect he craved. It was very sad."

"But surely Russell and George must have done something terrible for Atherton to have cut them off so completely."

Dora sighed deeply.

"I can't help thinking it was the incident with the pants," she said. "Oddly enough, it began with an act of kindness. Atherton could actually be quite kind as long as you did things his way. In honor of my birthday he had flown us all to New York for a week-end. On the second night we were going out to a fish house down-town. We met downstairs in the hotel lobby. Atherton took one look at George and ordered him to go upstairs and change his pants."

"What was wrong with his pants?" asked Molly.

"Nothing," said Dora. "That was the point. Oh, they were a little casual, I suppose, but there wasn't anything really wrong with them."

"Then why did Atherton want him to change?"

"It was just Atherton's way of dominating people, forcing them to his will. But George was a grown man now, a doctor. He refused to change his pants, said it wasn't necessary. Atherton insisted. The argument escalated until Atherton declared that if George wouldn't change his pants, Atherton would cut him out of his will. That's when Russell spoke up. He said that Atherton was being ridiculous. Atherton replied that unless Russell supported his opinion, he would be cut out of the will, too."

"George didn't change?"

"No, he didn't. And Russell refused to take Atherton's side. I remember thinking it was a very important moment, a rite of passage for the boys. Of course they were grown men then, but this was the first time they had really stood up to their father. I never dreamed that Atherton was actually serious about disinheriting the boys. Besides, Henry always warned me about any changes Atherton wanted to make to his will. But Atherton tricked us all and went to that man in Boston. I really do think it was all because George wouldn't change his pants."

"My God," said Molly, shaking her head at the senselessness of it.

"There was really no way to win with Atherton," said Dora, her voice level, her eyes hard. "You either did it his way or he cut you out. That's why I'm still here, I'm ashamed to say. I always did it his way. I was too afraid, too dependent upon him to do anything else."

She fell silent as the clatter of orthopedic Oxfords signaled Mrs. McCormick's return from the kitchen. She carried a silver tray with a silver Queen Anne tea service and a plate of cookies.

The four of them nibbled cookies and sipped tea and chatted about nothing in particular for another fifteen minutes. Dora went on about gardening and the weather. Nell ate a few cookies and wouldn't make eye contact. McCormick was very subdued.

To get her mind off Atherton Gale and all the people who had died, Molly focused her thoughts on the tea set. She was dying to pick up the creamer and investigate the hallmarks on the bottom but could see no polite way to do so. All she received for her interest was a second cup of tea, which Dora insisted on pouring for everyone.

By the time the clock in the living room chimed nine-thirty, Molly was ready for bed. The days started early at Gale Castle and there wasn't much reason to stay up very late. Nell was yawning, too.

"Will you excuse us, Dora?" said Molly, rising from the table. "It's been a long day."

"Of course, my dear," said Dora. "You children run along to bed. I'll help you clean up, Mrs. McCormick."

"Good night then," said Molly. "Thank you for dinner."

McCormick grunted a perfunctory farewell. Molly and Nell headed toward the stairs and to their room.

In the upstairs hall strange shadows played over the suits of armor and the house groaned like an old wooden ship. Gale Castle no longer seemed such an interesting place, Molly decided. There was too much death here, and somewhere a murderer walked free.

"It's pretty wild about Mrs. McCormick and Troutwig, don't you think?" Molly said later, after she had brushed her teeth and was getting into her nightgown. "And how about Atherton and the pants? McCormick was right. The man was insane."

Nell had already changed into her nightdress. She made no move to get into bed, however. She sat on the overstuffed chair in their room, a worried expression on her face.

"You're not scared about Atherton's ghost, are you?"

Nell glanced up and nodded.

"There's no such things as ghosts, you know."

Nell nodded her head again, though it wasn't clear whether she was agreeing with Molly or saying that there were.

Molly went to the door of their room and locked them in. Dora was right. You couldn't be too careful these days, even here in Vermont on an island in the middle of nowhere. Maybe David Azaria was right, too. Maybe they should think about getting out.

"I suppose that Atherton Gale does have a lot of influence around here for a dead person. But he's not going to hurt us, believe me."

Nell didn't look convinced.

Molly shrugged and got into bed. There would be plenty of time tomorrow to worry about Atherton Gale and where to spend the rest of their lives. She was so tired she could barely keep her eyes open and more confused than she had ever been in her life.

Molly reached over and turned off the lamp on the night table. Nell didn't move from the chair. In the moonlight that streamed through the window she looked like some kind of gossamer angel.

"Come on to bed," Molly murmured.

Nell got up from the chair after a moment, but instead of getting into her bed on the other side of the night table she crossed the room and sat down on the floor of the big cedar closet.

"Come on, Nellie," said Molly with a sigh. "You're going to be all stiff and sore if you don't come to bed. You can't sleep in the closet."

But Nell didn't move. The last thing Molly remembered before she feel asleep was hearing the closet door squeak closed.

Seventeen

Molly was awakened by a gunshot and a scream.

Her head thick with sleep, she frantically felt around in the darkness for the bedside lamp. There were terrible sounds coming from the floor in front of her, like two animals fighting. What in God's name was going on?

After what seemed liked eons but couldn't have been more than a few seconds, Molly finally found the switch and turned it on. A small yellow cone of light opened to reveal a frantic scene. Nell and another smaller figure were on the floor, wrestling over a snub-nosed, blue-black revolver that was now aimed at the ceiling.

"Nell!" Molly cried. "What are you doing?"

The voice that answered didn't sound human. It was a hideous guttural rasp, like some wild animal in pain. What was more strange, the horrible noises were organized into words that Molly could somehow understand. They were coming from Nell.

"She . . . killed . . . Mommy. She . . . killed . . . Mommy!"

The gun fired again, and pieces of plaster fell from the ceiling.

Nell jerked her upraised hand back. There was another shrill scream, and the gun suddenly went sailing across the room. It skidded over the uncovered hardwood floor by the window and disappeared behind an old-fashioned steam radiator.

Molly practically leaped out of bed. Nell was now on top of her struggling opponent, pinning her arms against the Turkoman rug.

"Nell, you're talking! Nellie, stop."

"She . . . shot . . . Mommy," came the awful voice from Nell again, as Molly reached the two and tried to separate them. "I . . . saw. I . . . remember."

"Please," cried the small figure, who Molly could now see, looking almost like a child in her blue-and-white-checked flannel robe. "You're hurting me."

It was Dora Gale.

"Nellie, let go!" exclaimed Molly. She finally broke her sister's grip on the tiny old woman and pulled them apart. She couldn't believe that Nell was talking. She didn't want to believe what Nell had said.

"I . . . saw . . . her," rasped Nell, glaring at Dora. "She killed her. I . . . was in the closet. I remember. And now she came . . . again. With . . . the gun. To . . . kill . . . us, too."

Molly shook her head to try to clear it. None of this made any sense. Dora in their room with a gun? Nell talking? Was it a dream? Molly felt groggy, like she'd had way, way too much to drink. But she hadn't had anything to drink at dinner but tea. And this wasn't a dream.

"The poor thing, the poor, poor thing," said Dora in a shrill voice. "I couldn't sleep. I was just walking around, like I do sometimes at night. Your door was open. I heard a sound. I thought one of you might be sick. I came in and your sister jumped on me. She had that terrible gun."

"You . . . liar," screeched Nell, lurching toward Dora. Molly put herself in between them and stopped Nell before she could get her hands on the tiny old woman and tear her apart.

"Don't, Nellie," Molly shouted, embracing her sister. "Stop. Please, stop."

Nell struggled for a moment. Then her hard body relaxed in Molly's arms. She began to sob. Molly turned to Dora, her arms still around her sister.

"I locked the door before we went to bed," said Molly. "Nell wouldn't have opened it. She was frightened. That's why she was hiding in the closet."

"The door was open," said Dora, her voice higher, almost verging on hysterical. "I swear, Molly. Don't you believe me?"

"She . . . had . . . key," said Nell, angrily wiping the tears from her eyes. "In her . . . pocket."

Dora stood silently, where she was. Molly went over to her and reached into one pocket of the old lady's robe, then the other. In the second pocket was a key. Molly held it up.

"It's for my room," said Dora.

"Lie!" shouted Nell. She rushed over, grabbed the key from Molly's hand and went to the door with it. When she inserted the key into the lock, it turned.

"Many of the doors here have the same locks," said Dora. "Your sister is sick, Molly. She wanted to kill me. I'm terribly afraid she might have killed your cousin, James, too."

"No!" shouted Nell, but didn't move.

Nell's voice was still raw, horrible. It was a low alto, not the little girl's voice that Molly had last heard from her sister. Could Nell have suddenly begun speaking after so many years to tell a lie? But if she were telling the truth, it meant that Dora really had come to their room tonight to kill them. It also meant that Dora had killed Evangeline O'Hara Cole. Had she killed Jimmy Gale, too? Molly stared into Dora's frightened blue eyes.

"Why did you come to our room?" Molly demanded. "Was that your gun? Tell me the truth."

"I am telling the truth," protested Dora, her voice calmer now, more reasonable. "Nell is the one who's lying. She's ill."

"There's nothing wrong with my sister."

"We must get help for her. A psychiatrist."

"Tell me the truth," said Molly.

"It's my word against hers. Who wouldn't believe me over a crazy girl like that?"

Molly was stunned by the level of rage that welled up inside her. Nell wasn't crazy, but Dora was right. No one would believe Nell's word against hers. How could Molly get her to admit the truth? She walked over and suddenly found herself grabbing the old woman's hand and bending back her pinkie finger. It was what the bad mother had done to her daughter in David's play, to get the little girl to say she loved her.

"Please, Molly," said Dora. "You're hurting me."

"Tell me the truth or I'll break your fingers one by one, so help me God."

"I am telling you the truth," said Dora in a tiny voice.

Molly bent Dora's little finger back farther.

"You wouldn't really hurt me, Molly," said the old lady, trying to smile. "I know you wouldn't."

Molly released Dora's hand in disgust. Dora was right. It was just a bluff. Molly couldn't do it, even for Nell. She stood up and walked over to the bed, shaking her head.

Nell waited for only a moment. Then, before Molly could move a muscle to stop her, she calmly walked over to Dora, grabbed the old lady's pinkie finger and bent it backward as far as it would go.

"Tell," she said.

There was a sickening snap, like an old dead twig breaking. Dora shrieked in pain. Nell grabbed another finger and began bending.

"Tell!"

"All right," sobbed Dora. "I'll tell you, I'll tell you. Just stop. Please don't hurt me any more, Molly, please don't let her hurt me any more."

Nell released her grip. Molly came over and gently pulled her sister away. Then she sat down on the floor next to the old woman, who had begun to weep. So much for Nell not being able to hurt a fly, Molly thought; perhaps she didn't know her sister so very well after all. They were all probably in some kind of state of shock.

"You killed our mother," Molly said simply.

Dora nodded, holding her useless finger.

"I'm so sorry," she whimpered. "Please believe how sorry I am."

"But why? Why did you do it?"

"He was a monster. You can't know. You just can't know."

"Who was?"

"Atherton," said Dora, cradling her broken finger in her pale, almost translucent hand. "I lived with him for more than forty years. It was constant torment. Never knowing where you stood. Never being safe."

Dora paused, nursed her hand, sobbed. Molly waited in silence for her to continue.

"I've wanted to tell someone for so long. Wanted to, but I couldn't. There was no one I could trust."

"Tell . . . us," said Nell. "Tell everything."

"We're entitled to know," said Molly.

The old woman nodded. Then she began speaking in a subdued, defeated voice.

"I used to go through Atherton's desk when he was away. I needed to protect myself anyway I could, to understand what he was up to. He was so crazy, so unpredictable. A short while after the time that I told you about at dinner tonight, when we had gone to New York and George wouldn't change his pants, I found something terrible."

"The new will," said Molly. "The one that left everything to our mother."

"You know about that?"

Molly nodded.

"I couldn't believe what I was reading," said Dora. "It was so callous, so hideous of Atherton—cutting out our own sons like that in favor of some . . . stranger. And all because of something so ridiculous, a grown man not changing his pants. I couldn't bear it, after all those years I had spent with Atherton, after everything I had given up. Living at Gale Castle was already torture, it was like being in prison with the cruelest jailor imaginable, and now Atherton was going to punish me even more, punish me by cheating our children of their birthright."

"Did you try to talk to him about it?"

"What would have been the use?" said Dora, shaking her head. "Atherton wouldn't have listened. He'd just be furious that I had gone through his desk and found out his secret. He'd see it as treachery, betrayal. Atherton went insane if he thought someone was disloyal, and he was so very stubborn. For weeks I was in agony and despair, a helpless pawn in his game like everyone else. Then finally I couldn't stand it any longer. I made a plan. I told everyone I was going to visit my sister in Chicago, but I flew down to North Carolina, instead. I was only seventy-seven then. It was much easier to get around."

"How did you know where we lived?" asked Molly.

"I had found some letters that your mother had written to

Atherton in his desk, too," said Dora. "Your mother had gone on about her two girls, about you and Nell, and about how her husband spent all of his time drinking, so I knew what to expect. I waited outside your house in my rented car, wondering if I could really do what I had decided to do. The man who I knew must be her husband left the house early, got in his pickup truck and drove away. Then later I saw the two little girls leave and I knew she must be alone."

Molly swallowed hard. It had been Molly and Taffy going off to the movies that Dora had seen. Nell had still been inside, hiding in the closet.

"I didn't know that I could go through with it," Dora went on. "But I went to the door and rang the bell. Someone opened it. The next thing I knew, I was putting the gun back in my purse and walking back to the car. I don't remember pulling the trigger. I don't remember even seeing her."

"You . . . shot her," said Nell. "In her . . . head."

Dora let out a wail that was barely human.

"I'm sorry," she said. "I'm so sorry. It was a horrible thing to do, I know, but because of it, I thought, some good would finally come from the Gale fortune. I knew that, under the terms of the will I had seen, if this young woman died, then everything would go to worthy causes. Russell and George would still suffer, of course, but so many people could be helped by Atherton's filthy money. The children. The sick. The old. If you could look into their eyes as I have, you would understand how important it is to help those in need. That's the only thing that was in my mind, I swear to you. That's the only reason I could go through with it."

"But Atherton changed his will," said Molly accusingly. "You killed our mother for nothing."

Dora wept softly.

"I know, I know. My God, you can't begin to comprehend

how I've suffered all these years because of it. I had no idea that Atherton had made another will. When the man from Boston showed up after the funeral with it, I thought I would die. I prayed to die for the terrible thing I had done, but I couldn't. God made me live, and keep living, all these years to punish me. Oh, the guilt, the anguish I've felt. And Atherton made sure I couldn't get away. The trust only pays for my expenses as long as I stay at Gale Castle. I have no money of my own, no property, nothing. I'm still Atherton's prisoner here in this terrible place."

"My God," said Molly, shaking her head.

"You must understand how desperately I wanted to make amends for what I did to your mother, Molly, to cleanse my terrible sin. That's why I had the Gale family reunion last month. My children and I couldn't use Atherton's fortune to bring any good into the world, I knew, but maybe the Gales could. Of course, after what I had done to your mother I couldn't face your branch of the family, but I invited all of Atherton's other blood relatives. I tried to persuade them to do something decent with the money, so Atherton's greed wouldn't triumph over all of us, so that your poor mother wouldn't have died in vain. How naive I was. It was useless, of course. They were all just like Atherton. Venal. Greedy. Selfish. I could see that the Gale Trust would just end up going for jewelry and fast cars and divorce lawyers."

"And then their plane went down. How did you manage that?"

"But I didn't do anything," said Dora. "That's what this has been all about, don't you see? God struck down their plane with a bolt of lighting. At first I thought He was just teasing me further, giving death to everyone around me, while I had to go on. Then suddenly I realized that maybe He was showing me the way to redemption. There were now only a handful of people left between Atherton's fortune and all the good it could do. There was James.

And the two of you, the little girls. You must be all grown up, now, I knew. And there was Atherton Gale's daughter, Margaret. Your mother had mentioned her in the letter. She might still be alive, too.

"So you decided to kill all of us?"

"No," said Dora. "I just saw what was possible. And I began to hope again. Then one night, after the funerals for the Gales, I found myself alone with James. He was more insufferable than ever. So smug that he was Atherton's only heir. He even told me how he intended to spend the Gale Trust after I died. Trips to Las Vegas. Condos in Florida. It was sickening. So I told him about you and your grandmother. I told him your names and that you lived in Pelletreau, North Carolina. I told him that he'd have to split everything with the three of you, that he'd be only a quarter as rich as he had thought."

"But there were millions," said Molly. "There was more than enough for everybody."

"Twenty-five million dollars is a lot less than a hundred million," said Dora. "Especially to someone like James, who'd had hardly anything all his life, who'd had to watch his relatives live in the kind of luxury he could only imagine. I knew how bitter and angry James was, how greedy, how stupid. I played on all his weaknesses. I told him he wasn't much of a Gale or much of a man. If Atherton were in his place, I said, he would figure out a way so he wouldn't have to split the money with anybody. But that's all I did. I didn't know what James would do. I simply put it all in God's hands to do with as He would. I let myself be His instrument. We are all His instruments. I didn't have any real power over James."

"No," said Molly. "You just put a poisonous seed in his mind and hoped it would grow."

Dora bit her lip and nodded.

"When James told us he was going on a hunting trip down South," she said, "I began checking the Pelletreau *Times-Picayune* Web site on the computer Russell got me. A few days later I found the obituary for Margaret Jellinek. After another week, there on the front page was the story of how you and your sister had been killed in an explosion."

"It . . . was . . . Taffy," rasped Nell from the chair. "Taffy . . . and her friend."

"Yes, obviously it wasn't the two of you who had died," said Dora. "But I couldn't know that. I didn't need to check the Pelletreau newspaper any more. Now there was only James left, and I knew he was a murderer. God had indeed given me another chance. Killing James, executing a murderer, would not only serve justice, but by doing so I would assure that Atherton's money would do good after I was gone. And best of all, the poor woman I had shot, your mother, wouldn't have died in vain, as I had believed she had all these years."

"So you killed Jimmy."

Dora nodded.

"I drove down to his house that morning. The door was open. He was sitting there drinking a beer, watching cartoons on the television. Drinking a beer at ten o'clock in the morning, can you imagine? He didn't even look up when I came in, just mumbled, 'What do you want?' The boy had no manners at all. 'I want to make up for what I did seventeen years ago,' I said. 'Look at me when I speak to you, James,' I said. When he looked up, I shot him. I'm a very good shot. My first husband, Mr. Bowslater, taught me. I thought that was the end of it. I was so relieved. The burden of what I had done so many years before lightened for the first time. Then, that very night, you and Nell appeared right at my door. I thought I would die."

"That's why you had your attack," said Molly, turning and looking at her sister. "You recognized Dora."

Nell shrugged her shoulders.

"I just didn't want your mother to have died for nothing," said Dora. "You must believe me, Molly. I didn't want to harm anyone else."

"No, but it was all right if Jimmy did."

"He was God's instrument, just as I was. Don't you see? I acted the only way I could. I had to do something to make up for all the evil Atherton had done in the world, all the misery and hate he had brought to everyone. There are millions and millions of dollars in the Gale Trust. How could I let it go to feed the base desires of people who didn't need it?"

Nell had begun to sob again. Molly went over to her and put an arm around her shoulder.

"I'm not a bad person, Molly," said Dora, smiling a horrifyingly benign smile. "I didn't mean for your mother and your grandmother to die. I didn't want to hurt you and Nell, but you're the only ones left between the Gale Trust and the greater good. Don't you see? If I didn't kill you tonight, then everything would have been for nothing. All those people would have died for nothing."

"But no one had to die. You were the one who decided that they had to die."

"Every life has its purpose, Molly. We're not here to judge one another. Please try to see the larger picture and you'll understand. There's a greater good involved here and that was what I was trying to serve. You think about it, and you'll see I'm right. I did it for only the highest, most noble motive possible. I did it for charity."

"What gets me," said David Azaria, sipping a Coke a week later in Ralph's, the actor bar in New York City, "is how they could let her out on bail. Dora Gale killed your mother and your cousin Jimmy. She was responsible for the deaths of your grandmother and your friends in North Carolina, and then she tried to murder the two of you in your sleep. She's a menace to society."

"She's ninety-three years old," said Molly. "What purpose would there have been to hold her in some jail cell until her trial? Where is she going to go? What more harm can she do?"

It was ten to five on a Thursday—long past lunchtime but still a bit too early for dinner in New York. Ralph's was almost empty. The jukebox was silent. Molly and David, who had been to the Metropolitan Museum, had joined Tuck Wittington, who was killing time at Ralph's after an afternoon of commercial auditions. It was too late for David and Tuck to go home, but too early to go over to the theater for the night's show.

"So she's ninety-three, so what?" said David "Why should she be treated differently just because she's old? Dora Gale is every bit as much a killer as some kid who pops a gas station attendant during a holdup. More, if you ask me. This is one of the reasons why I got out of the legal business. There's no justice."

"Well, I certainly wouldn't have granted bail," pronounced Tuck Wittington. "There's magnificent justice in my court."

"You're an actor, Tuck," said David. "You don't have a court."

"Be that as it may," replied the old elf, "I have a pronounced sense of right and wrong, and Margaret Jellinek happened to have been a friend of mine. How on earth did that horrible woman ever think she could get away with such behavior?"

"If Nell hadn't been there to stop her, she probably would have, that's the scary thing," said David. "As it was, the case against her is very weak. Basically there's just Molly and Nell's word against hers. If Fishwig hadn't let her confess, she'd probably walk."

"Troutwig," said Molly. "And if it had been up to Mr. Troutwig, Dora wouldn't have confessed. He kept telling her not to say anything, but she insisted. She said she couldn't go on with all the deaths on her conscience."

"And so he pleads temporary insanity and gets bail," said David, shaking his head.

"She is insane," said Molly. "She was going to kill Nell and me for the sake of the American Cancer Society and the Salvation Army. Not that those aren't worthy causes, but still . . ."

"That old lady was about as insane as I am," said David with prosecutorial indignation. "Talk about premeditation! She had laced the tea you all drank with that stuff Russell had given her . . ."

"Melatonin," said Molly.

"Melatonin, right, a natural sleep hormone that would have left no traces in the body. She had planted the idea in the nurse's mind that the back door had been left open, so some unknown killer could have snuck in. She even waited until she was sure her sons had solid alibis so they wouldn't be suspects."

"Well, I think that Dora is going to experience almost perfect justice," said Molly. "Gale Castle was already like a prison for her. She might live another twenty years for all we know. That's what she's most afraid of, she told me, and I have a feeling that's what will happen. God will make her live for years and years, alone in that place she hates, shunned now by the friends who had always admired her, waiting for hearings and trials, being examined by shrinks right and left, with the burden of all she's done on her conscience."

"Well, if she lives long enough," said David, "maybe North Carolina will extradite her for your mother's murder. Of course, there's not much of a case against her there, either, except for her having possession of the murder weapon. Fishwig will probably be able to fight that for years, too."

The table fell silent for a moment. Molly tried to put the horrible picture of the police leading Dora away out of her mind by focusing on the memory of seeing Troutwig and Mrs. McCormick that same night surreptitiously kissing in an alcove behind a suit of armor. David sipped his Coke. Tuck admired his reflection in the mirror above the bar twenty feet away.

"I should have suspected Dora much earlier," said Molly. "When she answered the door, Nell had one of her attacks. I should have seen right then."

"I thought you said that the others all came to the door, too," said David.

"Yes," said Molly. "But I should have seen the pattern. I should have understood long ago what was setting Nell off. It was always little old ladies. Nell was having an attack every time she was surprised by a little old lady. Obviously it was from the trauma of seeing Dora shoot our mother. I just never made the connection. Nell didn't understand, either; I actually had to explain to her what had been happening."

"Where is Nell, anyhow?" asked David.

"Keeping bad company, I see," said Tuck, for at that very moment a group of dancers had entered Ralph's. You could tell they were dancers not only by their costumes—leotards, tight jeans, and dance bags—but also by the easy, athletic way they carried themselves. For a moment Molly couldn't pick Nell out among them, so well did she fit in.

The group made for a big table at the other side of the room, laughing and talking. Nell broke away and came over to the booth where Molly, David and Tuck sat.

"Guess what?" she said, beaming. "I got a job."

Molly looked up, stunned.

"What job?"

"Road company revival of *Barnum*. I'm an actor."

"You have lines?" said Tuck, incredulous.

Nell smiled and walked over to behind where Molly was sitting.

"A few," she said happily. "Mostly I just juggle and do acrobatics. And dance."

Her voice was stronger now, less raspy, but just as low. Molly didn't know why she should be surprised by Nell's soft North Carolina accent, but she was.

"It's a road company?" asked Molly, alarmed. "How long are you going to be gone?"

"Eight weeks, and maybe another eight after that if things work out. We're going to play at least twenty-two cites, some of them for only one night. Isn't it great?"

Nell threw her arms around Molly from behind.

"Yes," muttered Molly. "That's really wonderful. I'm very happy for you. When do you leave?"

"Three weeks. We start rehearsals on Monday."

"Ah, the actor's life for me," said Tuck. "Pack plenty of reading matter and a game of tiddlywinks is my advice to you. Life gets very boring out on the road. And the food is usually wretched."

Molly tried to think of something clever to say, but couldn't speak. Something was ending here, something that she had never thought would end.

"I gotta go over and sit with my friends," said Nell happily. "Hi, David."

"Hi, yourself," he replied, raising his Coke. "Congratulations."

"Don't wait up for me tonight."

"Where are you going?" asked Molly automatically, managing to find her voice. Since they had arrived in the city she and Nell had been staying at David's apartment, which wasn't nearly as big as he had claimed. The two sisters were sharing the bedroom and David was camped out on his sofa. It was a situation that couldn't continue, Molly knew. Apparently it wasn't going to if Nell was to leave in three weeks to go on tour. Molly felt a lump in her throat. It would be the first time the girls would have been separated since they were little. It would be the first time Molly would be alone with David.

"We're all going out to a club downtown," said Nell, grinning broadly. "I'll be back real late. Maybe not at all."

Molly wanted to stop her, to protect her from all the dangers that had to be waiting for a beautiful young woman out in the city, out in the world, but somehow that was no longer her job. It was time to let go.

"Have fun," said Molly.

Nell winked her eye and trotted off, looking so vibrant and full of confidence that Molly could barely recognize her.

"Ah, youth," said Tuck with a sigh. "I was young once, too, a hundred years ago. Happily, we elder statesmen have our charms, and if we're lucky we have gotten ourselves a steady Broadway gig so we don't have to go out on the godforsaken road. Twenty-two cities in eight weeks—and she's excited about this! I think I'll go have a pee."

Tuck rose solemnly from the table and floated off in the direction of the restrooms.

"Hi," said David softly when he was gone.

"Hi, yourself," Molly answered back.

"I liked how you handled that with Nell. I guess you've decided that the two of you can have lives of your own, after all."

"I guess," said Molly.

"She's a smart girl. And talented, obviously. She'll be fine."

Molly nodded.

"So what are you going to do with all the money?" said David, staring at her with his big earnest brown eyes. "We haven't talked about that yet, and I don't want it to be a problem between us."

"What money?"

"The Gale millions."

"I don't ever want to see a nickel of that money," said Molly, frowning. "My mother died because of it, and so did my friend, Taffy. I'll give it all to charity."

"No, you won't. That would justify everything that Dora Gale has done. Maybe you could set up a little antique shop on Madison Avenue or something. You probably wouldn't be able to afford anything too big, though, not the way rents are in this town. Or you could become a Broadway angel, invest in shows. You'd go through the whole bundle in no time at all."

"Well, I'm not going to worry about it now," said Molly. "We won't have anything as long as Dora is alive."

"You'll inherit sooner or later, though, and I think you should start thinking about ways to get rid of it. I don't like the idea of being a kept man."

"What makes you think I'd keep you?"

"Oh, I just have a hunch," he said. Under the table he gently placed a big hand on her knee.

Molly froze for a minute, then relaxed. There was nothing to be afraid of anymore. She placed her hand over David's and smiled in a way she didn't remember ever smiling before.

"You could be right," she said quietly. "Anything is possible, I suppose."